HITMAN ANDERS AND THE MEANING OF IT ALL

D1440249

ALSO BY JONAS JONASSON

The Girl Who Saved the King of Sweden

*The Hundred-Year-Old Man Who Climbed Out of the
Window and Disappeared*

HITMAN ANDERS AND THE MEANING OF IT ALL

JONAS JONASSON

Translated from the Swedish
by Rachel Willson-Broyles

4th ESTATE · London

HarperCollinsPUBLISHERS

4th Estate
An imprint of HarperCollins*Publishers*
1 London Bridge Street
London SE1 9GF
www.4thEstate.co.uk

First published in Great Britain by 4th Estate in 2016
This paperback edition published by 4th Estate in 2017
Originally published in Sweden as *Mördar-Anders och hans vänner
(samt en och annan ovän)* by Piratförlaget in 2015

3 5 7 9 8 6 4 2

HITMAN ANDERS AND THE MEANING OF IT ALL

You would have liked this one, Dad.
So it's for you.

PART ONE

AN UNUSUAL BUSINESS STRATEGY

CHAPTER 1

Daydreaming in the reception area of one of Sweden's most wretched hotels stood a man whose life would soon come to be filled with death and bodily harm, thieves and bandits.

The only grandchild of horse-dealer Henrik Bergman was, as always, channelling his paternal grandfather's shortcomings. The old man had been foremost in his field in southern Sweden; he never sold fewer than seven thousand animals per year, and each was first-class.

But from 1955, the traitorous farmers began to exchange Grandfather's cold- and warmbloods for tractors at a rate that Grandfather refused to comprehend. Seven thousand transactions became seven hundred, which became seventy, which became seven. Within five years, the family's multimillion-krona fortune had gone up in a cloud of diesel smoke. In 1960, the as-yet-unborn grandson's dad tried to save what he could by travelling around to all the farmers in the region and preaching on the curse of mechanization. After all, there were so many rumours flying about. Such as how diesel fuel would cause cancer if it got on your skin and, of course, get on your skin it did.

And then Dad added that studies showed diesel could cause sterility in men. But he really shouldn't have mentioned that. For one thing, it wasn't true, and for another, it sounded perfectly lovely to breadwinning but continuously horny farmers with three to eight children each. It was embarrassing to try to get your hands on condoms, not so for a Massey Ferguson or John Deere.

His grandfather had died not only destitute but kicked to death by his last horse. His grieving, horseless son took up the reins, completed some sort of course, and was soon employed by Facit AB, one of the world's leading companies in the production of typewriters and mechanical calculators. Thus he succeeded in being trampled by the future not once but twice in his lifetime, because suddenly the electronic calculator popped up on the market. As if to poke fun at Facit's brick of a product, the Japanese version fitted the inner pocket of a jacket.

The Facit group's machines didn't shrink (at least, not fast enough), but the firm itself did, until it shrivelled up into absolutely nothing.

The son of the horse dealer was laid off. To repress the fact that he had been twice cheated by life, he took to the bottle. Unemployed, bitter, always unbathed and never sober, he soon lost all his power of attraction in the eyes of his twenty-years-younger wife, who managed to stick it out for a little while, then another little while. But eventually it occurred to the patient young woman that the mistake of marrying the wrong man was possible to undo. 'I want a divorce,' she said one morning, to her husband, as he walked around their apartment, looking for something while clad in white underpants covered with dark stains.

'Have you seen the bottle of cognac?' said her husband.

'No. But I want a divorce.'

'I put it on the counter last night. You must have moved it.'

'It's possible it ended up in the drinks cabinet when I was cleaning the kitchen, I don't remember, but I'm trying to tell you I want a divorce.'

'In the drinks cabinet? Of course, I should have looked there first. How silly of me. So are you moving out? And you're going to take the thing that just craps its pants with you, right?'

Yes, she took the baby. A boy with pale blond hair and kind blue eyes. The boy who would, much later, be a receptionist.

For her part, the boy's mother had imagined a career as a language teacher, but the baby happened to arrive fifteen minutes before her final exam. Now she moved to Stockholm with her little one, plus her belongings and the signed divorce papers. She went back to using her maiden name, Persson, without reflecting upon the consequences for the boy, who had already been given the name Per (not that it's impossible to be named Per Persson or, for that matter, Jonas Jonasson, but some might find it monotonous).

Awaiting her in the capital city was a job as a traffic warden. Per Persson's mom walked up one street and down the next, receiving near-daily harangues from il-legally parked men, primarily those who could easily afford the fines they had just been saddled with. Her dream of being a teacher – of imparting the knowledge of which German prepositions governed the accusative or dative to students who couldn't care less – was interrupted.

But after his mom had spent half an eternity in a career that was meant to be temporary, it so happened that one of the many haranguing illegally parked men lost his train of thought in the midst of his complaint when he discovered that the person inside the traffic warden's uniform was a woman. One thing led to another, and they found themselves having dinner at a fancy restaurant, where the parking ticket was ripped in two around the time they partook of their coffee with a little something on the side. By the time the second thing had led to a third, the illegal parker had proposed to Per Persson's mom.

The suitor happened to be an Icelandic banker about to move home to Reykjavik. He promised his wife-to-be the moon and the stars if she followed him there. He would offer an Icelandic arm to welcome her son as well. But time had passed to such an extent that the little blond boy had become a legal adult and could make his own decisions. He counted on a brighter future in Sweden, and since no one can compare what happened after that with what might have happened instead, it is impossible to determine how right or wrong the son was in his calculations.

*

At just sixteen years old, Per Persson got himself a job alongside the studies he wasn't very engaged in. He never told his mother in detail what his work consisted of. And for that he had his reasons.

'Where you going now, boy?' his mom might ask.

'To work, Mom.'

'So late?'

'Yes, we're open for business most of the time.'

'What is it you do again?'

'I've told you a thousand times. I'm an assistant in … the entertainment industry. Where people have meetings and stuff like that.'

'What kind of assistant? And what is the name of—'

'Have to run now, Mom. See you later.'

Per Persson slipped away yet again. Of course he didn't want to share any details, such as the fact that his employer packaged and sold temporary love in a large shabby yellow wooden building in Huddinge, south of Stockholm. Or that the establishment went by the name Club Amore. Or that the boy's work involved handling logistics as well as acting as an attendant and inspector. It was important that each individual visitor find his way to the right room for the right sort of love for the right amount of time. The boy made up the schedule, timed the visits and listened through the doors (and let his imagination run free). If something seemed about to go awry, he sounded the alarm.

Around the time his mom emigrated and Per Persson finished his studies – in the formal sense as well – his employer chose to start a new line of business. Club

Amore became Pensionat Sjöudden: the Sea Point Hotel. It was not by the sea, or on any point. But as the owner of the hotel said, 'I gotta call this shithole something.'

Fourteen rooms. Two hundred and twenty-five kronor per night. Shared toilet and shower. New sheets and towels once a week, but only if the used ones looked used enough. Going from running a love nest to running a third-class hotel was not something the hotel owner truly desired. He had earned significantly more money when the guests had had company in their beds. And if any free time popped up in the girls' schedules, he himself could cuddle up with one for a while.

The only advantage of the Sea Point Hotel was that it was less illegal. The former sex-club owner had spent eight months in the slammer; he thought that was more than enough.

Per Persson, who had demonstrated his talent for logistics, was offered the job of receptionist, and he thought things could be worse (even if the salary couldn't). He was to check people in and out, make sure the guests paid, and keep an eye on bookings and cancellations. He was even permitted to be a bit pleasant, as long as his attitude didn't have a negative influence on the results.

It was a new business under a new name, and Per Persson's duties were different and more laden with responsibility than before. This prompted him to approach the boss and humbly suggest an adjustment to his salary.

'Up or down?' the boss wondered.

Per Persson responded that up would be preferable. The conversation had not taken the turn he desired. Now he was hoping at least to keep what he already had.

And so he did. The boss had, however, been generous enough to make a suggestion: 'Hell, move into the room behind the reception desk, and you won't have to pay rent on the apartment you took over after your mom left.'

Well, Per Persson agreed that this was one way to save a little money. And since his salary was paid under the table, he could also try to get social-welfare and unemployment benefits on the side.

Thus it happened that the young receptionist became one with his work. He roomed and lived in his reception area. One year passed, two years passed, five years passed and, to all intents and purposes, things did not go better for the boy than they had for his dad and grandfather before him. And the blame lay squarely with his late grandfather. The old man had been a millionaire several times over. Now the third generation of his own flesh and blood was standing at a reception desk, welcoming foul-smelling hotel guests, who answered to names like Hitman Anders and other horrid things.

This very Hitman Anders happened to be one of the long-term residents of Sea Point Hotel. His real name was Johan Andersson, and he had spent his entire adult life inside. He had never had an easy time with words or expressions, but early on in life he had realized that you could be very convincing by walloping anyone who disagreed with you, or appeared to be considering doing so. And walloping them again if necessary.

In time, this sort of conversation led to young Johan ending up in bad company. His new acquaintances urged him to blend his already violent argumentation techniques with alcohol and pills, and with that he was more or less done for. The alcohol and pills brought him twelve years in prison at the age of twenty, after he was unable to explain how his axe had ended up in the back of the region's leading distributor of amphetamines.

Eight years later, Hitman Anders was out again, and he celebrated his release with such fervour that he'd barely had time to sober up before he received fourteen more years on top of his previous eight. This time a shotgun had been involved. At close range. Right into the face of the person who had taken over from the guy with the axe in his back. An extraordinarily unpleasant sight for those who were called in to clean up.

In court, Hitman Anders maintained that he hadn't meant to do it. He didn't think he had, anyway. He didn't remember very much of the incident. Which was pretty much like his next stay in jail, after he'd cut the throat of a third pill entrepreneur because said entrepreneur happened to accuse him of being in a bad mood. The man with the soon-to-be-cut throat had essentially been correct, but this was of no help to him.

At the age of fifty-six, Hitman Anders was free again. In contrast to the earlier times, this was not a question of a temporary visit to the outside: this time it was permanent. That was the plan. He just had to avoid alcohol. And pills. And everything and everyone who had anything to do with alcohol and pills.

Beer wasn't so bad; it mostly made him happy. Or semi-happy. Or, at least, not crazy.

He had found his way to the Sea Point Hotel in the belief that the place still offered experiences of the sort one might have found lacking during a decade or three in prison. Once he'd got over his disappointment that this was not the case, he decided to check in instead. He needed somewhere to stay, after all, and just over two hundred kronor per night was nothing to argue about, especially given what arguing had often led to in the past.

Even before he collected his room key for the first time, Hitman Anders had managed to tell his life story to the receptionist who happened to land in his path. It included his childhood, even though the murderer didn't think it had any bearing on what had followed. His early years had mostly involved his dad getting drunk after work in order to tolerate his job, and his mom doing the same in order to tolerate his dad. This led to his dad being unable to tolerate his mom, which he demonstrated by beating her up at regular intervals, usually while their son watched.

After hearing the whole story, the receptionist didn't dare to do anything but welcome Hitman Anders with a handshake and an introduction. 'Per Persson,' he said.

'Johan Andersson,' said the murderer, promising to try to commit murder as little as possible in the future. Then he asked the receptionist whether he might have a pilsner to spare. After seventeen years without, it was no wonder his throat was a bit dry.

Per Persson had no intention of beginning his relationship with Hitman Anders by refusing him a beer. But as

11

he poured it, he asked if Mr Andersson might consider keeping away from alcohol and pills.

'That would probably lead to the least trouble,' said Johan Andersson. 'But listen, call me Hitman Anders. Everyone else does.'

CHAPTER 2

It's good to find happiness in little things. Such as the fact that months went by and Hitman Anders murdered neither the receptionist nor anyone else in the immediate vicinity of the hotel. And the fact that the boss allowed Per Persson to close the reception desk and take a few hours off every Sunday. As long as the weather – unlike most other things – was on his side, he took the chance to leave the premises. Not to kick up his heels: he never had enough money for that. Sitting still and thinking on a park bench, though, was always free.

That was where he was sitting, with the four ham sandwiches and bottle of raspberry cordial he'd brought with him, when he was unexpectedly addressed: 'How are you, my son?'

Before him stood a woman not many years older than Per himself. She looked dirty and worn out, and a white clerical collar gleamed around her neck, though there was a grimy stain on it.

Per Persson had never put much effort into being religious, but a priest was a priest, and he thought she deserved just as much respect as the murderers, drug addicts and plain old trash he saw at work. Or maybe even more. 'Thanks for asking,' he said. 'I suppose I've been better. Or maybe not, come to think of it. I suppose you could say my life is relatively not great.'

My goodness, he'd been too honest, he thought. Better put things right. 'Though I don't mean to burden the priest with my health and well-being. Just as long as I get something in my stomach I'll be fine,' he said, signalling the end of the conversation by opening the lid of his lunchbox.

The priest, however, did not register the signal. Instead she said she would certainly not be burdened by being of service – a lot or a little – if it would make his existence more tolerable. A personal prayer was the least she could do.

A prayer? Per Persson wondered what good the grimy priest thought a prayer might do. Did she think the heavens would rain money? Or bread and potatoes? Although … why not? He was loath to reject a person who only meant well. 'Thank you, priest. If you think that a prayer directed toward Heaven might make it easier for me to live my life, I won't put up any fuss.'

The priest smiled and made room for herself on the park bench next to the receptionist, who was enjoying his Sunday off. And then she began her work.

'God, see your child … What's your name, by the way?'

'My name is Per,' said Per Persson, wondering what God would do with that information.

'God, see your child Per, see how he suffers …'

'Well, I don't know that I'm suffering, exactly.'

The priest lost her stride and said she might as well start again from the beginning, as the prayer would do most good if she wasn't interrupted too much.

Per Persson apologized and promised to let her finish in peace and quiet.

'Thanks,' said the priest. 'God, see your child, see how he feels that his life could be better, even if he's not exactly suffering. Lord, give him security, teach him to love the world and the world shall love him. O Jesus, bear your cross by his side, thy kingdom come, and so on.'

And so on? Per Persson thought, but he dared not say a word.

'God bless you, my son, with strength and vigour and … strength. In the name of the Father, the Son and the Holy Spirit. Amen.'

Per Persson didn't know how a personal prayer should sound, but what he'd just heard sounded like a rush job. He was about to speak up when the priest beat him to it: 'Twenty kronor, please.'

Twenty kronor? For that?

'I'm supposed to pay for the prayer?' said Per Persson.

The priest nodded. Prayers were not something you just reeled off. They demanded concentration and devotion, they took strength – and even a priest, after all, had to live on this Earth as long as it was here, rather than in the Heaven she would eventually hang around in.

What Per Persson had just heard sounded neither devoted nor concentrated, and he was far from certain that Heaven awaited the priest when the time came.

'Ten kronor, then?' the priest tried.

Had she just lowered the price from not much to practically nothing? Per Persson looked at her more closely and saw something … else. Something pitiful? He made up his mind that she was a tragic case rather than a swindler. 'Would you like a sandwich?' he asked.

She lit up. 'Oh, thank you. That would be lovely. God bless you!'

Per Persson said that, from a historical perspective, pretty much everything indicated that the Lord was too busy to bless him in particular. And that the prayer He had just received as nourishment was unlikely to change that.

The priest appeared to be about to respond, but the receptionist was quick to hand over his lunchbox. 'Here,' he said. 'Best fed, least said.'

'God leads the humble in what is right and teaches the humble his way. Psalm Twenty-five,' said the priest, her mouth full of sandwich.

'What did I just say?' said Per Persson.

She really was a priest. As she gobbled up the receptionist's four ham sandwiches, she told him that she'd had her own congregation until the past Sunday, when she was interrupted in the middle of the sermon and asked by the president of the congregation council to step down from the pulpit, pack her belongings and leave.

Per Persson thought that was terrible. Was there no such thing as job security in the realm of the heavenly?

Certainly there was, but the president was of the opinion that he had grounds for his action. And it so happened that the entire congregation agreed with him. Incidentally, that included the priest herself. What was more, at least two of its members had thrown copies of the hymnal after her as she departed.

'As one might guess, there is a longer version. Would you like to hear it? I must say, my life has not exactly been a bed of roses.'

Per Persson considered this. Did he want to hear what the priest had spent her life sleeping in, if not a bed of roses, or did he have enough misery of his own to lug around without her help? 'I'm not sure that my existence will be made any brighter by hearing about others who live in darkness,' he said. 'But I suppose I could listen to the gist of it as long the story doesn't get too long-winded.'

The gist of it? The gist was that she had been wandering around for seven days now, from Sunday to Sunday. Sleeping in basement storage areas and God knows where else, eating anything she happened upon …

'Like four out of four ham sandwiches,' said Per Persson. 'Perhaps the last of my raspberry cordial would be good for washing down my only food.'

The priest wouldn't say no to that. And once she'd quenched her thirst, she said: 'The long and the short of it is that I don't believe in God. Much less in Jesus. Dad was the one who forced me to follow in his footsteps – Dad's footsteps, that is, not Jesus's – when, as luck would have it, he never had a son, only a daughter. Though Dad, in turn, had been forced into the priesthood by my grandfather. Or maybe they were sent by the devil, both of them – it's tough to say. In any case, priesting runs in the family.'

When it came to the part about being a victim in the shadow of Dad or Grandfather, Per Persson felt an immediate kinship. If only children could be free of all the crap previous generations had gathered up for them, he said, perhaps it would bring some clarity to their lives.

The priest refrained from pointing out the necessity of previous generations for their own existence. Instead she asked what had led him all the way to … this park bench.

Oh, this park bench. And the depressing hotel lobby where he lived and worked. And gave beers to Hitman Anders.

'Hitman Anders?' said the priest.

'Yes,' said the receptionist. 'He lives in number seven.'

Per Persson thought he might as well waste a few minutes on the priest, since she'd asked. So he told her about his grandfather, who had frittered away his millions. And Dad, who'd just thrown in the towel. About his mom, who'd hooked up with an Icelandic banker and left the country. How he himself had ended up in a whorehouse at the age of sixteen. And how he currently worked as a receptionist at the hotel the whorehouse had turned into.

'And now that I happen to have twenty minutes off and can sit down on a bench at a safe distance from all the thieves and bandits I have to deal with at work, I run into a priest who doesn't believe in God, who first tries to trick me out of my last few coins and then eats all my food. That's my life in a nutshell, assuming I don't go back to find that the old whorehouse has transformed into the Grand Hôtel, thanks to that prayer.'

The dirty priest, with breadcrumbs on her lips, looked ashamed. She said it was unlikely that her prayer would have such immediate results, especially since it had been a rush job and its addressee didn't exist. She now regretted asking to be paid for shoddy work, not least since the receptionist had been so generous with his sandwiches. 'Please tell me more about the hotel,' she said. 'I don't suppose there's an extra room available at … the friends-and-family discount?'

'Friends-and-family?' said Per Persson. 'Exactly when did we become friends, the two of us?'

'Well,' said the priest. 'It's not too late.'

CHAPTER 3

The priest was assigned room eight, which shared a wall with Hitman Anders's room. But unlike the murderer, whom Per Persson never dared to ask for payment, the new guest was required to pay a week up front. At the regular price.

'Up front? But that's the last of my money.'

'Then it's extra important it doesn't go astray. I could whip up a prayer for you, absolutely free of charge, and maybe it will all work out,' said the receptionist.

At that instant, a man with a leather jacket, sunglasses and stubble appeared. He looked like a parody of the gangster he presumably was, and skipped the greeting to ask where he could find Johan Andersson.

The receptionist stood up straighter and replied that who was or was not staying at the Sea Point Hotel was not information he could share with just anyone. Here it was considered a duty of honour to protect the guests' identities.

'Answer the question before I shoot your dick off,' said the man in the leather jacket. 'Where's Hitman Anders?'

'Room seven,' said Per Persson.

*

The menace vanished into the hallway. The priest watched him go and wondered if there was about to be trouble. Did the receptionist think there was anything she could do to help, as a priest?

Per Persson thought nothing of the sort, but he didn't have time to say so before the man in the leather jacket was back.

'The hitman is out cold on his bed. I know how he can be – it's best if he's allowed to stay like that for the time being. Take this envelope and give it to him when he wakes up. Tell him the count says hello.'

'That's it?' said Per Persson.

'Yes. No, tell him there's five thousand in the envelope, not ten thousand, since he only did half the job.'

The man in the leather jacket went on his way. Five thousand? Five thousand that apparently ought to have been ten. And now it was up to the receptionist to explain the deficit to Sweden's potentially most dangerous person. Unless he delegated the task to the priest, who had just offered her services.

'Hitman Anders,' she said. 'So he really exists. That wasn't just something you made up?'

'A lost soul,' said the receptionist. 'Extremely lost, in fact.'

To his surprise, the priest inquired whether this extremely lost soul was so lost that it would be morally sound for a priest and a receptionist to borrow a thousand kronor from him in order to eat their fill at some pleasant establishment nearby.

Per Persson asked what kind of priest she was if she was capable of coming up with such a suggestion, but he

21

admitted that the idea was tempting. Though there was, of course, a reason Hitman Anders was called Hitman Anders. Or three reasons, if the receptionist remembered correctly: an axe in a back, shotgun pellets to a face, and a cut throat.

The question of whether or not it was a good idea to borrow money secretly from a hitman was interrupted: the hitman in question had awakened and was now shuffling down the hallway towards them, his hair all over the place.

'I'm thirsty,' he said. 'I'm getting a payment delivered today, but it hasn't arrived yet and I have no money for beer. Or food. Can I borrow two hundred kronor from your till?'

This was a question, and yet it wasn't. Hitman Anders was counting on getting his hands on two hundred-krona notes at once.

But the priest took half a step forward. 'Good afternoon,' she said. 'My name is Johanna Kjellander and I am a former parish priest, now just a priest at large.'

'Priests are all a bunch of crap,' said Hitman Anders, without glancing at her. The art of conversation was in no way his forte. He continued to address the receptionist. 'So, can I have some money?'

'I can't quite agree with you on that,' said Johanna Kjellander. 'Certainly there are a few strays here and there, even in our line of work, and unfortunately I happen to be one of them. I would be happy to discuss that sort of thing with you, Mr ... Hitman Anders. Perhaps at a later date. At the moment I would rather discuss an envelope containing five thousand kronor that has just been delivered to the reception desk by a count.'

'Five thousand?' said Hitman Anders. 'It's supposed to be ten! What did you do with the rest, you goddamned priest?' The bleary and hung-over hitman glared at Johanna Kjellander.

Per Persson, who wished to avoid a priesticide in his lobby, was quick to add anxiously that the count had asked them to mention that the five thousand was a partial payment since only half the job had been completed. He and the priest at his side were innocent messengers, he hoped Hitman Anders understood …

But Johanna Kjellander took over again. 'Goddamned priest' had rubbed her up the wrong way.

'Shame on you!' she said, so sternly that Hitman Anders nearly did feel shame. She went on to say that he must certainly realize that she and the receptionist would never dream of taking his money. 'We're hard up, though – we really are. And while we're on the subject, I might as well ask, Hitman Anders, if you might consider loaning us one of those five lovely thousand-krona bills for a day or two. Or, even better, a week.'

Per Persson was astounded. First the priest had wanted to help herself to the money in Hitman Anders's envelope without his knowledge. Then she'd had him on the verge of flushing red with shame for having accused her of that very thing. Now she was entering into a lending agreement with the hitman. Didn't she have any survival instinct at all? Didn't she realize that she was putting both of them in mortal danger? Curse the woman! He ought to shut her up before the hitman beat him to it with something more permanent.

But, first of all, he had to try to clear up the mess she had just made. Hitman Anders had taken a seat, possibly out of shock that the priest, who in his world presumably would simply have stolen his money, had just asked to borrow what she hadn't had time to steal.

'As I understand it, Hitman Anders, you feel you've been tricked out of five thousand kronor. Is that correct?' said Per Persson, making an effort to sound fiscal.

Hitman Anders nodded.

'Then I must reiterate and emphasize that it was neither I nor Sweden's perhaps strangest priest here who took your money. But if there's anything – anything at all – I can do to aid you in this situation, don't hesitate to ask!'

'If there's anything I can do …' is the type of thing every person in the service industry likes to say but doesn't necessarily mean. That made it all the more unfortunate that Hitman Anders took the receptionist at his word. 'Yes, please,' he said, in a tired voice. 'Please get me my missing five thousand kronor. That way I won't have to beat you up.'

Per Persson did not have the slightest desire to track down the count, the man who had threatened to do something so unpleasant to one of Per's dearest body parts. Merely encountering that person again would be bad enough. But to ask him for money on top of that …

The receptionist was already deeply troubled when he heard the priest say: 'Of course!'

'Of course?' he repeated in terror.

'Great!' said Hitman Anders, who had just heard two of-courses in a row.

'Why, certainly we'll help Hitman Anders,' the priest went on. 'We here at the Sea Point Hotel are always at your service. For reasonable compensation, we are in all ways ready to make life simpler for anyone, from a murderer to a marauder. The Lord does not distinguish between people in that way. Or maybe he does, but let's stick to the matter at hand: could we start by learning more about which "job" we're referring to here, and in which way it seems to have been only half completed?'

At that moment, Per Persson wanted to be somewhere else. He had just heard the priest say 'We here at the Sea Point Hotel.' She hadn't even checked in yet, much less paid, but that hadn't stopped her initiating a financial transaction with a hitman in the hotel's name.

The receptionist decided to dislike the new guest. Beyond that, he had no better idea than to stand where he was, by the wall next to the lobby refrigerator, and try to look as uninteresting as possible. The person who arouses no emotion need not be beaten to death, was his reasoning.

Hitman Anders was pretty confused himself. The priest had said so much in such a short time that he hadn't quite followed it all (plus there was that business of her being a priest: that really mucked things up in and of itself).

She seemed to be suggesting some form of cooperation. That sort of thing usually ended poorly, but it was always worth a listen. It wasn't necessary to start with a good thrashing in *all* cases. In fact, surprisingly, it was often best to do that part last.

And so it came to be that Hitman Anders told them the details of the job he had done. He hadn't killed anyone, if that was what they were thinking.

'No, I suppose it's hard to half commit a murder,' the priest mused.

Hitman Anders said that he had decided to stop murdering people because it came at too high a price: if it happened once more, he wouldn't walk free again until he was eighty.

But the thing was, no sooner was he out in the world and had found a place to live than he had received a number of proposals from various directions. Most were from people who, for a substantial amount of money, wanted enemies and acquaintances cleared away, that is, murdered, that is, the thing Hitman Anders was no longer engaged in. Or, more accurately, never had been engaged in. Somehow it had all just ended up like that.

Aside from the proposed contract killings, he received the occasional assignment of a more reasonable nature, such as the most recent one. The object was to break both the arms of a man who had purchased a car from Hitman Anders's employer and previous acquaintance, the count, driven away in it and, later that evening, lost all the purchase money on blackjack instead of paying off his debt.

The priest didn't know what blackjack was – it wasn't a pastime either of her two former congregations had spent much time on during the fellowship hour after services. Instead they had had a tradition of playing Pick Up Sticks, which could be fun now and then. Anyway, the priest was more curious to know how the purchase of the car had taken place.

'Did he take the car without paying?'

Hitman Anders explained the legalities of Stockholm's less legal circles. In this particular case, the car in question was a nine-year-old Saab, but the principle was the same. Arranging one or a couple of days' credit with the count was never a problem. A predicament would arise only if the money wasn't on the table when the time was up. And when that happened the borrower, rather than the creditor, was the one with the predicament.

'Such as one involving a broken arm?'

'Yes, or two, like I said. If the car had been any newer, ribs and face would probably have been included in the order.'

'Two broken arms that became one. Did you miscount, or what went wrong?'

'I stole a bike and paid a visit to the thief with a baseball bat on the luggage rack. When I found him, he was holding a newborn baby girl in one arm, and he asked me to have mercy or whatever it's called. Since, deep down, I have a good heart, my mom always said I did, I broke his other arm in two places instead. And I let him put down the baby first, so she wouldn't get hurt if he fell over while I was doing my job. And fall over he did. I've got a mean wind-up with a baseball bat. Though now I think about it, I might as well have broken both his arms while he was wailing on the ground. I've noticed I can't always think as quickly as I'd like. And when booze and pills enter the picture, I don't think at all. Not that I can recall.'

The priest had registered one particular detail in this story: 'Did she really say that, your mom? That, deep down, you have a good heart?'

Per Persson was wondering the same thing, but he stuck to his strategy of blending in with the lobby wall as best he could, while remaining as quiet as possible.

'Yes, she did,' said Hitman Anders. 'But that was before Dad threatened to knock out all her teeth if she didn't stop jabbering on all the time. After that she didn't dare say much until after Dad drank himself to death. Oh dear, oh dear.'

The priest was in possession of a few suggestions for how a family can resolve its conflicts without knocking out each other's teeth, but there is a time and place for everything. At that moment she wanted to focus on summarizing the information Hitman Anders had given them, to see if she had understood it correctly. So, his most recent employer had demanded a fifty per cent rebate, invoking the fact that Hitman Anders had broken one and the same arm twice rather than two different arms once each?

Hitman Anders nodded. Yes, if by fifty per cent she meant half price.

Yes, that was what she'd meant. And she added that the count seemed to be a finicky sort. Nevertheless, both priest and receptionist were ready to help.

Since the receptionist was unwilling to contradict her, the priest continued: 'For a twenty per cent commission, we will seek out the count in question with the intention of changing his mind. But that's a minor detail. Our cooperation will not become truly interesting until *phase two*!'

Hitman Anders tried to digest what the priest had just said. There had been a lot of words, and a strange percentage. But before he got to his question about what 'phase two' might be, the priest was a step ahead of him:

The second phase involved further developing Hitman Anders's little operation under the guidance of the receptionist and the priest. A discreet PR job to broaden his customer base, a price list to avoid wasting time on people who couldn't pay, and a clear-cut ethics policy.

The priest noticed that the receptionist's face had gone as white as the refrigerator beside the wall he was pressing himself against, and that Hitman Anders had lost track of what was going on. She decided to stop talking so that the former could take in fresh oxygen and so the latter wouldn't get the bright idea of starting to fight instead of trying to understand.

'Incidentally, I must say I admire Hitman Anders for his good heart,' she said. 'Just think, that baby got away without a scratch! The kingdom of Heaven belongs to the children. We find testimony of this even back in the Gospel of Matthew, chapter nineteen.'

'It does? We do?' said Hitman Anders, forgetting that just thirty seconds before he had decided to give a good slap at least to the guy who wasn't saying anything.

The priest nodded piously and refrained from adding that, only a few lines later, the very same Gospel happened to say that you shall not murder, that you shall love your neighbour as yourself, and – apropos of the knocked-out teeth – you shall honour your mother, and, for that matter, your father.

The rising rage in Hitman Anders's face subsided. This was not lost on Per Persson, who finally dared to believe in a life after this (that is, he believed that both he and the priest would survive their current conversation with the guest in room seven). Not only did the receptionist start breathing again, he also regained the ability to speak and was able to contribute to the overall situation by managing reasonably well to explain to Hitman Anders what twenty per cent of something meant. The hitman apologized, saying he had become quite a wizard at counting years while in the slammer, but all he knew about percentages was that there were about forty of them in vodka and sometimes even more in the kind of stuff that was produced in random basements without any oversight. In some of the earlier police investigations, it had come to light that he washed down his pills with 38 per cent shop-bought hooch and 70 per cent home-brew. Now, police reports were not always to be trusted, but if they were right in that instance it's no surprise things went the way they did – with 108 per cent alcohol in his blood and the pills on top of that.

Inspired by the merry atmosphere that would soon prevail, the priest promised that Hitman Anders's business revenues were about to be doubled – at least! – as long as she and the receptionist were given free rein to act as his representatives.

At the same time, cleverly enough, Per Persson took two beers from the lobby refrigerator. Hitman Anders swallowed the first, started on the second, and decided that he had understood enough of what had been explained to him. 'Well, hell, let's do it, then.' The hitman terminated the second beer in a few rapid gulps, burped, excused himself and, as a kind gesture, handed over two of the five available thousand-krona notes with 'Twenty per cent it is!'

He stuck the three remaining notes in the breast pocket of his shirt and announced that it was time for a combination of breakfast and lunch at his usual place around the corner, which meant he didn't have time to discuss business further.

'Good luck with the count!' he said from the doorway before he vanished.

CHAPTER 4

The man who was called the count could not be looked up in the book of noble families. The fact was, he couldn't be looked up anywhere. He owed nearly seven hundred thousand kronor in unpaid taxes to the Tax Authority, but no matter how often the Authority pointed this out in letters mailed to his last known address on Mabini Street in the Philippines capital city of Manila, it never received any money in return. Or anything else. After all, how could the Tax Authority know that the address had been chosen at random, and that the notices ended up at the home of a local fishmonger, who opened them and used them to wrap tiger prawns and octopus? Meanwhile, the count actually lived in Stockholm with his girlfriend, who was called the countess and was a high-level distributor of various narcotics. Under her name, he ran five dealerships that sold used cars in the southern suburbs of the capital city.

He had been in the business since analogue days, when it was possible to dismantle and rebuild a car with a monkey wrench rather than a degree in computer science. But he had had an easier time than most in surviving the transition to digital, which was how one single dealership had become five in the span of a few years. In the wake

32

of this growth there arose financial discord between the count on the one hand and the Tax Authority on the other, bringing both joy and a certain amount of irritation to an industrious fishmonger on the other side of the globe.

The count was the sort of person who saw moments of change as opportunities rather than threats. Throughout Europe and the rest of the world, people were building cars that might cost a million kronor to buy, but only fifty to steal with the help of electronics and five-step instructions you could get on the internet. For some time, the count's speciality had been locating the whereabouts of Swedish-registered BMW X5s: his partner in Gdansk would send two men to fetch them and bring them to Poland, supplying them with a new history, then importing them again himself.

For a while this had brought in a net profit of a quarter-million kronor per car. But then BMW wised up and installed GPS trackers in every new vehicle, and the nicer used ones. They had no sense of fair play: they didn't even inform the car thieves in advance. Suddenly the police were standing in a middleman's warehouse in Ängelholm, gathering up both cars and Poles.

The count, however, made it through. Not because he was listed as living with a fishmonger in Manila, but because the seized Poles were far too enamoured of life to squeal.

Incidentally, the count had received his nickname many years earlier from his elegant manner of threatening customers who didn't pay up. He might use words such as 'I would truly appreciate it if Mr Hansson were to settle up his pecuniary accounts with me within twenty-four hours, after which I promise not to chop him into bits.' Hansson, or whatever the customer's name might have been, always found it preferable to pay. No one wanted to be chopped into bits, no matter how many. Two would be bad enough.

As the years passed, the count (with the help of the countess) developed a more vulgar style. This was the one that befell the receptionist, but the name had already stuck.

Per Persson and Johanna Kjellander set off to see the count to demand five thousand kronor on behalf of Hitman Anders. If they were to succeed, the murderer in room seven would be a future potential source of income for them. If they failed ... No, they must not fail.

The priest's suggestion of how they should handle the count was to fight fire with fire. Humility didn't work in those circles, was Johanna Kjellander's reasoning.

Per Persson protested, and protested some more. He was a receptionist with a certain talent for spreadsheets and structure, not a violent criminal. And even if he were to transform himself into a violent criminal, he would absolutely not start by practising on one of the region's foremost players in the field. Anyway, what sort of experience did the priest have with the circles she was referring to? How could she be so sure that a hug or two wasn't just the ticket?

A hug? Surely even a child could figure out that they would get nowhere if they tracked down the count and apologized for existing.

'Let me handle the sermonizing and everything will be fine,' said the priest, once they had arrived at the count's office, which was, as always, open on Sunday. 'And don't hug anyone in the meantime!'

Per Persson reflected that he was the only one of the two who was at risk of having a sexual organ cut off, but he was resigned in the face of the priest's courage. She was acting as if she had Jesus by her side rather than a receptionist. Nevertheless, he wanted to know what the literal meaning of fighting fire with fire might be, but it was too late to ask.

The count looked up from his desk when the doorbell rang. In stepped two people he recognized but, at first, couldn't quite place. They weren't from the Tax Authority, though – he could tell by the collar on one.

'Good day again, Mr Count. My name is Johanna Kjellander and I'm a priest with the Church of Sweden and, until very recently, the parish priest of a congregation we can leave out of this conversation. The man by my side is a long-standing friend and colleague ...'

In that instant, Johanna Kjellander realized that she didn't know the receptionist's name. He had been nice to her on the park bench, a bit stingier when it came to negotiations over the price of her room, relatively anonymous in the effort to bowl over Hitman Anders with

35

words, yet sufficiently brave to come along and rip the missing five thousand kronor out of the hands of the count, who stood before them now. He had probably mentioned his name as she was trying to trick him out of twenty kronor for a prayer, but it had all happened so quickly.

'My long-standing friend and colleague ... and he has a name too, of course. We all tend to be in possession of such a thing ...'

'Per Persson,' said Per Persson.

'As I was saying,' Johanna Kjellander continued, 'we have come here in our capacity as representatives of—'

'Aren't you the people I gave the envelope with five thousand kronor to a few hours ago, at the Sea Point Hotel?' The count was certain he was right. Surely there couldn't be that many female priests with dirty collars in the southern reaches of Stockholm. At least, not at the same time.

'That's exactly it,' said the priest. 'Only five thousand. Five thousand is missing. Our client, Johan Andersson, has asked us to come here to pick up the rest. He sends word that it would be best for everyone involved if his wishes were met. Because the alternative, according to Mr Andersson, is that the count will lose his life in an unpleasant manner, while Mr Andersson himself, as a result, will likely be locked up for another twenty years in addition to those he has already amassed for similar reasons. Or, as it says in scripture, "Whoever is steadfast in righteousness gives life, but whoever pursues evil will die." Proverbs, 11:19.'

The count pondered this. Coming here to threaten him? He ought to twist that collar around the priest's neck and cut off her oxygen. On the other hand, according to what the priest had just explained, doing so would turn the useful idiot Hitman Anders into a regular old idiot. The count would be forced to off the hitman before the hitman offed him, and that, in turn, meant that his favourite bone-breaker would no longer be available. He couldn't have cared less what the Bible did or didn't say on the matter.

'Hmm,' he allowed.

The priest kept the dialogue moving: she didn't want any to risk ending up in some sort of deadlock. So she explained Hitman Anders's reasoning when he had broken one and the same arm twice and allowed the other to remain in working order. In doing so, he had been acting in accordance with the ethical guidelines he had worked out jointly with his agents – the priest herself and her friend Per Jansson by her side.

'Per Persson,' said Per Persson.

According to these guidelines, it was out of the question to allow children to come to harm in the execution of his duties, and that was just what would have happened if Hitman Anders hadn't acted so resourcefully in a situation that had arisen without warning. Or, as the Lord commands in 2 Chronicles 25:4, 'The parents shall not be put to death for the children, or the children be put to death for the parents; but all shall be put to death for their own sins.'

The count said that the priest was good at talking nonsense. It remained to be seen how she planned to handle the matter in question, it being that the intended victim was currently driving around in and steering the very same damned car he hadn't paid for, with one arm but not the other encased in plaster.

'That is a conundrum we have considered in great detail,' said the priest, of the problem she had just been made aware of.

'And?' said the count.

'Well, we suggest the following,' said the priest, in the very instant she thought of the solution. 'You pay Hitman Anders the five thousand kronor you owe him from his previous assignment. At some later date, as we know, considering your line of business, you will need his help again. At that time, if those of us in upper management consider the job worthy of him, and I'm sure we will, we will accept the assignment according to the applicable price list, and we will also return to Object A: make sure that no babies are in the vicinity and break his arms. Both the one that has just healed and the other, which so infelicitously survived unscathed last time. And all this at no extra cost!'

It felt strange to negotiate with a priest and a – whatever the other person was – about this sort of thing, but the count found what he heard acceptable. He paid the five thousand, shook hands with the priest and the other man, and promised to get in touch when it was time to teach a lesson to whoever it might be for whatever it might be.

'And I suppose I ought to apologize to you, Per Jansson, for that bit about your dick,' he said, as a farewell.

'By all means,' said Per Persson.

'A limb for a limb ...' the priest happened to say, out of sheer momentum, but she stopped herself before she got to an eye for an eye and a tooth for a tooth, all in accordance with Leviticus 24.

'Huh?' said the count, who suspected that he had just been threatened, and threatening the count twice in the span of a few minutes was at least one and a half times too many.

'Nothing,' Per Persson said quickly, grabbing the priest by the arm. 'My little Johanna just happened to get lost in the Bible on our way out. My goodness, it's warm. Come along, sweetheart. Here's the door.'

CHAPTER 5

The priest and the receptionist didn't speak as they strolled away from their visit to the count. They were each gathering their thoughts from different directions.

The receptionist suspected that misfortune was headed their way. And so was money. And even more misfortune. And money. He was used to the misfortune part. Surely he would hardly notice more of the same. But he had never laid eyes on considerable amounts of money, other than in his nightmares about Grandfather. And yet he had to consult with the priest … Having people beaten up to order?

Johanna Kjellander appeared to be searching for a good answer, but the best she could come up with was that those who fear the Lord will be taught how they should choose.

'Psalm Twenty-five,' she added, without conviction.

The receptionist said that was one of the stupidest things he'd ever heard and suggested she start using her head instead of reciting quotes from the Bible as if they were in her very marrow. Especially considering that the marrow in question belonged to someone who believed in neither God nor the Bible. Not to mention that, in Per Persson's opinion, neither of the last two quotes had hit their mark. By the last one, had she meant that she and he had been dispatched by God to guide those with questionable morals to the correct path via Hitman Anders? In which case, why had God chosen a priest who didn't believe in him to lead the project? Along with a receptionist who had never even considered cracking open a Bible.

Slightly wounded, the priest replied that it wasn't always so gosh-damned easy to navigate through life. From her birth until about a week ago, she had been locked into a family tradition. She now found herself in a new role, in upper management over an assassin, but she couldn't say for sure whether that was the correct way to take revenge upon the God who didn't exist. She would have to feel her way forward, and maybe she'd come across a krona or two in proceeds during this trial period. Speaking of which, she wanted to thank Per Jansson or Persson for his resourceful intervention when her Biblical autopilot happened to reel off that bit about a limb for a limb in front of the count at the worst possible moment.

'By all means,' said the receptionist, not without pride.

He didn't comment on the rest. But it seemed likely that the priest and the receptionist had a few things in common.

They were back at the hotel. Per Persson handed over the key to room eight and said that he and the priest could discuss the room rate another time. Quite a bit had

41

happened for just one Sunday, and he was hoping to turn in early.

The priest thanked him in as worldly a fashion as she could manage. 'Thanks,' she said. 'Thanks for a nice day. I expect I'll see you tomorrow. Good night to you, Per. Good night.'

* * *

On the night following the day he had met, first, a priest, then a count, and subsequently become a consultant to the hitman he already knew far too well, Per Persson lay on his mattress in the room behind the reception desk and stared up at the ceiling. A broken arm here and there probably wouldn't be the end of the world, especially when they were dealing with people who deserved nothing better, and when it also enriched both the executor and his management.

The priest was one of the strangest people he had ever encountered. The receptionist was able to say this, even though he had encountered a lot of strange things in his years at the Sea Point Hotel – the hotel God had forgotten.

But she moved things forward, and she did so in a financially ingenious manner (even if she might have prepared her prayer on the park bench a little better – she had lost herself twenty kronor back there).

'I think I'll hitch my wagon to your train for a while, Johanna Kjellander,' Per Persson said to himself. 'I think I just will. You smell like money. And money smells nice.'

He turned off the bare lightbulb next to his mattress and was asleep in only a few minutes.

And he slept better than he had in a very long time.

CHAPTER 6

A company specializing in the field of assault and battery has more to deal with than you might expect. The allocation of income, of course, was originally set at eighty per cent to Hitman Anders and twenty per cent for the receptionist and the priest to divide between them. But one had to consider the cost of doing business as well. For example, Hitman Anders would need new work clothes when the old ones had become too bloody to salvage. There was no controversy there. But he also argued that the cost of the beer he consumed before each shift ought to be divided between the parties. He claimed he was unable to beat anyone to a pulp while sober.

The receptionist and the priest responded that, with a little practice, it would certainly be possible to commit assault while sober; it was just that Hitman Anders had never tried. They maintained their position that he ought instead to decrease his consumption of alcohol on days he was supposed to work.

Hitman Anders lost the beer negotiation. He did, however, convince the group that it was unreasonable to expect him to take public transport to work, or to make use of a stolen bicycle with a baseball bat on the luggage rack. It was unanimously decided that the firm would cover the cost of a taxi. The receptionist negotiated a fixed price with Taxi Torsten, a former regular at Club Amore. The girls had called him the Taxi Trick, which was the only reason the receptionist even remembered him. Per Persson looked up the former purchaser of sex and got straight to the point. 'What would it cost for you to act as a private chauffeur in the Greater Stockholm area for one or two hours on one or two afternoons a week?'

'Six thousand kronor per fare,' said Taxi Torsten.

'I'll give you nine hundred.'

'Done!'

'And you have to keep your mouth shut about anything you see or hear.'

'Done, I said.'

The group felt their way forward, with follow-up meetings every Monday. The original price list was constantly adjusted, based on Hitman Anders's stories of how troublesome various types of task had been to execute. The prices also varied based on the combinations ordered. A broken right leg cost five thousand kronor, for example, same as a broken right arm. But the combination right leg/left arm cost forty thousand rather than thirty. That had come to be after Hitman Anders had given a vivid description of how a person who had just had his right leg smashed to bits with the baseball bat flailed around on the ground, which meant it was a hell of a job to get at his left arm. Especially for the perpetrator in

45

question, who had a hard time telling right from left (as well as right from wrong).

They were also particular with the ethical guidelines. The first and most important one was that children must never come to harm, either directly or indirectly, by being forced to watch as Mommy or (for the most part) Daddy got a kicking.

The second rule was that any injuries that arose should, as far as possible, be of the sort that healed with time: one who had paid for his crime shouldn't have to limp his way through the rest of his life. This involved, to name one example, being judicious about a broken kneecap because it was well-nigh impossible to put back together again. One lopped-off finger, however, was acceptable. So were two. Per hand. But no more.

The most common order was for plain old broken arms and legs, with the help of the baseball bat. But sometimes the client wanted it to be clear, when looking at a person's face, that he hadn't minded his Ps and Qs, and then it was time for fists and brass knuckles, which led to just the right amount of fractured jawbones, nasal bones and zygomatic bones, preferably accompanied by a black eye and a split eyebrow (the last, incidentally, usually appeared all on its own).

Per Persson and Johanna Kjellander convinced one another that anyone who got a thrashing by way of their agency had had it coming. After all, each buyer had to argue his case carefully. So far, the only one they had refused was a recently freed heroin addict who, during psychodynamic therapy in prison, had come to realize that his ninety-two-year-old nursery-school teacher was to blame for everything. Hitman Anders thought there might be something in that, but Per Persson and Johanna Kjellander said the proof was lacking.

The heroin addict slouched helplessly away. To top it all, the old woman died of pneumonia two days later, thereby killing off every possibility for revenge.

* * *

The division of labour was such that Per Persson, who had to man the reception desk anyway, accepted incoming orders, named the price, and promised a decision within twenty-four hours. Thereafter he called Johanna Kjellander and Hitman Anders to a management meeting. The latter attended only occasionally, but each individual order could still be accepted by a vote of 2–0.

When payment in cash had been made, the assignment was carried out as stipulated, usually within a few days, always within a week. Although left sometimes turned into right and vice versa, the customer never had reason to complain about the quality of implementation.

'Your left arm is the one you wear your watch on,' the priest tried.

'Watch?' said Hitman Anders, who, since his first murder, had learned to tell the time in years and decades rather than hours and minutes.

'Or the hand you hold your fork in when you eat.'

'In the slammer I mostly ate with a spoon.'

CHAPTER 7

Life would have been good at the Sea Point Hotel if it weren't for the fact that the business hadn't really taken off. Rumours of Hitman Anders's excellence weren't spreading quickly enough to the right circles.

The only person in the group who had no problem working just a few hours a week was the protagonist. Hitman Anders, though he had sampled alcohol in all its forms, could not be accused of being a *work*aholic.

The receptionist and the priest regularly discussed how best to market his skills. Their conversations went so well that, one Friday evening, the priest went ahead and suggested they round things off with a bottle of wine in the receptionist's room (which essentially consisted of a chair, a wardrobe, and a mattress on the floor). It was a tempting idea, but Per Persson remembered their first encounter, when she had tried to trick him out of his money, far too vividly. He would go along with sharing a bottle of wine, but it would be best to continue holding their meetings where they usually held them, then go their separate ways.

The priest was disappointed. There was something harsh and lovely about the receptionist. She should never have put a price on the prayer back on that park bench.

Now that – to her own surprise – she was fishing for a little bit of love, that first encounter put her at a disadvantage.

But a shared bottle of wine there was, and maybe it was thanks to that bottle that they were able to agree that *media attention* would be an admittedly risky yet effective method of reaching their stated goals. It was decided that the hitman would give an exclusive interview to some suitable Swedish medium, and his unusual talent would become evident.

The receptionist read morning papers, evening papers, weekly papers, and magazines; he watched all sorts of programmes on various TV channels, listened to the radio – and decided that the best and most immediate results could be obtained from one of the two national tabloids. His final decision was *The Express*, because it sounded faster than *The Evening Post*.

Meanwhile, the priest explained the plan to Hitman Anders and practised patiently with him for his coming interview. He was fed information about the message they were reaching out with, what must be said, and what absolutely could not be said. The long and the short of it was that he would appear, in the newspaper, to be

1. for sale
2. dangerous, and
3. insane.

'Dangerous and insane … I think I can manage that,' said Hitman Anders, without sounding totally sure of himself.

'You have all the prerequisites,' the priest said encouragingly.

Once all the preparations had been made, the receptionist contacted the news editor at the chosen paper and said he was able to offer them an exclusive interview with the mass-murderer Johan Andersson, better known as Hitman Anders.

The news editor had never heard of any mass-murderer by that name, but she knew a good headline when she heard one. 'Hitman Anders' fitted the bill. She asked to hear more.

Well, Per Persson explained, the thing was, Johan Andersson had spent his entire adult life behind bars for recurrent murders. Perhaps it was an exaggeration to call him a mass-murderer, but Per Persson didn't dare to guess how many skeletons Hitman Anders had in his cupboard, beyond the ones he had gone to prison for.

In any case, these days the living murder machine was free, out in the world, and sent word via Per Persson that he would be happy to meet *The Express* to say he had become a better person. Or not.

'Or not?' said the news editor.

It didn't take more than a few minutes for the newspaper to look up Johan Andersson's pathetic history. Hitman Anders was not a name that had been used in the media previously, so the receptionist had prepared an exhaustive argument about how the name had come about and stuck during the man's most recent sojourn in prison, but his worry in this case was unwarranted. *The Express*'s reasoning was that if your name is Hitman

Anders, then your name is Hitman Anders. This was brilliant! The paper had its very own mass-murderer on the hook. That was better than any old sensational murder story.

A reporter and a photographer met Hitman Anders and his friends in the slightly pimped lobby of the Sea Point Hotel the very next day. His friends began by taking the reporter to one side to explain that the two of them must not figure in the piece because such exposure might jeopardize their lives. Did they have the reporter's word on this?

Young and plainly nervous, he had to ponder this for a moment. It would never do for outsiders to dictate the conditions of the paper's journalism. On the other hand, Johan Andersson was the subject of the interview. It seemed reasonable to leave out the tipsters. But it was tougher for him to comply with their demand for still images only, no audio or video recordings. Here, too, the receptionist invoked his own security and that of the priest, if on somewhat murkier grounds. The reporter and the photographer's faces clouded, but they accepted.

Hitman Anders described in detail all the ways he had killed people over the years. But, according to the prevailing PR strategy, he said nothing about being under the influence of drink or pills; instead he was supposed to list the things that might make him fly off the handle, that might make him turn violent again.

'I hate injustice,' he told *The Express*'s reporter, because he remembered the priest talking about that.

'I suppose pretty much everyone does,' said the still-nervous reporter. 'Is there any specific type of injustice you had in mind?'

Hitman Anders had gone through them with the priest, but his brain was at a standstill. Should he have had a breakfast beer to get himself into proper shape? Or had he already had one too many?

There was nothing he could do about the former, but the latter seemed unlikely. He snapped his fingers and got the receptionist to fetch him a fresh pilsner from the fridge. The hitman had it in his hand and open within fifteen seconds, and by the time half a minute had passed it was empty.

'Now, where were we?' said Hitman Anders, licking the beer foam off his lips.

'We were talking about injustice,' said the reporter, who had never before seen anyone down a bottle of beer so fast.

'Oh, right, and how I hate it, right?'

'Yes ... but what kinds?'

During all of their practising, the priest had learned that the hitman's sense of reason came and went of its own accord. Right now it was likely out for a stroll, all on its own.

And she was right about that. Hitman Anders could not for the life of him remember what it was he was supposed to hate. Plus, that last beer had really hit the spot. He was very close to just sitting there and loving the whole world instead. But, of course, he couldn't say so. All he could do was improvise.

'Yes, I hate ... poverty. And terrible diseases. They always get the good people in a society.'

'Do they?'

'Yes, the good people get cancer and stuff. Not the bad people. I hate that. And I hate people who exploit ordinary folk.'

'Who are you thinking of?'

Yes: who was Hitman Anders thinking of? *What* was he thinking? Why was it so terribly difficult for him to recall what he was supposed to say? Just take that part about killing. Was he supposed to claim that he didn't kill people any more, or was it the other way around?

'I don't kill people any more,' he heard himself saying. 'Or maybe I do. Everyone on my hate-list should probably watch out.'

Hate-list? he asked himself. *What hate-list? Oh, please, don't let the reporter ask a follow-up question about ...*

'Hate-list?' said the reporter. 'Who's on it?'

Dammit! Hitman Anders's brain was spinning fast and slow all at once. *Have to gather my thoughts ... What was it again?* He was supposed to appear ... insane and dangerous. What else?

The priest and the receptionist did not pray to any higher power for their hitman to find his way: they considered themselves to have far too poor a relationship with the power in question. They did, however, stand there hoping. Hoping that Hitman Anders would land on his feet somehow.

Over the shoulder of the *Express*'s reporter and through the window, Hitman Anders could make out the neon logo of the Swedish Property Agency on a building a hundred yards down and across the street. Next to it was a small suburban branch of Handels-banken. He could hardly see it from where he sat, but he knew it was there, because how many times had he stood there smoking in the bus shelter outside, waiting for the bus that would take him to the nearest den of iniquity?

In the absence of sufficient order inside his head, Hitman Anders allowed himself to be inspired by what he saw before his eyes.

Estate agent, bank, bus stop, smoker ...

He had never owned a rifle, or a revolver, but that didn't mean he couldn't shoot from the hip. 'Who's on my hate-list? Are you sure you want to know?' he said, lowering his voice, speaking a little more slowly.

The reporter nodded, his expression grave.

'I don't like estate agents,' said Hitman Anders. 'Or bank people. People who smoke. Commuters ...'

With that, he had included everything he'd seen and remembered across the street.

'Commuters?' the reporter said in surprise.

'Yes – do you feel the same?'

'No. I mean, how can you hate commuters?'

Hitman Anders seemed to settle into playing the role of himself, and he made the most of what he'd happened to say. He lowered his voice a bit more and spoke even more slowly: 'Are you a *commuter-lover*?'

By now, the reporter from *The Express* was truly scared. He assured the man that he did not love commuters: he and his girlfriend both biked to and from work and, beyond that, he hadn't given a lot of thought to what sort of attitude he ought to have towards commuters.

'I don't like cyclists either,' said Hitman Anders. 'But commuters are worse. And hospital workers. And gardeners.'

Hitman Anders was on a roll. The priest thought it best to break in before the reporter and his photographer realized he was messing with them, or that he had no idea what he was saying, or a little of both.

'I'm afraid you'll have to excuse us, but Hitman Anders, I mean Johan here, needs his afternoon rest, with one yellow and one orange pill. It's important to make sure that nothing goes wrong later this evening.'

The interview hadn't gone as planned, but with a little luck they could still make it work in their favour. The priest was just sorry that the most important part hadn't been said, the part she had repeated twenty times to her hitman. The advertisement, so to speak.

And then a miracle happened. He remembered! The photographer was already sitting behind the wheel in the *Express* car and the reporter had one foot in the car, but Hitman Anders hailed them: 'You know where to find me if you need a kneecap broken! I'm not expensive. But I'm good.'

The *Express* reporter's eyes widened. He thanked him for the information, pulled his other leg into the car, rubbed his right hand across his uninjured kneecap, closed the door, and said to his photographer: 'Let's go.'

* * *

The Express's posters the next day read:

Sweden's most dangerous man?
HITMAN
ANDERS
In an exclusive interview:
'I WANT
TO KILL AGAIN'

The quote was not an exact reproduction, but when people couldn't express themselves in a manner that worked on a poster, the paper had no choice but to write what the interviewee had probably meant instead of what he or she had actually said. That's called creative journalism.

In the four-page spread, the newspaper's readers discovered what a horrid person Hitman Anders was. All the atrocities he had confessed to in the story but, above all, his potentially psychopathic tendencies: the way he hated everyone from estate agents to hospital workers to … commuters.

The hatred Hitman Anders harbours for large parts
of humanity seems to know no bounds. In the end,
it turns out that no one, absolutely no one, is safe.

For Hitman Anders's services are for sale. He offers to break a kneecap, any kneecap at all, on behalf of *The Express*'s reporter, for a reasonable fee.

Besides the main article about the meeting between the brave reporter and the hitman in question, the newspaper included a supplementary interview with a psychiatrist who devoted half of the discussion to emphasizing that he could speak only in general terms, and the other half to explaining that it was not possible to lock Hitman Anders up because, from a medical perspective, he was not documented to be a danger to himself or others. Certainly he had committed crimes but, from a legal perspective, he had atoned for them. It was not enough just to *talk* about the further atrocities one could imagine committing in the hypothetical future.

From the psychiatrist's argument, the newspaper inferred that society's hands were tied until Hitman Anders struck again. And it was probably just a matter of time.

By way of conclusion, there was an emotional column by one of the paper's best-known faces. She began: 'I am a mother. I am a commuter. And I am scared.'

After the attention from *The Express*, requests for interviews streamed in from all imaginable quarters of Scandinavia, and the rest of Europe. The receptionist accepted a handful of international papers (*Bild Zeitung, Corriere della Sera*, the *Daily Telegraph, El Periódico* and *Le Monde*) but nothing more. The questions were posed in English, Spanish or French, and went through the linguistically gifted priest, who didn't bother to respond with what Hitman Anders had said but with what he ought to have said. Letting him loose in front of a TV camera or a journalist who understood what he was saying was out of the question. The trio would never be able to recreate the luck they had had with *The Express*. Instead, by allowing other Scandinavian media outlets to reproduce quotes from *Le Monde*, for example (formulated by the hitman, distorted and refined by the priest), the right material got out.

'There certainly isn't anything wrong with your talent for PR,' said Johanna Kjellander to Per Persson.

'It would never have worked without your gift for languages,' Per Persson offered in return.

CHAPTER 8

The man who had now become Hitman Anders to a whole people and half a continent woke up at around eleven each morning. He would get dressed, in the event he had undressed at bedtime, and walk down the hallway for breakfast, which consisted of the receptionist's cheese sandwiches with beer.

After that he would rest for a while before he started to feel true hunger around three in the afternoon. Then he would make his way to the local pub for Swedish home-cooking and more beer.

This was assuming it wasn't a workday, and workdays had become more and more frequent since all the media attention. The business he ran with the receptionist and the priest was going as well as could be expected. There were jobs on Monday, Wednesday, and Friday; Hitman Anders had no desire to work any more than that. In fact, he didn't really have any desire to work as much as he did, especially since there ended up being so many more broken kneecaps than planned. Of course, that was what he'd accidentally offered in the newspaper, and it seemed that most of those who ordered sundry limb-maimings had imaginations too limited to come up with something of their own.

The hitman tried to arrange his assignments to take place immediately after the home-cooking but before he had got tanked up for the evening. With the taxi ride there and back, a job was often completed within about an hour. It was important to keep the balance of drunkenness steady. If he had too many beers before work, things would go awry. A few beers more, and he risked a mess of a more dramatic nature. Though not as dramatic as it would have been if he had added spirits and pills to the menu. He could tolerate the idea of eighteen additional months in prison. But not eighteen additional years.

The hours between breakfast at eleven and lunch at three were best in the event that the priest and the receptionist had something to tell their business partner. Around that time, Hitman Anders had recovered from the troublesome hangover, while the current day's excesses had not yet taken hold.

The meetings might occur spontaneously, but they kept a regular appointment on Mondays at eleven thirty in the hotel's small lobby, which happened to have a table with three chairs in one corner. Anyway, Hitman Anders would appear at the Monday meeting as long as he hadn't passed out in some strange place in the city and therefore couldn't make it.

The meetings all followed the same routine. The receptionist would serve a beer to Hitman Anders and a cup of coffee each to himself and the priest. Thereupon followed a conversation about newly scheduled orders, upcoming activities, financial development, and other such matters.

The only real problem with their business was that the hitman, despite all the good advice he had received, was seldom correct about which was left or right when it came to broken arms and legs. The priest tried new tips, such as: right was the side you used to shake hands. To this, however, the hitman responded that he wasn't very used to shaking hands. He was apt to raise a glass if the atmosphere was friendly and find both of his hands busy at the same time if it wasn't.

Then it occurred to the priest that they could write a big L on Hitman Anders's left fist. Surely that would solve the problem. The hitman nodded in approval, but he thought that to be on the safe side they might as well follow up with an R on the other.

This idea turned out to be both brilliant and stupid: what was L for Hitman Anders, of course, was R for the person who had the great misfortune to be standing in front of him. So the plan didn't work until the hitman's left fist was misleadingly marked with an R and vice versa.

The receptionist was pleased to be able to say that their client network was broadening, that client complaints had nearly ceased since left and right fists switched places, and that they had received orders from Germany, France, Spain and England. Not Italy, however: they seemed capable of handling things on their own down there.

The question was whether they should expand their operations. Was it time for the company to enlist some new recruits? Might Hitman Anders know of a suitable candidate, someone who could break arms and legs but knew where to draw the line? Assuming the hitman himself planned to stand firm on his decision not to work more than one or two hours per day, three days a week.

Hitman Anders perceived a tone of criticism in those words and responded that it was possible he was not as interested in accumulating piles of money as the receptionist and priest were, and that he had the good sense to value meaningful free time. Working three days a week was plenty, and he absolutely did not want any rowdy youngster going around windmilling his arms and disgracing Hitman Anders's good name while the hitman enjoyed time off.

And speaking of all those countries they had just rattled off, he had just one thing to say: *not on your life!* Hitman Anders was no xenophobe, that wasn't the problem – he firmly believed in the equal worth of all people: he wanted to be able to say 'hi' and 'good morning' and behave politely in front of whomever he was about to beat to a pulp. After all, wasn't that the very least a fellow human being could expect?

'That's called respect,' Hitman Anders said sulkily. 'But maybe you two have never heard of it.'

The receptionist made no comment on the hitman's view of the amount of respect it took to exchange pleasantries with someone you were about to beat half to death. Instead he said acidly that he was aware that Hitman Anders was not amassing piles of money. After all, a few nights ago a jukebox had ended up flying through the window of the hitman's favourite pub just because it happened to be playing the wrong music. 'How much did *that* meaningful free time cost you? Twenty-five thousand? Thirty?' Per Persson asked, feeling a degree of satisfaction in daring to pose the question.

Hitman Anders said that thirty was pretty close to the truth and that that had not been the most meaningful incident of his life. 'But what kind of person puts money into a machine to listen to Julio Iglesias?'

CHAPTER 9

To Per Persson, it was an objective truth that he had been cheated by life. Since he didn't believe in a higher power and since his grandfather was long dead, he had no one and nothing specific at whom or which to direct his frustration. So, early on, from behind his reception desk, he had decided to dislike the entire world, everything it stood for, and everything it contained – including its seven billion inhabitants.

He had no immediate reason to make an exception for Johanna Kjellander, the priest who had initiated their relationship by trying to cheat him. But there was something about her misery that reminded him of his own. And before their first day together was over, they had hastily broken bread (that is, the priest had eaten all of the receptionist's sandwiches) and on top of that had had time to become partners in the torpedo industry.

They'd shared an affinity from day one, even if the receptionist had had a harder time seeing it than the priest did. Or maybe he'd just needed more time.

When they had been in business for close to a year, the receptionist and the priest had earned about seven hundred thousand kronor, while the hitman had made four times that. The receptionist and the priest had eaten and drunk well together now and then, yet just over half their earnings remained, neatly hidden in a pair of shoeboxes in the room behind the reception desk.

The rather squarely inclined Per Persson complemented the daring, creative Johanna Kjellander, and vice versa. She liked his aversion to his existence; she saw herself in it. And in the end he, a man who had never loved anyone, including himself, could not defend himself against the insight that another person on Mother Earth had realized that the rest of humanity was completely useless.

After a visit to Södermalm to celebrate the advance payment for contract number 100 – an extra-lucrative one, for a double leg-and-arm fracture, an unspecified number of cracked ribs, and a rearranged face – the duo returned to the hotel. The mood was such that Per Persson found himself asking whether Johanna remembered the time a number of months earlier when she'd suggested they round off the evening in his room.

The priest remembered her question and his negative response.

'I don't suppose you'd consider re-asking the question, here and now?'

Johanna Kjellander smiled and asked in return whether it would be possible to receive an advance ruling before doing so. After all, no woman wanted to be told, 'No,' twice in a row.

'No,' said Per Persson.

'No what?' said Johanna Kjellander.

'No, you won't get a "no" if you ask again.'

The summit on the mattress between two of the nation's potentially most bitter people turned out to be a sheer delight. When it was over, the priest gave a short and, for the first time, sincere sermon on the themes of faith, hope and love, where Paul had considered love to be the greatest of them all.

'He seems to have had the right idea,' said the receptionist, who was perfectly giddy over the realization that it was possible to feel as he felt, whatever the feeling was.

'Well,' said the priest, drawing out the rest, 'Paul uttered a lot of nonsense too. Like woman was created for man and shouldn't speak unless spoken to, and that men shouldn't lie with other men.'

The receptionist skipped the part about who had been created for whom but said he could only recall a single instance, two at the most, in which it would have been best for the priest to remain silent rather than speak. Regarding who should lie with whom, he preferred the female priest over their male hitman by a long shot, but he couldn't see what Paul had to do with it.

'For my part, I'd rather sleep with a bike rack than with Hitman Anders,' said the priest. 'But otherwise I'm in complete agreement with you.'

When the receptionist wondered what the Bible had to say about a sexual relationship between a woman and a bike rack, the priest reminded him that bicycles hadn't been invented in Paul's time. Neither, probably, had the bike rack.

And no one had anything more to add to that. Instead they began another summit that was just as non-hateful as the one they'd just archived.

* * *

For a while, everything seemed to be heading in the right direction. The priest and the receptionist joyfully and contentedly shared their genuine dislike of the world, including the entirety of the Earth's population. The burden was now only half as great, since each of them could take on three and a half billion people rather than seven billion alone. Plus (of course) a considerable number of individuals who no longer existed. Among them: the receptionist's grandfather, the priest's entire family tree, and – not least! – Matthew, Mark, Luke, John, and everyone else in the book that had persecuted (and continued to persecute) Johanna Kjellander.

While the currently newly in-love couple had earned their seven hundred thousand kronor, Hitman Anders had, according to the contract, brought in 2.8 million. But since he could keep a whole pub going for half the night all by himself, he never had more than a few thousand-krona notes in savings. He burned through what came in at approximately the same rate it came in. If his money ever happened to grow into a pile of cash worthy of the name, it tended to be an extra-lively time at the pub, such as when the jukebox had gone through the window.

'Couldn't you just have pulled the plug out of the wall?' the pub owner said, a bit cautiously, to his ashamed regular the next day.

'Yes,' Hitman Anders admitted. 'That would have been a reasonable alternative.'

This sort of incident actually suited the receptionist and the priest quite well, because as long as Hitman Anders didn't do what they did – that is, fill boxes with money – he would need to dispense justice on behalf of those who could afford to have justice dispensed according to their own definition of the concept.

What the receptionist and the priest didn't know was that, during the past year, Hitman Anders had been experiencing an increasing sense that life was hopeless. Incidentally, he was barely aware of it. He had spent his whole life reasoning with other people via his fists. It wasn't easy to talk to oneself in the same fashion. So he sought out alcohol earlier in the day and with greater emphasis than before.

It had helped. But it took constant replenishing. And his situation was not improved by the way the priest and the receptionist had started walking around side by side, smiling happily. What the hell was so damn funny? That it was only a matter of time before he ended up back where he belonged?

Perhaps it was just as well to put himself out of his misery, hasten the process, off the first prize idiot he saw, and move into the slammer for another twenty or thirty years – the exact fate he had resolved to avoid. One advantage would be that the priest and the receptionist would probably have grinned their last grins before he got out again. New love was seldom as new and loving two decades later.

One morning, in an unfamiliar and awkward attempt to gain insight, the hitman asked himself what it was all about. What, for example, had the jukebox incident really been about?

Of course he could have pulled the plug. And then Julio Iglesias would have gone silent while his jukebox fans went on a rampage. Four men and four women around a table: in the best case it would have been enough to slug the mouthiest of the men; in the worst case, he would have had to bring down all eight. With even a tiny amount of bad luck, one wouldn't have got up again, and there would have been those twenty additional years in prison just waiting for him, plus or minus ten.

A more practical solution might have been to allow the eight fools to choose the music they liked. Unless it was an indisputable truth that a line had to be drawn at Julio Iglesias.

For Hitman Anders, lifting the jukebox and heaving it out of the window, thus bringing the evening to an end for him and everyone else, had allowed his destructive self to take control of his extremely destructive self. It had worked. It had been expensive, but – crucially – it had allowed him to wake up in his own bed, rather than in a jail cell awaiting transport to somewhere more permanent.

The jukebox had saved his life. Or he had saved it himself, using the jukebox as a weapon. Did this mean that the road back to prison was not as inevitable as his inner voice had started harping on about? What if there was life *beyond* violence, and, for that matter, life with no jukeboxes flying through the air?

In which case – how could he find it, and where would it lead?

He thought. And opened his first beer of the day. And soon the second. And he forgot what he'd just been thinking, but the knot in his stomach was gone, and cheers to that!

Beer was the water of life. The third in succession was almost always the most delicious.

Whoopty-ding!

He thought.

CHAPTER 10

Then came the day when it was time for the group to make good on their debt to the count. The victim this time was a customer who had test-driven a Lexus RX 450h over the weekend and managed to get it stolen.

So he said.

In reality, he had hidden it in Dalarna, at the home of his sister who, instead of thinking carefully, took a photograph of herself behind the wheel and posted it to Facebook. Since everyone on the site knows someone who knows someone who knows someone, it didn't take the count many hours to learn the truth. The deceitful customer didn't even have time to work out that he'd been exposed before his face had been ruined and every more or less accessible tooth knocked out. Thanks to the age of the car and its intended price tag (it was new and expensive), one kneecap and one shin were goners as well.

It was one routine job among many but, according to the agreement made nineteen months earlier, the price was to include two broken arms for the guy who had played blackjack too poorly for his own good and half got away with it, thanks to a baby.

Hitman Anders carried out this job, too, with precision (both arms were always easier than just one, since he didn't have to pick the correct one). And that would probably have been the end of it, had it not occurred to him to consider the kind thing the priest had said the first time they met. It was something about how *nice* it had been for Hitman Anders to respect a small child.

The priest had referred to the Bible, of all things. What if there was more of the same inside that book? After all, it was fatter than the devil. Stories that could make him … feel good? Become someone different? Because there was something that came and went inside his head, something he had thus far done his best to drink away.

He would talk to the priest the very next day, and she could tell him. The *next* day. First the pub. It was already four thirty in the afternoon.

Unless …

What if he were to drop in at the hotel after all and ask the priest to explain this and that about this and that first, then drink away the eternal knot in his stomach? He wouldn't have to say much while she talked: he could just listen. And a person could always drink at the same time.

* * *

'Listen, priest, I need to talk to you.'

'Do you need to borrow some money?'

'Nope.'

'Is the beer in the refrigerator gone?'

'Nope. I've just checked.'

'Then what do you want?'

'To talk, I just said.'

'About what?'

'About how God and Jesus and the Bible and all that stuff work.'

'Huh?' said the priest. Who perhaps, even then, should have suspected that a terrible mess was in the offing.

The priest and the hitman's first theological discussion began with Hitman Anders saying he understood that she knew pretty much everything about religion. Maybe it would be best if she started from the beginning …

'From the beginning? Oh, well, they say that in the beginning God created the heavens and the Earth, and that it happened about six thousand years ago, but there are some people who think that—'

'No, dammit, not that beginning. How did it begin for you?'

The priest was surprised and delighted instead of being on her guard. She and the receptionist had been in agreement for some time that they would dislike everyone and everything together, rather than each on their own. But they had never truly shared their life stories with one another, not beyond the superficial facts. When the occasion arose, they preferred to devote their time to the delightful things two people can do rather than to bitterness and its causes.

At the same time – she was learning now – Hitman Anders had been ruminating on his own. This was, of course, a potential catastrophe, because if he were to start reading books about turning the other cheek when his job was rather the opposite, breaking jaws and noses on Monday, Wednesday and Friday, well, where would that leave their business plan?

Perhaps a casual onlooker might be of the opinion that the priest ought to have grasped this from the start. And that she ought to have warned the receptionist. But, as it happened, there was no casual onlooker present, and the priest was only human (as well as a pretty dubious intermediary between man and God). If someone wanted to hear about her life, even if that someone was a half-deranged assailant and murderer, she was happy to oblige. And that was that.

So she invited Hitman Anders to hear the story of her life, the story no one but her pillow had ever heard before. She was aware that he would offer the same intellectual response as the pillow from IKEA, but this was overshadowed by the fact that someone wanted to listen to her.

'Well, in the beginning my father created Hell on Earth,' the priest began.

She had been forced into the trade by her father, who, naturally, opposed female priests. Not because female priests went against God's will, that was up for debate, but because women belonged in the kitchen and also, from time to time, at the request of their husbands, in the bedroom.

What was Gustav Kjellander to do? The priesthood had been passed down from father to son in the Kjellander family since the late 1600s. It had nothing to do with belief or a calling. It was about upholding tradition, a position. That was why his daughter's argument about not believing in God didn't hold much sway. She *would* become a priest, according to her father, or he would personally see to it that she was damned.

For several years now, Johanna Kjellander had wondered how it could be that she had done as he'd said. She still didn't know, but her dad had had her under his thumb as long as she could remember. Her earliest memory was of her father saying he was going to kill her rabbit. If she didn't go to bed on time, if she didn't clear up after herself, if she didn't get the right grades at school, her rabbit would be put to death out of mercy because a rabbit needed a responsible owner, one who led by good example, not someone like *her*.

And mealtimes: the way Dad would reach slowly across the table, grab her plate, stand up, walk to the bin and throw her dinner into it, plate and all. Because she had said something wrong at the dinner table. Heard the wrong words. Given the wrong answer. Done the wrong thing. Or just *was* wrong.

Now Johanna Kjellander wondered how many plates it had been over the years. Fifty?

Hitman Anders listened to her with great concentration, because you never knew when there might be something worth taking in. The story about her dad didn't count: it had been clear to the hitman from the start that the old man needed a good thrashing, and that would probably take care of that. Or he could have a second thrashing, if necessary.

In the end, Hitman Anders was forced to say so, in order to put a stop to the priest's complaints. After an eternity she had got no further than her seventeenth birthday, when her dad had spat at her and said, 'O God, how much must you hate me to give me a daughter, to give me this daughter. You have truly punished me, Lord.' Her dad didn't believe in God any more than she did, but he did believe in tormenting others with God's help.

'Please, priest, can I have the old man's address so I can go over there with the baseball bat and preach some manners to him? Or a lot of manners, it sounds like. Should we say both right and left? Arms or legs, that's up to you.'

'Thank you for the offer,' said the priest, 'but it comes too late. Dad died almost two years ago, on the fourth Sunday after Trinity. When I got the news, I was up in the pulpit giving a sermon on forgiveness and not judging. But it turned out a bit different. I stood there and thanked the devil for taking my father home. It was not well received, you might say. I don't remember everything but I'm pretty sure I called my dad a word that relates to the female genitals …'

'Cunt?'

'We don't need to get into the details, but they inter-rupted me, pulled me down from the pulpit, and showed me the exit. Although I already knew where it was, of course.'

Hitman Anders really wanted to know which dirty word it had been, but he had to content himself with learning that the priest's choice had unleashed a sensa-tional moment in which two of the congregation's most devoted lambs had thrown their hymnals at her.

'Then it *must* have been …'

'Now, now!' said the priest, and continued her story. 'I took my leave and wandered around until the next Sunday, and that was when I found our mutual friend Per Persson on a park bench. And then I met you. And one thing led to the next and now we're sitting here, you and I.'

'Yes, we are,' said Hitman Anders. 'Now can we get back to what the Bible says about stuff so that this conversation goes somewhere?'

'But *you* were the one who wanted … you wanted me to tell you about my—'

'Yeah, yeah, but not a whole novel.'

CHAPTER 11

Johanna Kjellander's need to share with someone –
anyone at all! – the essential facts about her upbringing
caused her to remind Hitman Anders that *he* had come
to *her* and must behave accordingly. In short, he was to
zip his lips until she had finished.

Hitman Anders was not a person one could boss
around, but since she put a beer out for him while she
said this, he let her have her way. 'Thanks,' he said.

'I told you to be quiet.'

Johanna had been abused since the very first day of her
life in every way except physically. She weighed seven
pounds and five ounces when her father had touched his
daughter for the first and last time. He had lifted her up,
held her slightly more firmly than was necessary, brought
her face to his, and hissed into her ear: 'What are you
doing here? I don't want you. Do you hear me? *I don't
want you.*'

'How *could* you, Gustav?' said Johanna's exhausted
mother.

'I am the one who decides what I can and cannot do,
do you hear me? You will never contradict me again,'

said Gustav Kjellander to his wife, handing back the baby.

His wife heard and obeyed. During the next sixteen years, she never once contradicted her husband. Instead, when she could no longer stand herself, she walked straight into the sea.

Gustav was enraged when his vanished wife's body washed up on the shore two days later. As previously mentioned, he was never violent, but Johanna saw in his face that he could have killed her mother there and then if she hadn't already been dead.

'I need to take a shit soon,' Hitman Anders interrupted her. 'Is there much left?'

'I already told you to zip it while I'm talking,' said the priest. 'Do the same with your behind, if you must, because you're not going anywhere until I've finished.'

Hitman Anders had never seen her so decisive. And his visit to the bathroom wasn't that urgent – he was just bored. He sighed and let her continue.

Three years after her mother's death, it was time for Johanna to leave home for higher studies. Her father made sure to keep a firm grip on her, just as he'd always done, with letters and phone calls.

Priesthood is not the sort of status you can attain in a day. Johanna had to collect a substantial number of academic points in theology, exegesis, hermeneutics, religious pedagogy and other subjects just to be accepted into the final semester at the Church of Sweden's pastoral institute in Uppsala.

The closer the daughter got to complying with her father's demands, the more frustrated her father became about the state of things. Johanna was and remained a woman: in essence she was unworthy to carry on the family tradition. Gustav Kjellander felt trapped between the importance of upholding a centuries-old tradition on the one hand and betraying his forefathers – because Johanna was a daughter rather than a son – on the other. He pitied himself, hating God and his daughter in equal measure, just as he knew that God (if he existed) hated him, and his daughter would, too, if she dared.

The only rebellion Johanna was capable of was hardly worth the name. She devoted all her intellectual power to despising God, to not believing in Jesus, and to seeing right through all the stories in the Bible. By demeaning the pure, evangelical Protestant faith, she demeaned her father. And yet, by not telling anyone else that she was an active non-believer, she succeeded in being ordained one rainy June day. It wasn't just rainy. It was also very windy, on the verge of a storm. It was only thirty-nine degrees Fahrenheit – in June! Hadn't there even been a little hail?

Johanna scoffed inwardly. If the weather on her ordination day was God's way of protesting at her career choice, was that the best he could do?

Once the rain and hail had passed, she packed her bags and returned home to Sörmland. First to a congregation at arm's length from her father and overseen by the same. Four years later, as planned, she took over the Kjellander family congregation as parish priest. Her dad retired, probably with the intention of running the show anyway, but he got stomach cancer and – just think! – it turned out he could be defeated after all! What God had spent a whole life failing to do (if he'd even tried), the cancer had taken care of in three months. Thereupon, spontaneously and straight from the pulpit, his daughter bade him welcome to Hell. When she used that word for the female sex organ, applying it to the man who had personified the congregation for thirty-three years, it was the nail in the coffin.

'Can't you just say once and for all whether or not it was "cunt"?' said Hitman Anders.

The priest looked at him with a face that said, 'Did you not receive express orders to keep your mouth shut?'

The congregation's experiment with a woman as a parish priest was over. Her dad was dead; the daughter was free. And unemployed. And, after a week on the streets, dirty and hungry.

But four ham sandwiches and a bottle of raspberry cordial later, she had both a new home and a new job. It paid well from the start, and even after two years the money just kept improving. And, of course, she had also found love! If only the hitman sitting across from her didn't insist that they talk about the Bible ...

'Right, the Bible,' said Hitman Anders. 'If you're done blathering, maybe we could get to the point.'

The priest took offence at the hitman's lack of interest in her story and her fate in life. And at the fact that he'd spoken at all, in violation of the rule currently in effect.

'Would you like another beer?' she asked.

'Yes, please! Finally!'
'Well, you can't have one.'

CHAPTER 12

One of the central tenets of newly minted theology graduate Johanna Kjellander's active non-belief had been that the four gospels were unquestionably written long after Jesus's death. If there was a man who could walk on water, make food out of nothing, help the lame to walk, drive demons from man into pig, and even get up and walk around after having been dead for three days – if there was a man like that (or a woman, for that matter), why would it take one, two or more generations before someone bothered to write down all the things that that man had done?

'No fucking idea,' said Hitman Anders. 'But he made lame people walk? Tell me more!'

The priest noticed that the hitman found the miracles more compelling than the doubt, but she didn't give up. She explained that two of the four evangelists had had a third evangelist's writings in hand as they wrote. No wonder their testimonies were similar. But the last one, John, had made up a load of stuff on his own *a hundred years* after Jesus had hung on the cross. He suddenly claimed that Jesus is the way, the truth, and the life, that he is the light of the world and the bread of life and everything in between.

'The way, the truth, and the life,' said Hitman Anders, with a certain reverence in his voice. 'And the light of the world!'

The priest continued, saying that parts of the Gospel of John, by the way, were not even written by John. Someone had made up new bits as much as three hundred years later, including a famous scene where Jesus talks about how he who is without sin should cast the first stone. The guy who came up with that, whoever he was, was probably trying to say that no one is without sin, because there never ended up being any stone-throwing, but the question is what this story had to do with the Bible.

'Three hundred years! Do you understand?' said the priest. 'That's worse than if I were to sit down today and make up how things *actually* went during the French Revolution, and who said what – and then have all the world's historians reading, nodding, and agreeing with me!'

'Yeah,' said Hitman Anders, without listening to any more than he wanted to. 'Jesus is definitely right. Who on earth is without sin?'

'But that's not really my point—'

The hitman stood up right in the middle of the priest's sentence. The pub seemed to be calling. 'See you Wednesday at the same time, okay?' he said.

'On Wednesday I don't think I can—'

'Great. Bye.'

CHAPTER 13

The meetings between priest and hitman were held more and more frequently. At first, the priest had seen no reason to inform her receptionist of them, and after a while it was more that she didn't dare to tell him. She did everything in her power to keep their talks from evolving in the direction they nevertheless evolved in. Hitman Anders started to express dissatisfaction with himself, saying that he wanted to be led by the priest and God to become a better person. If Johanna Kjellander hinted that she didn't have the time or the energy, he threatened her with refusal to work and/or a beating.

'Not a big one, just a little one at first,' he said, to smooth things over. 'After all, we're colleagues. And it says in the Bible that—'

'Yeah, yeah,' said the priest.

Her only remaining option was to drag God through the dirt, thereby making Hitman Anders think worse of him. Thus she claimed, citing the Book of Job, that the main similarity between Hitman Anders and God was that they both killed people but, unlike God, Hitman Anders spared the children.

'Once he killed ten children in one blow, to show Satan that it wouldn't make the children's dad lose faith.'

'Ten kids? What did their mom say?'

'Although her main purpose in life was to remain silent and obedient, it's said that she took offence. And just imagine – I can understand why. But after a few ups and downs, God gave ten new children to this nice dad. I expect his grumpy wife had to give birth to them, or else they came in the mail. It doesn't mention anything about that.'

Hitman Anders was quiet for a few seconds. He was searching his memory for a reasonable way to explain this, even if that was not exactly how he put it in his mind. The priest saw that he was shaken: there was hope!

The former hitman first mumbled that at least the Lord had sent ten *new* children ... That was good, right? To this the priest replied that perhaps God wasn't quite the right hand-holder if he couldn't see that children, in relation to their parents, are not as interchangeable as car tyres.

Car tyres? In Job's day? But by now Hitman Anders had thought up a better way forward: 'What was that expression you used the other day when I had a go at you for throwing around difficult words?'

Oh, no! The priest knew what the hitman was getting at. 'I don't remember,' she lied.

'No, you said that the ways of the Lord are ... unfathomable.'

'I ought to have called him fickle, or seriously disturbed. I apologize ...'

'And then you said that *God's wisdom is infinite and cannot be understood by man*, didn't you?'

'No – I mean yes – I mean I said that people tend to hide behind such wording when they need to explain the inexplicable. Like, for example, God's ability to tell the difference between ten children and four car tyres.'

Hitman Anders continued to listen only to that which he wanted to hear. And he argued accordingly: 'I remember a prayer my mom taught me when I was little – you know, the piece of shit with the knocked-out teeth. She wasn't quite so horrible at first, before the booze took over – how did it go? "God, who holds his children dear, Watch over me as I lie here …"'

'So?' said the priest.

'What do you mean, "So"? You heard it for yourself. God loves the children. We are all his children, by the way. I read that just yesterday while I was on the throne and—'

The priest stopped the hitman mid-sentence. She didn't need to hear the other half. He'd already tricked her into giving him a copy of the New Testament and he had left it on a stool in the first-floor bathroom. Presumably he'd landed in the Gospel of John. Be that as it may, she had no ammunition left, apart from the central theological issue, the one that asks how the world can be as it is if God is good and all-powerful. This conflict was as talked to death as everything else, but perhaps Hitman Anders had never considered it before, Maybe there was a chance that …

At some point, the priest was interrupted. Hitman Anders stood up and said what he said.

And with that, catastrophe had become a reality.

'I'm not going to beat people up any more. Or drink alcohol. From now on, I'm placing my life in Jesus's hands. I want the payment for my last job, the one I did yesterday, and I'll give the money to the Red Cross. Then we'll go our separate ways, as they say.'

'But … you can't do that,' said the priest. 'I won't allow—'

'Won't allow? Like I said, I'm not going to beat people up anymore. But I'm sure Jesus would think it was fine to make two exceptions – you and the receptionist.'

CHAPTER 14

Then followed a night and a morning in which the priest got no sleep to speak of. As the sun began to shine through the blinds, she realized she had no choice but to wake the receptionist and confess the facts: she had accidentally caused Hitman Anders to find Jesus, and Jesus, in turn, had caused Hitman Anders to give up alcohol and beating people up for money.

Effective immediately.

Starting now, the only people on Earth whose heads he would even think of harming a hair on were theirs. And harm them he would, if they didn't acquiesce to his demands.

'His demands?' wondered the bleary receptionist.

'Well, we owe him thirty-two thousand kronor, and he wants us to pay up so he can give it to the Red Cross. I think that was it.'

The receptionist sat up. He felt an urge to become very angry with someone, but he wasn't sure whom. Grandfather, the priest, Hitman Anders and Jesus were closest to hand. Yet he knew that there was no point.

Might as well get up, have breakfast, stand at his bloody reception desk, and think logically to see where that might lead.

So their assault-and-battery business no longer had anyone to do the assaulting and battering, which meant they could not expect any further income. His revenge on Grandfather had been interrupted – unless Hitman Anders changed his tune. For that to happen, they would have to guide him away from God, Jesus and the Bible, the trio that was such a bad influence on him, and move him back towards alcohol, pubs and kicking his heels.

Per Persson barely had time to convey these thoughts to the priest before the former hitman arrived – at least two hours earlier than ever before.

'God's peace be with you,' he said, instead of asking for beer and sandwiches as had been his habit until now.

It couldn't be easy to go from being an alcoholic to a teetotaller in the span of one day. The receptionist suspected that an inner battle was raging in Hitman Anders, even if Jesus was still holding his own. This led Per Persson to launch a plan as hasty as it was treacherous. Hasty and treacherous plans were usually the priest's speciality, so the receptionist soon felt extra proud when the outcome was as intended.

'I understand you'll have a cheese sandwich, as usual, but surely you'll want communion rather than beer, as one who walks with Jesus.'

Hitman Anders understood the part about the sandwich, but not the rest. He had never seen a church from the inside and, as luck would have it, he had no idea what communion was.

'Half a bottle, I'm guessing, since it's still morning,' said Per Persson, placing some red wine next to the plastic-wrapped sandwich.

'But I don't drink alcohol.'

'I realize that – anything but communion wine is out of the question. The blood of Jesus. Would you like me to remove the plastic from Jesus's body for you?'

The priest realized what the receptionist was trying to do and came to his aid. 'We didn't quite get that far in our Bible study,' she said. 'But I'm sure, Hitman Anders, that you take your faith seriously and don't want to neglect consuming the body and blood of Jesus. As is becoming more and more common in our secular world.'

Hitman Anders had no idea what a secular world was, and he didn't understand the connection between Jesus and plonk – but he thought he grasped that, in the name of Jesus, he could down half a bottle of wine with his cheese sandwich. Which would be fantastic, because something along those lines happened to be just what his insides were screaming for. Leaving all the drinking behind had been a hasty decision. 'Well, no one's perfect,' he said, 'least of all those of us who are new to our faith. I realize I have no choice now that I walk with Jesus. But he and I actually met each other last night – doesn't that mean I'm half a bottle behind?'

There it was. A small success amid all the misery. By now, Hitman Anders was convinced that he who truly walked with Jesus had better start with morning and afternoon communion and proceed with a more substantial evening communion before it was time for a free-for-all night-time communion starting sometime after nine p.m. He kept the thirty-two thousand kronor he'd been planning to donate to the Red Cross so he could invest it in the blood of Jesus.

But his refusal to work still stood. Four orders lay waiting, all accepted just before Hitman Anders and Jesus ran into each other. After that, the receptionist had been rather vague when contacted by potential clients. He'd said, 'We're fully booked at the moment,' or 'We're experiencing a temporary disruption in service.' But he couldn't keep it up indefinitely. Was it time to give up the business? There was quite a bit of money in the shoeboxes, after all – not for that striking hitman, but enough for the receptionist and his fairly beloved priest.

Yes, the fairly beloved agreed. There were no signs of improvement – that is, worsening – in Hitman Anders's belief in God. So the priest saw no reason for herself and the receptionist to keep dealing with him. For all she cared, the hitman and Jesus could continue to walk side by side, preferably off a cliff if one happened to get in their way.

She could also live without the Sea Point Hotel, she said, but she added that she had become awfully used to Per Jansson's company. It was like it was the two of them against everything else, and she would be happy to share both the shoeboxes and her life with him for all eternity, if he saw fit.

There was something special about a woman who, like himself, didn't fully understand the purpose of fighting life's battles. Yet they fought well alongside each other against everyone and everything. So Per Persson was also keen to continue along the path upon which they already walked, on the condition she would eventually remember his name.

CHAPTER 15

The shoeboxes in the room behind the reception desk contained nearly six hundred thousand kronor for the priest and the receptionist to share. This was their joint savings. In addition, there was a hundred thousand kronor in advance payments for work not yet completed; they would be forced to return those since there were no indications that Hitman Anders and Jesus would have a falling out.

The repayment of thirty thousand plus thirty thousand plus forty thousand to three of Greater Stockholm's semi or full-blown gangsters was not something the receptionist was looking forward to. Partly because it meant a hundred thousand kronor less in the kitty, and partly because the clients had obviously been expecting results for their money, not money back with no interest. The general character of their clientele, broadly speaking, was not the most accommodating, the most flexible or understanding. There was a good chance the receptionist and the priest would encounter unpleasantness when they explained that Hitman Anders had stopped beating people up.

'It might be best to mail the money back with an explanation, then flit,' the receptionist mused. 'No one knows our names, we won't be leaving a lot of clues behind – we'd hardly be able to find ourselves if we started looking.'

The priest absorbed what he had said in silence. He understood that she might need time to think – after all, they were talking about provoking three hoodlums in one way or another. The receptionist went on: 'We could also consider keeping the money for ourselves – those three are going to be furious anyway. We really do have an excellent chance of staying under their radar. I've always been paid under the table, and I'm not listed as a resident anywhere, as far as I know. I didn't even have time to put your name down in the ledger before you turned yourself from a hotel guest into a business proprietor and my partner. The whole world knows the name of the guy in room seven, but we'll leave Mr Suddenly Saved here, of course. I'm sure he'll have fun explaining to all three clients that Jesus vetoed our operation and his former colleagues moved without leaving a forwarding address. Plus, in their haste, they happened to take all the clients' money.'

The priest still hadn't said anything.

'Am I thinking about this in the wrong way?' asked the receptionist.

The priest gave a friendly shake of her head. 'No,' she said, 'you're not. You're thinking the right way, but a little too defensively. As long as we're going to swindle the type of people no one in their right mind would swindle – why not swindle them all? For as much as they can manage? And preferably a little more. A hundred thousand is good, but I'm sure you'll agree that … say … ten million is better?'

The priest smiled a Mona Lisa smile at the receptionist, who gave a tentative smile in return. It had been just over two years since she'd approached him on that park bench in the hope of swindling him out of twenty kronor for a prayer in substandard packaging. This had led to their becoming, first, enemies, then partners, then friends, and eventually a couple. And now they were going to take off together. It felt great. *That* part felt great. But all the rest of it (grandfather, dad, mom, the millions, and the thieves), how did that feel?

Ten million was a hundred times more than a hundred thousand.

How much greater was the risk? And what did she expect they would do with the money together, other than, in the best case, love each other for richer rather than for poorer?

The receptionist didn't have time to pose the question, because Hitman Anders came down the hall, humming. 'The Lord be with you,' he said, in such a mild voice that the receptionist was irritated.

Fortunately, he was able to take out the invoice he had prepared as revenge for everything. 'For two years and thirty-six weeks Mr Andersson has not settled his bill,' he said. 'Two hundred and twenty-five kronor per night. That makes two hundred and twenty thousand kronor, if we're generous.'

In the good old days anyone who had suggested payment for lodging in such a way would have risked a thrashing, but that was no longer the case.

'But, dear, sweet receptionist,' said Hitman Anders, 'one cannot serve both God and Mammon.'

'That may be, and if it is, then I'll start with Mammon,' said the receptionist, 'and we'll see if there's time left over for the other guy later.'

'Good one,' the priest interjected.

'Wouldn't it be better if you started by giving me a cheese sandwich?' said Hitman Anders. 'Remember that you must love your neighbour as yourself, and I haven't had anything to eat yet. Or *the body of Jesus*, as we say.'

The priest was irritated by the former hitman, too, and she knew her Bible: '"Blessed are you who are hungry now," Luke six, verse twenty-one,' she said.

'Oh,' was the receptionist's follow-up. 'I wouldn't want to ruin Mr Andersson's level of blessedness. I'm sure not providing a sandwich is the least I can do for him. I wonder if there's anything else I can avoid assisting him with? If not, I wish him a pleasant day.'

Hitman Anders snorted, but he realized he wouldn't get anything to eat unless he went to the pub. He was hungry, so he rushed off, mumbling that the Lord kept an eye on all our doings and that the priest and the receptionist ought to decide where they stood while there was still time.

Thus the priest and the receptionist were alone once more. The priest explained what she had been thinking: 'Well, instead of admitting that the nutter who just left has got religion, we can spread the word that the exact opposite is the case: that Hitman Anders is more ferocious than ever, that he no longer has any limits. For a certain period of time, we'll accept orders for murders, broken kneecaps, poked-out eyes, whatever, as long as it's expensive. And then we'll take off.'

'You mean … disappear? Without having poked out any eyes?'

'Not a single one – not even glass ones! Partly because we don't do that sort of thing. Partly because we don't have anyone to do it for us …'

The receptionist made some calculations. How long could they accept orders without actually undertaking the work? Two or three weeks? Plus one or two more, with the excuse that Hitman Anders was ill, and we apologize for the delay. Say, four weeks altogether. If they really went on the offensive, they could collect money for six or seven murders, twice as many complicated fractures, and twice as many traditional assaults.

'You said ten million,' said the receptionist, who was in charge of finances and contracts. 'I'd say more like twelve.'

Ten to twelve million kronor on the one hand; a seriously enraged Greater Stockholm underworld on the other.

On the one hand again: the receptionist and the priest would have vanished without a trace – after all, no one knew their names or who they were. On the other: the gangsters would never stop looking for them.

'Well, what do you say?' asked the priest.

For the sake of artistic expression, the receptionist remained quiet for another few seconds. Then he copied the priest's Mona Lisa smile and said their only chance of ever finding out whether they ought not to have done what they were about to do was to do it.

'So it's on?' said the priest.

'It's on,' said the receptionist. 'May God be with us.'

'What?'

'It was a joke.'

CHAPTER 16

Fourteen point four million kronor later, the receptionist and the priest each packed a large, newly purchased suitcase, one yellow and one red, for their scheduled and permanent departure that afternoon.

The market had responded enthusiastically to the firm's new, more violent offerings. The priest and the receptionist were surprised by how many people wanted to pay to have those around them cleared out of the way. The last, just a few days earlier, had been a feeble man who told them about a neighbour who had built a chicken run 4.2 metres from the property line, violating the stipulated 4.5 metres. And when the feeble man pointed this out, the neighbour had made faces at the feeble man's wife. The feeble man was far too feeble to be capable of pounding justice into his neighbour, and if someone did it for him the neighbour would go for the feeble man as soon as he recovered. So the neighbour had to be cleared out of the way once and for all.

'For the sake of a chicken run?' said the receptionist. 'Why don't you complain to the city? Rules are rules, aren't they?'

'Yes, but it turns out that chicken wire doesn't count as a fence, so technically he was in the right.'

'And for that he has to die?'

'He made faces at my wife,' the feeble man clarified.

The priest could tell that the receptionist was about to forget that the neighbour with the chicken wire would be spared, and the only thing that would happen if they made a deal was that the feeble man would find himself with feeble finances as well. So she broke in and changed the subject: 'How did you hear about Hitman Anders and his available services?'

'Well, first there were the articles in the newspapers, and I made a mental note of it because this isn't the first time he's upset me, my neighbour. And when the situation became acute, all I had to do was ask how to get here at … well, slightly shady places …'

The story sounded plausible. The priest informed him that justice, in this case, would cost eight hundred thousand kronor.

The feeble man nodded, pleased. That was all his life savings, but it was worth it. 'You'll have the money on Wednesday. Will that do?'

Yes, it would. Their departure had been planned for the Thursday that had now arrived. All the priest and the receptionist knew about their joint future was that it was fully financed, that it was about to start – very soon, today – and that it did not include any recently saved former hitmen.

'Are you going somewhere?' Hitman Anders asked, on his way out to fill his belly with some of Christ's body and (above all) blood. Incidentally, he almost always went all the way into the capital city's most central neighbourhoods these days, changing pubs as often as was necessary. Out in the suburbs there was no longer anyone to spread the Word to, not without getting abuse in return. People in his home district had learned that the former hitman was now harmless, so when he insisted on reading aloud from Holy Scripture while Arsenal was playing Manchester United on TV they dared to tell him to get lost.

The suitcases were visible through the door from the other side of the reception desk, but luckily the same was not true of the piles of money they were about to be filled with.

'Was there anything else?' asked the receptionist, who did not consider himself duty-bound to report to the striking hitman. Not to mention that, by now, there were only a few more hours until he would never have to see him again.

'No, that's all. Go in peace,' said Hitman Anders, making up his mind to try one of the neighbourhood pubs in Södermalm. That area was overflowing with beer, but the hitman was sure he could find himself a glass of plonk instead.

He took a seat at Soldaten Švejk on Östgötagatan and ordered two glasses of Cabernet Sauvignon. The waitress soon arrived with a tray and placed one glass before Hitman Anders, who drained it as she wondered where to put the other. The hitman exchanged his first glass for the second and ordered glasses three and four. 'As long as you're here, miss.'

The blood of Jesus mixed with that of Hitman Anders, granting him a Christ-like tranquillity. He looked around the place and made eye contact with a stranger. Wait ... There was something familiar about him. A man in his forties, with a pint in his hand. Well now, if it wasn't one of the guys from his most recent stint in prison – his *last* stint! They had been in the same support group ... Wasn't he the guy who never stopped talking? Gustavsson or Olofsson or something?

'Hitman Anders! Nice to see you,' said Gustavsson or Olofsson.

'Same to you, same to you! Gustavsson, isn't it?'

'Olofsson. Can I sit down?'

Of course he could, no matter what his name was, because Hitman Anders had immediately identified him as a potential convert. 'I walk with Jesus now,' was his friendly opening.

The reaction was not what he had expected. Olofsson started laughing, and when Hitman Anders continued to be earnest, he laughed even harder. 'Well, hello to you, too!' he said at last. He took a big gulp of beer.

Hitman Anders was just about to ask what was so funny when Olofsson lowered his voice and said: 'I know you're going to off Ox.'

'Huh?'

'Don't worry, I won't say anything. My own brother is the one who ordered the hit. It'll be terrific to be rid of him. What a fucking swine! You remember what he did to my sister?'

Ox was a big stupid gangster among many others, in and out of prison, so huge that he thought he had the right to beat up anyone who wouldn't do his bidding. He had once attacked his own girl in accordance with the same logic. She, in turn, was not exactly one of God's greatest gifts to the world: she worked as a home carer and spent a lot of her time making copies of the keys to old people's homes to give to her brothers. They would wait for a bit, then go over and empty the house in question of any valuables. If the old people were at home they took the opportunity to scare the shit out of them.

But Ox had been of the opinion that the keys should go to him, and for this reason he beat first his girlfriend, then one of her brothers to a pulp. At that very moment, the other brother was sitting across from Hitman Anders at a Stockholm pub and thanking him for …?

'What do you mean, off Ox? I'm not going to off anyone. I just told you, I walk with Jesus.'

'With who?'

'Jesus, for Christ's sake. I'm saved.'

Olofsson looked at Hitman Anders. 'Then what about my brother's eight hundred thousand? You've already had the money.'

Hitman Anders asked Olofsson to calm down. He who walks with Jesus does not contract to kill his neighbour on the side, and that was that. Olofsson would have to look for his brother's eight hundred thousand somewhere else.

Somewhere other than in the pocket where the money had evidently ended up? Olofsson was no coward. He stood up and took a step toward the pig who was about to cheat his brother out of almost a million kronor. *And wasn't that bastard drinking wine to boot?*

One second later, Olofsson was sprawled on the floor. Recently saved or not, Hitman Anders couldn't turn the other cheek. Or even the first. Instead he fended off Olofsson's attack with his left arm (or was it his right?) and knocked him out with a straight right (or maybe left). This turning-cheeks thing was something he'd have to work on in the future.

The waitress came back with two more glasses of wine, caught sight of Olofsson, and inquired as to what had happened. Hitman Anders explained that his friend had had a little too much, but he was sure to come around very soon, and the last thing he'd done before he'd dropped off was promise to pay for both of them.

Then he knocked back one of the glasses from the waitress's tray and said that the guy asleep on the floor would probably want the other when he woke up. Hitman Anders stepped over Olofsson, thanked the waitress, and took off. He was on his way to a specific hotel in the southern reaches of Greater Stockholm where, at that very moment, suitcases were being packed, one red and one yellow, for what one might assume would be a departure later that day.

'With how much money?' Hitman Anders mumbled to himself.

He was, to be sure, a slow thinker and then some. And no one could say that he had much in the way of a gift for words.

But he wasn't stupid.

CHAPTER 17

One hour more and they would never have had to see that foolish hitman ever again. But at the pub Hitman Anders had met the wrong person and drawn the right conclusion. And that was why he was now standing in the centre of the room, next to the yellow suitcase and the red one, opening them and finding banknotes everywhere.

'Well?' was what he said.

'Fourteen point four million,' said the receptionist, in a resigned tone.

The priest tried to save her life and the situation: 'Four point eight million of it, of course, belongs to you. You can spread it around however you like: the Red Cross, the Salvation Army, and wherever else seems right. It's important to us that we don't leave you empty-handed. A third of it is for you. Definitely!'

'For me?' said Hitman Anders.

'For me' was all his brain could handle in that moment. It had been so much simpler before, when he hadn't had to think so much. All he would have had to do was:

1. beat the priest and the receptionist to a pulp
2. take the suitcases full of money
3. leave.

But these days it was more blessed to give than to receive; it was easier for a camel to go through the eye of a needle than for someone who was rich to enter the kingdom of God. And you weren't supposed to covet either one thing or the next.

Although … no, there were still limits. And he heard Jesus speak to him. 'Get rid of these two fakers, these Pharisees who have been using you for so long. Take all their money and start afresh somewhere else.'

Those were Jesus's exact words, and Hitman Anders conveyed them to the priest and the receptionist.

At that point, the receptionist began seriously to despair; he felt that it would soon be time to get down on his knees and beg for his life. Meanwhile, the priest was mostly just curious.

'Did Jesus really speak to you? Just think, in all my years as an ambassador between Heaven and Earth, he never said a word.'

'You don't think that might be because you're a fraud?' said Hitman Anders.

'I suppose that could be it.' The priest nodded. 'If I survive the next few minutes, I'll try to check with him. Just one quick question before you start getting rid of us.'

'Yes?'

'What does Jesus say you should do after that?'

'Take the money and go, as I told you.'

'Yes, of course that's right. But more specifically? Practically everyone in this country knows who you are. You realize that, don't you? You'll be recognized every-where. And you have almost every half- and full-blown criminal in the area after you. Did you tell Jesus about that?'

Hitman Anders was silent. And then he was silent a little longer.

The priest assumed he was trying to make contact with Jesus again, and perhaps was not receiving a response. If so, she said, Hitman Anders should not take it personally: maybe something had just come up for Jesus. He had so much to do: fill empty nets with fish, bring widows' dead sons back to life, drive demons out of men who couldn't speak ... There was proof to be found in chapter five of Luke and chapter nine of Matthew if Hitman Anders didn't believe her.

The receptionist squirmed. Was this really the best time to provoke him?

But Hitman Anders didn't feel provoked. She was right! Jesus must have his hands full all the time. He would have to work this out on his own. Or ask someone else for advice. Like, for example, the goddamned priest. 'Do you have any suggestions?' he asked sullenly.

'Are you asking me or Jesus?' wondered the priest, and was met with an angry look from the receptionist: *Don't go too far!*

'I'm asking you, for Christ's sake,' said Hitman Anders.

Ten minutes later, the priest had managed to get the story of what had happened at Soldaten Švejk out of him: about how the valiant hitman had laid a threatening Olofsson brother out cold ('first a left block and then a straight right, and that was that'), and about the conclusion the hitman had drawn from the conversation that had preceded the knockout – that is, that the priest and the receptionist were in the process of cheating the pants off their business partner.

'Former business partner,' the receptionist attempted. 'This all started when you went on strike.'

'I found Jesus! Is that so goddamn hard to understand? And just for that, you fucked me over!'

The priest broke in to put a stop to the fight they didn't have time for. She agreed with the hitman's description of the state of affairs, even if he might have chosen a different expression. But now it was time to look to the future and act quickly, since there was no way of knowing when Hitman Anders's friend from the pub would choose to get up off the floor, gather up his fury and take off. Probably in a beeline to his brother to inform him of this and that.

'A little while ago you asked if I had any suggestions of how we could move forward. The answer is yes!'

The best plan was for them to leave together. The priest and the receptionist's task would be to protect Hitman Anders from discovery, with all that that implied. They would divide up the money in the suitcases in a brotherly and sisterly fashion; after all, there was a little over five million each if they included the priest and the receptionist's more honestly saved money (not much more honestly, but a little).

They weren't quite sure where they would go, but the receptionist had visited Hitman Anders's old acquaintance the count the day before and purchased a small camper-van; there was room for all three of them to live in it for a limited amount of time, even though it was originally meant for just two.

'A camper-van?' Hitman Anders said. 'What did you pay for it?'

'Not much,' the receptionist confessed.

Per Persson had driven away in the vehicle with the promise that Hitman Anders would call in the following Friday to pay for it and also give details of the execution of the double murder the count had ordered.

'The double murder the count had ordered?'

'Yes, it's ordered and paid for, but not committed. One of the count's main competitors in car dealing, and ditto for the countess, but in the pill-pushing trade. I imagine they want fewer dogs in the race, and they thought it was worth one point six million.'

'One point six … which is now in this yellow suitcase?'

'Yes, or the red one.'

'And the count and countess won't be getting their murders?'

'Not unless Jesus insists you return to work, and we have no reason to hope he will. They will, however, have had a camper-van stolen from them too. There's a chance the count and countess will soon be the clients who are angriest with us, in company with a number of other angry clients. So perhaps we ought to set out on our journey to an unknown destination.'

At that moment, it was not easy to be named Johan Andersson. And nothing was made easier by the fact that he was better known as Hitman Anders, that he was recently saved – and that his only friends in the world seemed to be the two sincere enemies who suddenly wanted to move into a camper-van with him instead of being beaten to death.

Jesus continued to remain about as talkative as the Wailing Wall, while the priest and the receptionist chattered on. Despite everything, they seemed to have come up with the only reasonable solution he could think of.

'Can I tempt you with a half-bottle of the blood of Jesus for the road?' the receptionist tried.

Hitman Anders made up his mind. 'Yes, you may. Or a whole bottle on a day like this. Come on, let's go.'

CHAPTER 18

Ex-con Olofsson, the man who'd been knocked out by a freshly saved prison colleague at a pub in Södermalm, came to after only a few minutes. He was rude to the ambulance crew who had just arrived, swore at the poor waitress who wanted to be paid, threw the remaining glass of Cabernet Sauvignon at the wall, and staggered off. In less than half an hour he was at the home of his brother Olofsson (it is not unusual, in ex-con circles, to skip people's first names). As soon as the little brother had explained the situation to his big brother, Olofsson and Olofsson immediately took off for the Sea Point Hotel to dispense justice.

The hotel appeared deserted. There were a couple of confused guests standing in the lobby, wondering where the receptionist might be: they couldn't access the keys to their rooms. Another guest had been waiting to check in for at least ten minutes. He told Olofsson and Olofsson that he had rung the lobby bell to no avail, and when he had called the hotel from his mobile phone, he had been the closest person available to answer the phone on the desk.

'Have you two booked a room as well?' asked the man.

'No,' said Olofsson.

'We haven't,' said Olofsson.

And then they left, grabbed a can of gasoline from the car, walked to the back of the building, and set it alight.

To make a point.

What sort of point was unclear.

Things often turned out like that when the brothers were together. Olofsson was almost as temperamental as his brother.

One hour later, the incident commander from Huddinge fire station decided there was no point in calling for reinforcements. The property was engulfed in flames and lost, but there was no breeze and the conditions were otherwise favourable, so no nearby property was in danger. All they could do was to allow the hotel to finish burning. It was impossible to be certain at the moment, but witness statements indicated that no one had been trapped inside, and that two unknown men had purposely started the fire. Legally, this was tantamount to arson.

Given that no one seemed to have come to harm, the newsworthiness of the event should have been limited, from a national perspective … if an alert night-shift editor at *The Express* hadn't remembered where the interview with the guy known as Hitman Anders had been held. That must have been a year or three ago by now, but the hitman had lived there. Might he still? After some hasty but effective journalistic work, the next day's poster was drafted:

War in the underworld:
HITMAN
ANDERS
On the run from
ARSON
ATTACK

Two full pages in the paper, including, among other things, a full recap of how mortally dangerous Hitman Anders was said to be, accompanied by speculation about the causes of what was presumed to be an attempted murder. Plus the assumption that the hitman, who had not died in the fire, might be somewhere out there – on the run! – looking for a new place to settle. Perhaps somewhere near you!

A frightened nation is a nation that buys evening papers.

* * *

According to the receptionist, the fact that the Sea Point Hotel had burned to the ground was perfectly wonderful for two reasons and seriously unfortunate for one. The priest and Hitman Anders asked him to elucidate.

Well, first and foremost, the hotel owner, that old porn-lover and cheapskate, had lost his main source of income, which was great! If the receptionist remembered correctly, the owner had also considered it unmanly to pay several thousand kronor per year to insure the premises. Which meant he had no fire insurance: even better.

'Unmanly?' said the priest.

'Sometimes the line between manliness and sheer stupidity can be razor-thin.'

'What do *you* think, in this case?'

The receptionist gave an honest answer: given how things had turned out, it seemed stupidity had won the match, though manliness had been in the lead for quite some time.

The priest refrained from digging deeper into masculine wisdom and foolishness. Instead she asked her receptionist to continue his theme of good versus bad.

Right. It was also good that all the fingerprints, personal effects and anything else that might have identified the receptionist and the priest had also gone up in smoke. The priest and the receptionist were more incognito than ever.

More or less like Hitman Anders – only the exact opposite. The newspapers, with *The Express* in the lead, were repeating the story of the dangerous man and piling on very good pictures of him. There was no chance that the hitman would be allowed to leave the camper-van with anything less than a blanket over his head. And there was no chance that he would be allowed to leave the camper-van *with* a blanket over his head, because just think of the attention it would attract. In short, Hitman Anders was not allowed to leave the camper-van.

* * *

The next day, the newspapers offered a second helping in the form of further information about Sweden's most exciting person of the moment. The rumours of his crimes had spread so far that at least a handful of the diaspora of small-time criminals telephoned a contact at the newspaper to earn a thousand kronor in tip money: 'Yeah, listen, that bastard went and took advance payment to off people, and then he scarpered with the dough but didn't do the jobs. Easy money, heh heh, but how much longer d'you think he'll live *now*?'

CHAPTER 19

It would be an exaggeration to call it 'roving,' but the camper-van headed south without overthinking its destination. Away from Greater Stockholm was one of the basic ideas. Keeping in motion was another. After two days they were in the Småland city of Växjö, heading for the more central parts of town in the hope of finding a hamburger bar for an early lunch.

Blazing from the newspaper posters outside kiosks and shops, headlines warned that the dangerous and likely desperate hitman might be in the vicinity. By plastering a whole country with posters of this sort, it stood to reason that the premise held true somewhere, for example in Växjö.

The priest and the receptionist didn't have a very solid image of what their common future would be like. But the half-finished one did not include living in a smallish camper-van with a moody, recently saved, alcoholic hitman who was being pursued by a large percentage of the nation's criminal element.

The posters and front pages all over Växjö, full of giant photographs of an angrily glowering Hitman Anders, prompted the priest to mumble that it would be a while before she and the receptionist got the chance to do some private cuddling.

'Aw,' said Hitman Anders. 'Cuddle away. I can cover my ears.'

'And your eyes,' said the priest.

'My eyes too? Can't I ...'

At that moment, the camper-van passed a sight that pushed Hitman Anders's thoughts in a different direction. He ordered the receptionist to turn around, because there was ...

'A restaurant?' asked the receptionist.

'No, screw that. Turn around! Or go around the block – just make it snappy!' said Hitman Anders.

The receptionist shrugged and did as he was told. Soon the hitman's suspicions were confirmed – he had seen a charity shop owned by the Red Cross. It was a quarter past ten in the morning, and Hitman Anders was in his most loving mood, having been encouraged by the romantic conversation that had just taken place.

'Five million belongs to me, right? One of you go into that shop and give them five hundred thousand kronor in Jesus's name.'

'Are you nuts?' said the priest, although she believed she knew the answer.

'For a rich man to give money to a poor man – is that nuts? And this coming from a priest? You're the one who suggested a few days ago at the hotel that my money could go to the Red Cross and the Salvation Army if I so desired.'

The priest responded that she had been trying to survive one situation at the time, and that now she was trying to survive a different one. And that meant the outcomes might vary. She and the receptionist's unknown identities must be protected at all costs.

'Surely you realize we can't just walk in and say, "Here, have some money." They might have security cameras, or someone might take a picture on their phone, or they might call the police, who would find us and the camper-van. I can give you any number of reasons if you just let me have a few seconds to—'

That was as far as the priest got. Hitman Anders opened the yellow suitcase, grabbed two large piles of money, closed the suitcase, opened the side door of the camper-van, and stepped out.

'Back in a tick,' he said.

With a few long strides, he was inside the shop. The receptionist and the priest thought they could see a tumult through the window, but it was hard to tell … Was someone putting their hands into the air? Then there was an uproar that could be heard all the way out on the street, something smashing to pieces …

Within thirty seconds, the door opened again and out came Hitman Anders, but no one else. He leaped nimbly, for his age, into the camper-van, shut the door, and suggested the receptionist make a getaway, preferably a quick one.

Per Persson alternated between cursing and turning left, turning right, driving straight through a roundabout, driving straight through another roundabout, driving straight through yet another roundabout (that's what it looks like in Växjö), taking the second right out of a fourth and fifth roundabout, and driving straight and for a long time out of the city, followed by a left turn onto a forest road, another left, then yet another left.

There he stopped, in a clearing in an apparently deserted Småland forest. Judging from the activity in the rear-view mirror during the journey, no one had followed them. But that didn't mean the receptionist wasn't angry. 'Shall we take a vote of how fucking stupid that was, on a scale between one and ten?' he asked.

'How much money was in those bundles?' asked the priest.

'I don't know,' said Hitman Anders. 'But I trust that Jesus picked up the right amount for me.'

'Jesus?' said the still-upset receptionist. 'If he can turn water into wine, surely he can conjure up money without having to steal it from us. You tell him I said—'

'There, there,' said the priest. 'Everything seems fine. But I do agree that the world's almost unparalleledly stupid former hitman could have behaved differently from start to finish. Now tell us what happened in the shop.'

'Unparalleledly?' said Hitman Anders.

He didn't like it when he didn't understand something, but he let it go in favour of the new – to him – information that Jesus had made wine out of water. *Will I ever get that far in my own faith?* he wondered.

CHAPTER 20

After the ordeal at the Red Cross shop, the only option was to drive a left-hand circuit around Lake Helga and continue south without coming too close to the same town again. Their early lunch ended up consisting of service-station hot dogs and instant mashed potato. After lunch, there was no trouble until they reached the outskirts of Hässleholm in northern Skåne. There Hitman Anders signalled a stop at Systembolaget, the state-controlled drinks outlet, as he was beginning to suffer withdrawal symptoms from the wine that maintained contact between himself and Jesus. He had also failed thus far to transform the bottle of spring water he had found in the vehicle into anything potable. But practice made perfect, as the saying went.

The priest, who had taken over driving duties, was not happy with the hitman's demands. She would have preferred to put more distance between them and the debacle in Växjö before taking on another city centre, but she did as he said, since one of the few things worse than Hitman Anders was a sober Hitman Anders.

The receptionist made no protest either, for approximately the same reasons. The hitman was assigned the task of hiding in the very back of the little camper-van (where, for reasons unknown, he had been chatting with a bottle of water for some time), while the receptionist undertook a short stroll into the shopping centre that housed this particular drinks outlet. And a short stroll it was indeed, for the priest had been lucky enough to get the best parking spot, directly outside.

'I'll come straight back,' said the receptionist, 'and, you there, don't leave the camper-van! What kind of wine do you want, by the way?'

'Anything, as long as it's red and has a bit of a kick. Jesus and I aren't too picky. We don't like to waste money on communion if we don't have to. It's better to think of those who—'

'Yeah, yeah,' the receptionist said, and walked away.

Not much time had passed since Hitman Anders had learned from the priest that the ways of the Lord are unfathomable. Now he could see, through the curtain that covered the back side window of the camper-van, how true that was. For who did he see, not five metres away, but a Salvationist, strategically placed outside the much-frequented Systembolaget. She stood there with a collecting box in her hand, scraping up a few kronor now and then.

The priest, sitting behind the wheel, her thoughts else-where, did not foresee the danger. Hitman Anders silently gathered a pile of money of a similar size to last time, placed it in the plastic bag from the service-station, and opened the door quietly so he didn't alert her. Then he waved his hands until the Salvationist noticed him, with-out, as luck would have it, recognizing the most dangerous man in the country. She took the necessary steps up to the camper-van once she realized that she was the target of this man and his sign language. When she was beside him, Hitman Anders whispered to her through the half-open door, thanking the Salvationist for her work in the service of the Lord. And then he handed her the bag of money.

Hitman Anders thought the Salvationist looked worn out. She could probably use a word of comfort while he was at it.

'Rest in peace,' he said kindly, but a bit too loudly, then closed the door.

Rest in peace? The priest behind the wheel had time only to be shocked by what she saw, shocked again by the image of an elderly Salvationist staggering backwards after she, in turn, saw what she had just received as a gift, and shocked a third time as the Salvationist in question bumped into the receptionist with two bags of communion wine in his hands.

The bottles survived. The receptionist apologized to the Salvationist. But what was the matter? Was the lady feeling unwell?

Then he heard the priest's voice from the front side window of the camper-van. 'Forget the old bag! Get in the car right now! The idiot's done it again!'

CHAPTER 21

Just over three hundred miles north-east of Hässleholm, a businessman in car sales was having a discussion with his girlfriend. Both of them – like the majority of the nation – had had the chance to read the articles about the hitman who had cheated the underworld out of money.

The car salesman and his lawfully unwedded were among those cheated. And possibly among the least forgiving. Partly because forgiving was not in their nature, and partly because, in addition to all the money they'd lost, they'd been robbed of a camper-van.

'What do you say we cut him up into pieces, a little at a time, starting from the bottom and working our way up?' said the man who, in criminal circles, was called the count.

'You mean we'll like carve him up, just slowly enough, while he's still alive?' said his countess.

'More or less.'

'Sounds good. As long I can do some of the carving.'

'Of course, my darling,' said the count. 'All we have to do is find him.'

PART TWO

ANOTHER UNUSUAL BUSINESS STRATEGY

CHAPTER 22

After the incidents with the Red Cross and the Salvationist, the priest drove northwards again. After Växjö and Hässleholm, Malmö was the next logical landing point for anyone who might be looking for them. For this reason, the priest, the receptionist and the hitman were on their way in the opposite direction.

Hitman Anders was snoring on a mattress on top of the two suitcases at the very back of the vehicle when the priest turned off at a rest stop by a lake somewhere around the border of Halland and Västergötland. She stopped, turned off the engine, and pointed at a barbecue area down by the water.

'Meeting,' she said quietly, so as not to wake Hitman Anders.

The receptionist nodded. He and the priest walked down to the lake and each sat on a rock by the barbecue area. Both felt that this might have been a pleasant moment if only everything weren't so *un*pleasant.

'I hereby declare this meeting open,' said the priest, still quietly, so that the newly saved hitman in the camper-van definitely wouldn't hear her.

'Then I declare it duly announced,' the receptionist whispered back. 'And I regret that not everyone obeyed the summons. What do we have on the agenda?'

'There's only one issue,' said the priest. 'How will we get rid of that sleeping nuisance in the van, without losing our own lives in the process? And preferably while our money continues to belong solely to us. Not to Hitman Anders. Or to the Salvation Army. Or to Save the Children. Or to whomever or whatever we might encounter moving forward.'

The first idea that seemed like it might take hold was to hire a contract killer and assign him or her the task of doing away with their own version of the same. The problem was that there were a few too many people in those circles who might find out that they had just been cheated by the priest and the receptionist in Hitman Anders's name.

No, it was too risky to get a murderer to murder their murderer. Not to mention verging on immoral. Instead the priest thought of the simplest possible solution. What would happen if they just drove off as soon as Hitman Anders had left the vehicle to take a leak on some tree or another?

'Well,' said the receptionist. 'What would happen is probably … that we would be rid of him?'

'And we would still have all our money,' the priest added.

It was as simple as that! Why, they should have thought of this back at the Växjö Red Cross. 'Back in a tick!' Hitman Anders had said as he exited the camper-van. The priest and the receptionist had had an entire thirty seconds to gather their thoughts, come to the proper conclusions – and drive away.

An entire thirty seconds! they realized, nine hours later.

The meeting was over. The decision was unanimous: they would not be too hasty; they would wait and see what happened. Lie low for three days, take in what the media was reporting about the incidents in Växjö and Hässleholm, and gather details about how badly Hitman Anders had managed to frighten the nation, whether their identities remained protected, and how much effort was being put into pursuing them.

And after that: take action, using the knowledge they had gained as a foundation. All with the clear goal of separating themselves and their suitcases from the man who was currently snoring in the camper-van.

They had parked in such a way that the van was not visible from the road. Provisions could be obtained at a service-station a mile or so away. The receptionist offered to walk there and back while the priest guarded Hitman Anders; her primary task was to prevent him darting into the woods to give away a million or two if someone happened by.

CHAPTER 23

The two financial gifts in Växjö and Hässleholm were initially treated as criminal acts, high-priority ones at that, given that they had been committed by a person who was said to be the most dangerous man in Sweden: 475,000 kronor was seized from the Red Cross in Växjö, and 560,000 from the Salvation Army in Hässleholm. The police in the two southern Swedish towns were cooperating with each other.

The establishment in Växjö was the type of shop to which people donate things, others purchase them, and the profits are sent to one of the world's most miserable corners. On the day in question, there were two employees and just as many customers in the shop when the door opened and the nationally famous so-called Hitman Anders stepped in with a threatening expression. At least, his expression was considered threatening by at least one of the two customers, who screamed and ran smack into a shelf full of porcelain. The two employees threw their hands into the air to signal their surrender and that they preferred to stay alive, while the remaining customer, one long-since-retired Lieutenant Henriksson from the eighth company of the former Kronoberg Regiment, armed himself with a broom that cost forty-nine kronor.

Hitman Anders began by wishing 'God's peace upon this house,' while his sudden presence caused the exact opposite. Then he placed a large stack of banknotes on the counter before the two employees, their hands in the air, and said he wished they would use their arms, and more specifically their four hands, to accept and attend to this money in Jesus's name. By way of conclusion, he wished them a pleasant day and left as suddenly as he had arrived. He might have said, 'Hosanna,' as he walked out of the door, but the employees were not in agreement about that; one was sure that it had been a sneeze instead. After that he jumped into a white van or a similar vehicle, but only the second of the two employees thought he had seen it happen. The rest of those present were looking at the woman under the pile of broken porcelain. She had started to crawl out, pleading, 'Don't kill me, don't kill me ...' of the man who, at that point, was no longer on the premises.

The incident in Växjö was over so fast that no one could testify to the presence of any camper-van. All four people in the shop, however, had recognized Hitman Anders. Lieutenant Henriksson assured anyone who would listen that he would have attacked the assailant if necessary, but the party in question had likely suspected that and beaten a hasty retreat without completing his mission, except for the part about the money he'd left behind.

The other customer, the woman who had ended up under a shelf of porcelain, could not be questioned by the police or the media. As far as she was concerned, she had survived an attempted homicide by Sweden's foremost mass murderer and was currently in hospital, her whole body trembling. She did manage to say, 'Catch that monster!' to the reporter from *The Småland Post*, who then found himself lost and wandering the ward she was on, before being gently turned away by the charge nurse.

The employees with their hands in the air were informed, after a preliminary interview with the police, that they were not to make a statement to the media or anyone else. This order came from the publicity office at the Red Cross's headquarters in Stockholm. Anyone who wanted to hear about the two women's experience must instead call the acting press secretary, who was, at the moment, some three hundred miles away. The press secretary, in turn, was well educated in not saying anything that might bring harm to the Red Cross brand, and since any connection to the man called Hitman Anders risked doing just that, she chose to say nothing. That 'nothing' might have sounded something like this.

Question: What have the employees said about their encounter with Hitman Anders? Did he threaten them? Were they afraid?

Answer: In connection with incidents such as this one, our thoughts are with the hundreds of thousands of people around the world who are in need of and receive humanitarian aid from the Red Cross.

In the case of the Salvationist, the witness statements were more plentiful and more detailed. For many years, the railway hub of Hässleholm has been best known for how easy it is to get away from. So everyone – citizens, politicians, and journalists – was extra-engaged in the fantastic events that had taken place outside the shopping centre.

The witnesses from the pavement outside Systembolaget were very willing to be interviewed by the media and questioned by the police. One female blogger published a post on the theme of how she was likely single-handedly responsible for preventing a massacre just by coming around the corner and frightening away the perpetrators in the nick of time. When she was called in to give a statement, it turned out that the only thing she could say for certain was that Hitman Anders and his henchmen had fled in a red Volvo.

The best witness was the real-life RV fanatic who'd happened to be standing beside the Salvationist. He swore on his life that a woman had been behind the wheel of the camper-van, and that it was a 2008 Elnagh Duke 310. All he had to say about the woman behind the wheel was that the model in question includes a driver's side airbag. No matter how much the hungry reporter from the local paper and the slightly more exasperated investigator with the police asked, they could not unearth more about the driver than that she 'looked like women usually look', and that, for some reason, the wheel rims had not been original.

The chairman of the city council took the initiative and opened a crisis centre at the town hall. Any citizens who felt they had been directly or indirectly affected by Hitman Anders's ravages were welcome. The chairman had called in two doctors, one nurse, and a psychologist from his own circle of acquaintances. When not a single citizen showed up, he anticipated a political fiasco, got into his car, and picked up the Salvationist from her home. The Salvationist was in the process of making mashed turnips and didn't want to leave, but in light of all the considerations that must be taken, this could not be taken into consideration.

Thus the media could report on the crisis centre opened on the chairman's initiative, the fact that the shocked Salvationist was receiving help to return to a normal life, to the extent possible, and that when it came to information about how many other citizens had sought care and support, the chairman invoked the rule of confidentiality he had just enacted.

The truth – that the Salvationist was not shocked in the least, just hungry – never came to the notice of the general public.

CHAPTER 24

On day three, things started to turn around. First the police released a statement saying that the investigation against Johan Andersson had been put to rest. The man who had given a total of just over one million kronor was indeed a known criminal, but he had paid for his crimes and owed no money to the authorities. Furthermore, no third party had professed a claim on the money, and the banknotes could not be traced to any previous crime. The Red Cross and the Salvation Army could once again take possession of the gifts of 475,000 and 560,000 kronor respectively. It is not illegal even for murderers to give away money left and right.

To be sure, some witness statements mentioned that Johan Andersson had acted threateningly, or had at least *looked* threatening. But in opposition to this, there was the Salvationist's stubborn view, namely that Hitman Anders had beautiful eyes and a heart of gold must beat inside him. She refused to take his 'Rest in peace,' given in farewell, as a threat. The investigator in charge muttered to himself that she was probably right not to and closed the case.

'Rest in peace yourself,' he said to the investigation materials, then stuck them into the archive for closed cases in the basement of the police station.

During those same three days, someone had managed to start a support page in Hitman Anders's name on Facebook. After twenty-four hours, it had twelve members. After forty-eight, 69,000. And before it was time for lunch on day three, it surpassed a million.

The general public must have worked out what was going on around the same time as the tabloids *The Express* and *The Evening Post* did. Namely, the following.

A murderer had encountered Jesus and, as a result, tricked the underworld out of money in order to give to those in need. Like Robin Hood, only better, was the sudden opinion of an entire nation (minus a count, a countess, and a few others in the darkest corners of Stockholm and its immediate surroundings). *A miracle of God!* was the opinion of a number of the religiously inclined, enough to lead to the creation of a comparable Facebook movement with Biblical overtones.

And, furthermore, 'I think the man with the terrible nickname has shown courage, strength, and generosity. I hope that in his future endeavours he spares an extra thought for vulnerable children,' Her Majesty the Queen happened to say, during a live television gala broadcast.

'I can't believe this is happening,' said the receptionist, when the priest told him that the wife of the head of state had indirectly asked Hitman Anders to send half a million kronor to Save the Children or her own World Childhood Foundation.

'Would you look at that?' said Hitman Anders to the priest. 'To think I went and got royally addressed. Well, as we know, the ways of the Lord are unfathom— What was it again?'

'—able,' said the priest. 'Now get into the camper-van, you two. We're leaving.'

'Where are we going?' asked the receptionist.

'No idea,' said the priest.

'Maybe we'd be welcome in the palace,' Hitman Anders mused. 'I'm sure they have plenty of empty rooms.'

CHAPTER 25

The priest turned off at another sufficiently deserted rest area on the outskirts of Borås to discuss their impending and absolutely necessary change of vehicle. Instead what arose was a 100 per cent chance for the priest and the receptionist to be rid of the unwanted portion of their baggage once and for all.

Because the camper-van had no sooner stopped than Hitman Anders opened the door and hopped out.

'Aaaah,' he said, stretching his arms and body. 'I'll be jiggered if I'm not going have a little stroll in God's beautiful creation!'

Yes, he certainly would be. Jesus had given his approval at once, but he also pointed out that the air was chilly and it would probably be a good idea to bring along a bottle of something warming. For example, a far too cold Pinot Noir.

'I'll be gone for half an hour. Or even longer if I find any porcini mushrooms, *Boletus edulis*, along the way. Just so you know, in case you want to have a spot of hanky-panky while I'm out,' Hitman Anders said, as he put the bottle into his back pocket and departed.

When he was out of eye- and earshot, the priest said to the receptionist: 'Who taught him what porcini mushrooms are called in Latin?'

'Not me. I didn't know it until just now myself. But who *hasn't* taught him that you can't find them in April?'

The priest was silent. Then she said: 'I don't know. I don't know anything any more.'

The plan had been to take the first possible chance to separate themselves and the money permanently from the man who was, at that moment, wandering around nearby on the hunt for mushrooms that were at least four months away.

But now there was a note of fatigue in the conversation between the priest and the receptionist. Or of resignation. And it was mixed up with a faint hint of …

What?

Possibilities?

Should they just take off now, as fast as the campervan allowed, when so many parameters had shifted in such a short space of time? Like the fact that Hitman Anders had gone from being Sweden's least favourite person to its most favourite in just a day or two.

They needed a fresh analysis of the situation. Suddenly they were driving around with a man whose fame rivalled that of Elvis Presley.

'Although Elvis is dead,' the receptionist mused.

'From time to time I find myself thinking that life would be more peaceful if Hitman Anders were keeping him company. Preferably along with most of the rest of humanity, but what can you do?' said the priest.

The inherent threats of being in Hitman Anders's vicinity were clear. But the same went for the possibilities. A person who dearly loved money couldn't just dump the next Elvis in the nearest ditch.

'Let's wait for Mr Wandering-Around-in-the-Woods to come back and then I think we should start by driving into Borås to buy a bigger camper-van, as different from this one as we can find,' said the receptionist.

The priest agreed. Logistics was more Per Persson's speciality than her own. But then she changed her mind. 'Or else we start by doing what he suggested.'

'Who?'

'The mushroom-picker.'

'You mean … hanky-panky?'

Yes, that was what she meant.

CHAPTER 26

The priest and the receptionist walked arm in arm into the offices of Borås's leading, and possibly only, RV dealership. They called each other 'darling' and 'dearest,' respectively, in the presence of the dealer and gave the impression of being more or less genuine. This took place while Hitman Anders was hiding two blocks away with the vehicle that had nearly reached the end of its life. Without mushrooms, but with a Bible and a bottle of communion for company.

Both the priest and the receptionist fell for a Hobby 770 Sphinx. Not least because of the option for a *chambre séparée*.

The price, 660,000 kronor, was not an issue. Or, rather, it was.

'Cash?' said the dealer, looking discouraged.

This was the type of situation that brought out the best in the priest. She started by loosening the scarf that had hidden her clerical collar until that moment. And then she asked what was wrong with cash. The day before, the police had had to give back the very cash that *Hitman Anders* – God bless him! – had donated to the Red Cross and the Salvation Army.

The dealer was, of course, fully up to date on the

nation's number-one news story and hesitantly admitted that the priest had a point. But 660,000 kronor?

If he thought the amount was troublingly high, she was sure they could agree on a lower one. In which case the difference would, of course, be given in full to the international work done by the Church of Sweden. 'Which, incidentally, has no problem with cash payments. But if this dealership doesn't want to sell a vehicle to be used in our battle against hunger, I suppose we'll have to look elsewhere.'

The priest nodded in farewell, took her receptionist by the arm, and began to walk away.

Ten minutes later, all the paperwork was done. Priest and receptionist got into their new camper-van and drove away – upon which the receptionist was finally able to ask: 'Our battle against hunger?'

'I was improvising. Listen, I'm hungry. What do you say to the McDonald's drive-thru?'

* * *

Everyone who longed to meet the new national hero Hitman Anders (and that was a lot of people!) took an extra look each time an RV happened to pass. The more professionally inclined private investigators posed questions like: Was that a 2008 Elnagh Duke 310 that just drove by? And, if so, what kind of wheel rims did it have? Were they original or not?

The trio would shake off the pros by ditching the count's vehicle, and that was the next item on their agenda.

But for the blissfully ignorant a camper-van was a camper-van. Change of vehicle or no, the priest, the receptionist, and the people's hero would constantly be subjected to the eyes of curious citizens. Could Hitman Anders be seen in the front seat? Was that a woman (who, according to witness testimony, looked as women usually look) behind the wheel?

The only solution was to leave the count's camper-van behind and to do so as vociferously as possible. And, to be on the safe side, at a good distance from Borås.

After a drive through a fast-food joint followed by a trouble-free stop at Systembolaget and another at a service-station, to fuel both humans and vehicle, the journey continued on towards the north-east. The plan for the next day was locked, loaded, and ready to go.

Hitman Anders had been an endless nag ever since the Queen had suggested he give away another half-million kronor in Jesus's name. To the children this time! The priest and the receptionist had finally given in. Not so much for the children's sake, but because they could take the chance to make a scene when they left the count's camper-van behind. They could do it outside the headquarters of Save the Children in Sundbyberg, north of Stockholm.

After a number of run-throughs, Hitman Anders said he understood the plan. Three run-throughs later, the priest and the receptionist started to believe him. All that remained was the journey there.

The receptionist sat behind the wheel of the old camper-van; the priest was in the new one, with Hitman

Anders hidden behind the curtains in the company of his Bible.

Somewhere near the halfway point, the entourage stopped for the night. Hitman Anders snored in one vehicle; the priest and receptionist would soon do the same in the other, but first … Well, a couple had to cuddle when the opportunity arose.

* * *

One had to give Hitman Anders credit – he would sit for long periods, paging through his Bible. He especially liked to collect quotations that included examples of generosity. It had felt so good to give. And now he felt the same about the gratitude that washed over him via newspapers and social media.

Night became morning: time to cruise on towards Sundbyberg. The priest returned to the vehicle that contained Hitman Anders and found he was already awake, with his nose in Exodus.

'Good morning to you, Mini-Jesus. You haven't forgotten the plan, have you?'

'Just think how much of a beating that would have earned you only a few weeks ago,' said Hitman Anders. 'No, I haven't forgotten. But I want to write the letter to Save the Children myself.'

'Well, get to it, then. We have just a few hours to go. That book you're reading is several thousand years old, not likely to change.'

The priest was feeling annoyed for no reason. It was

no use provoking the saved man. It was just that … this was never the way it was supposed to turn out … The hitman wasn't supposed to be part of her life with the receptionist … and their little group was not supposed to be attracting the attention of Sweden and parts of the rest of the world.

But that was how it was. And she had to find her footing in this new situation. After all, there was some power to be found in the fact that the hitman had become a superstar and Scandinavia's most admired man of the moment. A power that could lead to something good – that is, money – in the priest and the receptionist's tiny personal war against humanity. Or whichever label one wanted to attach to their lifelong battle.

But every war (even those waged against existence as such) required soldiers to fight it. And soldiers were most useful if they were kept content.

'Sorry,' said the priest to Hitman Anders, who was already in the process of authoring his letter.

'Sorry for what?' he said, without looking up.

'Sorry I was so irritable,' said the priest.

'Were you?' said Hitman Anders. 'I finished my letter. Want to hear? "Dear Save the Children. In Jesus's name I want to give you five hundred thousand kronor so more children can get saved. Hallelujah! Exodus 21:2. Regards, Hitman Anders PS: Now I'll get in my red Volvo and drive away."'

The priest grabbed the hitman's Bible, looked up Exodus 21:2, and wondered what he was trying to get across with 'When you buy a male Hebrew slave, he shall serve for six years, but in the seventh he shall go out a free person, without debt.'

Hitman Anders said he had liked the part about being set free for free … Didn't the priest think there was something generous about that?

'After six years as a slave?'

'Yes?'

'No.'

The letter was more than a little stupid, but that wasn't a battle the priest wanted to fight. The part about the Volvo, Hitman Anders said, was a way to make people stop looking for him in a camper-van.

The priest said she'd understood that.

* * *

And then they arrived. The priest parked the count's camper-van at an angle, halfway up on the pavement, just outside the entrance to Save the Children on Landsvägen 39 in Sundbyberg. They left a parcel that said 'To Save the Children' in the driver's seat. Inside the package: Hitman Anders's letter, with 480,000 kronor (because he had miscounted).

While the priest and the receptionist waited around the corner with the camper-van that must not be linked to Hitman Anders at any price, the hitman walked through the doors, took the lift up, and was greeted by a friendly woman at the reception desk who didn't immediately recognize him.

'God's peace,' said Hitman Anders. 'They call me

Hitman Anders, although I'm not a hitman anymore and I don't do other stupid stuff either, at least not on purpose. Instead I hand out money to good causes in Jesus's name. I think Save the Children is a good cause. I want to give you half a million kronor … Well, actually, I want to give you more, but for now it's half a million and that's not exactly cat piss. Excuse my language. You learn so many bad words when you're inside. Where was I? Oh, yeah, the money's in a parcel in my camper-van, and it's parked outside … Well, it's not my camper-van. The name of the man who owns it is the count, no, it's not, but he's called the count, and you're welcome to give the camper-van back to him later on as long as you take the money out first. Well, I guess that's it. I wish you a blessed day in Jesus's name … Hosanna!'

With the concluding 'Hosanna!' Hitman Anders gave a pious smile and turned around to take the lift back down. All while the woman at the reception desk continued to not say a word.

Once he was out on the street, the hitman walked around the corner and was very thoroughly gone by the time the police's sniffer dog indicated, one and a half hours later, that the parcel in the front seat of the white camper-van outside the entrance to Save the Children was safe to open.

While the dog worked, the police tried to coax the bewildered woman into telling them what Hitman Anders had said beyond 'Hosanna'.

* * *

'Hitman Anders Strikes Again!' read one of the many headlines but, ambiguity notwithstanding, no one misunderstood the context. Everyone was in the know; everyone was aware that a killer was on the loose and that this killer handed out money to those in need instead of dispatching them.

Yet another PR success, with one minor flaw: Save the Children had received not the promised half-million kronor, but only 480,000. Oh, well, they were still happy.

The police's coaxing of the woman at the desk had brought results. After a few hours, she had managed to share just about everything Hitman Anders had told her. This included the nonsense about how the camper-van was owned by a count who wasn't a count. This information ended up in the newspapers as well, and led not only to the restoration of the camper-van to its owner (officially, it belonged to one of the countess's dealerships) but also to a literate civil servant with the Tax Authority, who was able to open a dormant tax case, find the count, and serve him a notice of unpaid back taxes for 1,064,000 kronor.

'We said we were going to carve him up slowly, from the bottom up, right?' said the count.

'Yes,' said his countess. 'Very slowly, please.'

* * *

Given the circumstances, the priest was satisfied with this development. While she, the receptionist, and their new Elvis continued to travel around in a camper-van (albeit of a different sort), all of the hero's fans were now looking for a red Volvo. What was more, a certain blogger in Hässleholm had completely lost her grip and gone to stand outside the local police station, shouting, 'A red Volvo! I told you I saw a red Volvo!' until she was chased off with the help of a dog.

At this point, as the priest saw it, they had two paths to choose from. One was that which they had already discussed: make sure to separate the priest, the receptionist, and the suitcases from the hitman and go up in smoke. That would be the most peaceful choice.

The other path was to reap the fruits of the hitman's enormous popularity. And the priest had thought of a way to make that happen.

'Start a church? And name it after Hitman Anders?' said the receptionist. 'The Church of Hitman Anders?'

'Yes. Or maybe we'll get rid of the "hitman" part. That could easily send the wrong signal,' said the priest.

'Why would we start a church? I thought your life – like my own – was based on hating as many people as possible as much as possible, including God, Jesus, and all of that.'

The priest muttered that it's difficult to hate what doesn't exist, but the receptionist was perfectly correct beyond that.

'But this is about running a business,' she said. 'Have you ever heard the word "collection"? Elvis is back. And he loves to give away money. Who doesn't want to be like Elvis?'

'Me?'

'Who else?'

'You?'

'Who else?'

'Not many people,' the receptionist admitted.

CHAPTER 27

Starting a church is not as simple as purchasing premises and unlocking the door. Not in Sweden. In the country that hasn't been at war for more than two hundred years, people have had plenty of time to think up regulations for most things of a peaceful nature. There are, for example, clear stipulations that must be followed by anyone who has experienced a divine revelation and wants to share it with others in an organized fashion.

The priest happened to know that the authority in charge of petitions to start a religious community was Kammarkollegiet, or the Legal, Financial, and Legislative Services Committee. Since she, the receptionist, and their intended religious leader had no address other than a camper-van, she chose to visit the committee in question, on Birger Jarlsgatan, in central Stockholm.

She nodded good morning, and said she wished to start a new faith community because she had seen the light.

The official at the committee, a man of upper middle age, had dealt with many seers of lights in his eighteen years at the same place of work, but he had never before had a customer come calling. 'All right,' he said. 'In that case, all you have to do is "see" a few forms and complete them in the appropriate manner. To which address may I send them?'

'Send?' said Johanna Kjellander. 'But I'm standing here among you, as the Lord almost puts it in Leviticus.'

The Kammarkollegiet official happened to be an organist in the Church of Sweden and had a good memory, so he was on the verge of responding that the same book said that a person who did not follow the statutes of God would be struck by terror, consumption, fever, and more besides. Blindness, if he remembered correctly.

The official's problem was that at no point had the Lord stipulated the necessary forms must be sent by mail, so now that a real live addressee was standing in front of him for the first time, he could hand them over in person.

As the official spent a brief moment reflecting on this, the priest (nimbly as ever) had time to switch to another angle of attack. 'I forgot to introduce myself,' she said. 'My name is Johanna Kjellander and I am a former parish priest. In my previous role, I was expected to serve as the congregation's bridge between the worldly and the heavenly, but all the while I was aware of my own inadequacy. Now I have found the bridge in question. The real one!'

The official did not allow himself to be carried away. Even if this was his debut for direct contact with an applicant, he had seen a lot over the years, including one group who wanted to register their belief that the root of all goodness could be found in a windmill in north-western Värmland. In fact, their last two members had frozen to death up there one winter, while the contents of the windmill had not intervened in the least.

The salient point about those frozen believers (before they froze, that is) was that they had statutes, a governing council, and clear objectives, like gathering for common prayer and meditation outside the windmill each Sunday at three p.m. Thus there was no reason to reject the sect's petition. Meditating each Sunday in zero-to-ten-degrees air and five feet of snow was religious enough.

The committee official decided that the rules allowed him not only to hand over the forms, which he had already pulled out, but to be helpful as well.

And thus he filled in everything that could be filled in for the former parish priest; he asked all the obligatory questions and made certain that they received proper answers. When it came to the name of the new religious community, the official informed the priest of the requirements. The name must differentiate the community's activities from those of others, and it must not be in poor taste or contrary to law and order.

'With that in mind, what would you like your religion to be called?'

'The Church of Anders. After our spiritual leader.'

'I see. What might his last name be?' asked the official, absently.

'His name isn't Anders, it's Johan. Johan Andersson.'

The official looked up from his forms. He read his evening tabloid each day on the way home from work, and this caused him to say spontaneously (and a mite unprofessionally): 'Hitman Anders?'

'He has been given that name in certain contexts. Beloved children have many names.'

The official cleared his throat and apologized for getting personal, then nodded and said that this was such a true observation, about beloved children and so on … Thereupon he informed her that it cost five hundred kronor to start the Church of Anders and he preferred payment via bank transfer.

The priest placed a five-hundred-krona note in his hand, yanked the stamped forms from his other hand, thanked him for the good service, and walked out to the waiting camper-van.

'Pastor Anders!' she said, as she climbed in. 'You need new clothes.'

'And a church,' said the receptionist.

'But how about some communion first?' said the pastor.

CHAPTER 28

All at once there was a lot to organize, and as soon as possible.

It fell to the priest to cobble together a powerful message and prepare Pastor Anders to make use of it. She considered this quite taxing, and said as much to her receptionist. At first he didn't understand. Surely it didn't matter what their superstar said, did it? As long as it sounded a little religious, which it usually did nowadays every time the hitman opened his trap. Elvis wants to give away money, and everyone wants to be like Elvis: wasn't that how the equation was supposed to work?

Yes, it was true that their plan was based on Hitman Anders's words filling the yellow and the red suitcases again, and with any luck the suitcases would be joined by another pair, whose colours were beside the point. But this could not be accomplished with a single crazy sermon. Rather, they needed an ongoing seemingly religious idea week after week. And this idea had to be based on something better than the pastor of the church standing in the pulpit alternately saying 'Hosanna' and bending down to take a gulp of wine. What was more, their project must not be too dependent on a single person.

'What do you mean? The Church of Anders without Anders?'

Pretty much.

'You're thinking of the count and the countess?'

'Yes. And close to twenty other gangsters with varying degrees of rank. There's no way for us to know whether it will take three minutes or three months for one of them to get him. But once it happens, he'll have preached his last.'

'And then what?'

'Our activities must go on, in the fond memory of our founder. There has to be a second well-prepared voice to take over once Pastor Anders is no longer with us. Someone who can grieve and remember along with the flock of the so tragically departed shepherd. Who can continue to bring in money in his honour, after his death.'

'You're talking about yourself now, right?' said the receptionist, who was starting to catch on.

The complication, for the priest, rested in which message she would be forced to inherit on the day Pastor Anders left his earthly life for a journey either upward or downward. Johanna Kjellander's fate in life was, once and for all, such that she would have an exceptionally difficult time returning to the pulpit even to pretend to carry on the Kjellander tradition. Truly, anything but that.

The receptionist felt he should not involve himself in details concerning the religious aspects of the church they had just started. He also understood the priest's dilemma, but he had to remind her that Jesus seemed to walk at

158

Hitman Anders's one side, and perhaps they couldn't place just anyone on the other.

The priest had already realized that Jesus had to be part of the plan in some fashion or another, no matter what else happened. This also went for communion, or an equivalent alcohol level in the blood of their preacher-in-chief.

The receptionist gave his priest a comforting hug and said that she would surely find a reasonable solution. Perhaps *with* Jesus but *without* the gospels?

'Hmm,' said the priest, thoughtfully. 'Everyone who searches finds. Matthew seven, verse eight.'

An overhaul of personal security was already high on the receptionist's to-do list. The priest's worries led him to do another lap of thinking. The truth was, they were about to expose not only Hitman Anders but also themselves to the sort of people who would rather see them all dead than anything else.

There was a risk that it would be a piece of cake to off Hitman Anders as he was preaching peace, joy and love. The pastor had already thought of that, and his death would be bad enough from a financial perspective. But, given their plan, the priest and the receptionist themselves would have to step out of the shadows, and there was no guarantee whatsoever that they would survive. If all three of them were to kick the bucket, it would be no exaggeration to say that their business plan didn't hold water. And they could hardly avoid such a development by sending apologetic postcards to counts, countesses, and other people they'd cheated.

'You're thinking a bodyguard, it seems,' said the priest.

'I *was* thinking a bodyguard,' said her receptionist. 'Now I'm thinking a team of bodyguards.'

The priest praised him for that and wished him luck as he strove to secure for them a long and preferably happy life. And she felt he might as well include Hitman Anders in this, as long as he remained financially relevant.

'But you'll have to excuse me now. I have a religion to make up, *with* Jesus but preferably *without* God,' she said, with a smile, then gave her receptionist a kiss on the cheek.

CHAPTER 29

Bodyguards, the right building, set up the bank transfer, telephones, phone numbers, email … The receptionist certainly had a lot on his plate. In his capacity as marketing manager, he was also thinking along the lines of Facebook, Twitter, Instagram …

Thus far, Facebook had not been his favourite scene. He had his own account, but he had only one friend, and that was his mother in Iceland; she had stopped responding to him some time ago.

There was no way for her son to know that she had moved and ended up in a barracks at the edge of Europe's largest glacier, Vatnajökull. This had occurred after the husband-slash-banker had made a serious blunder in Reykjavik and felt the need to escape to the ends of the world along with his still sufficiently attractive wife (if only she weren't so damned angry all the time). Her husband said it would be best to stay put until things cooled off in Reykjavik, London and, really, everywhere else. There was something about a statute of limitations, that everything would be fine as long as three years went by first.

'Three years?' said the receptionist's mother.

'Yes, or five. The legal situation is a touch unclear.'

The receptionist's mother asked herself what she had done with her life. 'I have removed myself to a barracks next to a glacier on an island where no one understands anything I say, even if I did come across someone to speak to. God! Why have you done this to me?'

It's not clear whether it was, in fact, God who answered. But after the despairing woman's question came a dull yet vigorous rumble. An earthquake. Right under the glacier.

'I'm afraid Bárðarbunga is waking up,' said her husband.

'Bardar who?' asked the wife, though she wasn't sure she wanted to know the answer.

'The volcano. It's four hundred metres below the ice. It's been dormant for a hundred years, so I imagine it's thoroughly rested …'

Since there wasn't any internet service in the receptionist's mother's barracks even before the volcanic eruption, the son had no contact with his sole Facebook friend. Thus he had limited experience of how the media platform worked, with sharing and all of that. But he quickly discovered that he had a talent for it:

Church of Anders
More blessed to give than to receive

A nice touch, if he said so himself. And an image of a backlit Hitman Anders, Bible and iPad in hand.

'What do I need this computer for?' the hitman had protested, when the picture was taken.

'It's not a computer, it's an iPad, and it's to contrast the old with the new. Our message is for everyone.'

'And what was it again?'

'That it's better to give than to receive.'

'So true, so true,' said Hitman Anders.

'Not really, but still,' said the receptionist.

As soon as the priest had put together the religious message to be preached, the receptionist could add the finishing touches. But he already disliked the 'Like' button, because it gave people the ability to give something a thumbs-up instead of going to the trouble of sending in a hundred-krona note. Or even a twenty.

Finding a location was another concern. The receptionist searched for hangars, barns, warehouses, and all sorts of places before he realized he didn't need a sledgehammer to swat a fly.

All they had to do was buy a church.

There had been a time when the Evangelical Lutheran State Church ruled supreme in Sweden. It was forbidden to believe in anything else, it was forbidden to believe in nothing at all, and it was forbidden to believe in the right God in the wrong way.

The Church was at its nadir in the eighteenth century, but it was challenged now and again by a Pietist who, with inspiration from horrid foreign lands, believed that a person ought to be allowed to experience a bit of *enthusiasm* about religious life, something more than just the cut-and-dried Lutheran ways.

Enthusiasm? The State Church made sure to have

anyone whose beliefs were right but wrong arrested and sentenced before things got out of hand.

Most of them apologized and got off lightly in that they were merely deported. But now and again someone stood his ground. The most stubborn of these was named Thomas Leopold. Instead of falling into line, he said a prayer for the judge in the courtroom, thus annoying the judge to such an extent that Leopold received seven years' imprisonment in Bohus Fortress.

When even that did not cause Pietist Leopold to give in, they added five years at Kalmar Fortress, and then just as long at Danviken Hospital.

After seventeen years, one might think that Leopold would have softened around the edges, but no such luck.

All they could do was give up. He was sent back to Bohus, locked up in the cell where his prison journey had begun, and then they threw away the key.

It was twenty-six more fretful years before Thomas Leopold finally had the good sense to die, at the age of seventy-seven. It certainly was a sad story, but it demonstrated the resolve of the State Church. Order and discipline, services on Sunday.

But the severe eighteenth century turned into a significantly milder nineteenth. A few free churches were allowed to exist for real, not just in secret. And then came misery upon misery: the Freedom of Religion Act in 1951 and the separation of Church and State fifty years later.

So, there had been a time when you would get forty-three years in prison (before you died and were carried off) because you didn't believe in the correct thing. Just two hundred and fifty years later, five thousand Swedes left the State Church each month with not so much as a parking ticket in punishment. They could go wherever they liked, or nowhere; this was guaranteed by law. Those who remained attended Sunday services not because they didn't dare do otherwise, but because they really and truly wanted to. Or, like most people, they didn't go.

Congregations merged at the same rate as they shrank. The consequences of the eighteenth century becoming the twentieth meant, in the end, that empty churches stood all over the proud kingdom of Sweden, and fell into ruin, unless great investments kept them in good order.

Of course, large amounts of money was something the Church of Sweden did possess. Its cumulative capital lay somewhere just short of seven billion kronor. But the annual dividends brought a ridiculously low three per cent, since for many years the Church had virtuously (and a little reluctantly) refused to invest in oil, tobacco, alcohol, bombers, or tanks. A portion of that three per cent was reinvested in the Church's own operations, but if it's raining on the priest that doesn't mean the bell-ringer will get wet. Or, translated loosely: the individual congregations were often on their last legs. Anyone who looked one of these up and offered a bag containing three million kronor in cash in exchange for taking over a church building that was nothing but a boarded-up money pit – that person would find an audience.

'Three million?' said the Reverend Mr Granlund, who suddenly realized all the lovely things he could do with that money in the parish's main church, which was also in need of sprucing up.

Sure, the asking price was set at 4.9 million, but the building had already been for sale for more than two years with no interested parties.

'Did you say the Church of Anders?' wondered Granlund.

'Yes, after our main pastor, Johan Andersson. A fantastic life story. Truly a miracle of God,' said the receptionist, thinking that if God did exist he would probably aim a bolt of lightning down at his head any second now.

'Yes, I've been following that in the papers,' said the cleric. He was thinking that there would be advantages to having another Christian community take over. It was, after all, a holy building, and in this way it could continue to be so.

Granlund obtained full negotiation rights from his congregation and decided to accept the three million. The church building was of considerable size; it had passed its best-before date about a hundred years earlier; it was far too close to European Highway 18, and it had a cemetery scattered with gravestones, all at least fifty years old. Granlund thought about the graves and how lucky it was that no one had been buried there for so long. How restful could it be to have your final resting place right next to one of Sweden's most heavily trafficked main roads?

And yet he happened to bring up the matter of gravestones with his potential buyers. 'Do you intend to respect the peace of the burial grounds?' he wondered, well aware that there were no legal restrictions on doing the exact opposite.

'Of course,' said the receptionist. 'We won't dig up a single grave. We're just going to even it out a little on top and put down some asphalt.'

'Asphalt?'

'Car park. Shall we settle this now? A speedy deal: we get access on Monday, and cash in hand for you now as long as I can have a receipt.'

Granlund regretted asking about the gravestones and decided to pretend he hadn't heard the answer. He extended his hand. 'Deal,' he said. 'Mr Persson, you've got yourself a church.'

'Lovely,' said Per Persson. 'I don't suppose you'd consider joining our faith, sir? It would be quite a feather in our cap. We'll throw in a free parking space if you like.'

Granlund had the feeling he was bringing misfortune upon the building he had just unloaded. He and the congregation most assuredly did need the three million kronor. But that didn't mean they had to suck up to the buyer. 'Get out of here, Persson, before I change my mind,' he said.

CHAPTER 30

And then there was the bodyguard issue.

Although the receptionist had spent his entire adult life surrounded by hooligans big and small, he felt inadequate when it came to contacts in the underworld. Because, after all, that was probably the best place to find their security team. The sort of people who would lash out if the count, the countess, and the likes of them popped up. Not the sort of people who would ask questions first or try to talk sense into them.

One person who had spent plenty of time inside was, of course, Pastor Anders. The receptionist asked him to think about it, and the pastor thought until his brain creaked. Unfortunately his brain creaked rather early on so he, too, failed to come up with a good security solution. On the other hand, he provided the interesting reflection that an awful lot of his fellow prison buddies had experience of working as bouncers in bars.

'Well, well,' said the receptionist. 'Do you know any of their names?'

'Yes ... Holmlund,' Pastor Anders mused. 'And Moose ...'

'Moose?'

'Well, people call him Moose. His real name is different.'

'I had a feeling that might be the case. Can we give Moose a tinkle?'

'Nope. He's in. For a long time. Homicide.'

'What about Holmlund?'

'He's the one Moose offed.'

The receptionist's mood soon improved: Pastor Anders was able to point out the two or three gyms in Greater Stockholm that were most commonly frequented by customers of the bouncer/ex-con variety. The receptionist called Taxi Torsten (to avoid driving around in a campervan) and went from gym to gym on the hunt for an entry point to the force in question.

He didn't find what he was looking for at the first or the second. After all, he couldn't walk up to just anyone and ask if he had been a bouncer and also spent time inside. By the time he got to the third gym, he was starting to despair. In contrast to the first two, it boasted a man here and there who looked sufficiently bouncer-like, and who might well have stood outside a bar, freezing his arse off. But, of course, it was impossible to tell who might have been locked up for something extremely violent, and who wouldn't hesitate to act in an acute situation.

Taxi Torsten had followed him into the third gym without being asked; it was so damn boring to wait in the car.

He had gained a rough insight into the problem during the drive, so he made himself useful. He walked up to the youngster at the desk, introduced himself as Taxi Torsten, and said: 'Who would you say we shouldn't start something with, out of all your guests here today?'

The youngster looked at Taxi Torsten. 'Taxi Torsten?' he said, instead of answering the question.

'Yes, that's me. But who should we definitely not start something with?'

'Are you here to start something?' said the youngster.

'No, far from it! That's why we want to know who we absolutely should not provoke, so that our visit doesn't go wrong.'

The youngster appeared to want to escape from both conversation and locale. He didn't know what to say or do, but at last he pointed out a tall and heavily tattooed man in a preacher curl machine across the room. 'He's called Jerry the Knife. I don't know why and I want it to stay that way. But I have noticed that everyone else is afraid of him.'

'Excellent!' said the receptionist. 'Jerry the Knife, you say? Great name!' The receptionist thanked him for his help and indicated to Taxi Torsten that he had conducted himself admirably but should go now and wait at the entrance. This was something for Per Persson and Jerry the Knife to deal with privately.

The receptionist waited until Jerry the Knife took a break from working his biceps. 'I understand you're Jerry the Knife?'

Jerry the Knife looked cautiously but not angrily at Per Persson. 'I'm Jerry No Knife at the moment,' he said. 'But things could still go poorly for you, depending on what you want from me.'

'Super!' said the receptionist. 'My name is Per Persson and I represent a gentleman called Hitman Anders. Perhaps you've heard of him.'

Jerry the Knife was having a difficult time maintaining his generally surly and uninterested expression, because this conversation was becoming both unusual and exciting. Where might it lead?

'Hitman Anders, that guy who got Jesus … and a bunch of enemies to boot,' Jerry the Knife reflected.

'I hope you're not one of them …?' said the receptionist.

No, Jerry the Knife had no bone to pick with Hitman Anders. They had never met, never been in the same prison at the same time. But it stood to reason that there were other people after him. Not least that count and his crazy old lady.

Yes, that was just it. Hitman Anders was embarking on a new career as the preacher of his own church. That sort of thing required a certain level of investment and it would be too bad if he suddenly had to meet his maker much earlier than anyone had budgeted for. That was why Per Persson was currently troubling Mr Jerry, knife or no. In short, might Mr Jerry consider taking on the mission of keeping Hitman Anders alive for as long as possible? And while he was at it, he might do the same for Per Persson and a priest named Johanna Kjellander. 'A delightful woman, incidentally.'

Jerry the Knife noted that Per Persson's relationship to Hitman Anders was of a businesslike nature and appeared to be sound. He himself was employed as a doorman at a relatively dull spot in the city and would be happy to trade it in for a new job. He identified his role in the situation as 'no coward'; he could probably stare down the count in his sleep. What did Per Persson have in mind for terms of employment?

Per Persson had not completely thought through the issue of bodyguards. He had approached the task of finding an 'in' to the world where bodyguards could be sourced with a certain amount of desperation. And now, partly thanks to Taxi Torsten of all people, he was standing across from Jerry the Knife – about whom he knew no more than that he had a decent vocabulary and the ability to express himself, and that he seemed impressively calm as he looked forward to protecting Hitman Anders from the count and the countess, the *hoi* and the *polloi*.

Time was of the essence. Without consulting his dear priest, he decided that Jerry the Knife was just the man they were looking for.

'I'm offering you a job as head of the security team you will create and have ready to go as soon as possible. Your recruits will be paid handsomely, and you'll get double that. If you accept the offer, my last question is, when can you start?'

'Not immediately,' said Jerry the Knife. 'I have to shower first.'

CHAPTER 31

Now they had permission to start a faith community, they had a church (paving of the cemetery was under way), they had a pastor and a reserve pastor, and they had a security team under construction. They also had an immediate threat, primarily thanks to the count and countess. Beyond that, the priest had misgivings; they still didn't have a clear, alternative religious message.

She would have liked very much to take a step, or several steps, back from the teachings of evangelism. To mix the blood of Jesus with fresh blood from somewhere else. Like Muhammad, for example. The priest knew her stuff. His real name was al-Amin – the trustworthy. And he was called Mustafa – the chosen one. There was something nice about the thought of a prophet of God, rather than the idea that God himself got Mary pregnant while poor Joseph stood by and watched.

But Jesus and Muhammad on either side of Hitman Anders – no, that would never work. It was as hopeless as another of the priest's ideas: running God and Jesus parallel with Scientology. The latter involved a method of spiritual rehabilitation to fix nearly everything, and that was the sort of plan a person could make good money on. *For one thousand kronor we will liberate your thoughts. For five thousand we will think for you.* Or something along those lines.

It was just that the Scientologists drove a hard line about aliens and other weird stuff. Even if Jesus could, in some respects, be seen as an alien, these were two faiths that would be difficult to adapt to one another. The most difficult part might be the age of the Earth: six thousand years, according to the Bible; at least four billion, according to Scientology. Even if they met halfway, the Biblical genealogies would have to be extended by two billion years, and who had time to do that?

In truth, she had known it all along: she was stuck with the Bible Hitman Anders had embraced and now guarded so tenderly. Since the Church of Anders was primarily, secondarily and tertiarily a commercial enterprise, the pastor decided to grin and bear it. After all, Christianity continued to be fairly widespread in Sweden. It wouldn't be a great leap for those who wanted to upgrade to the Church of Anders. The distinguishing feature of the Church would be that they had a superstar in the pulpit (as long as they could keep him alive), and that the pastor made sure to pan every grain of gold out of the Bible so that he could implement them properly.

Johanna Kjellander's personal favourite was the one Matthew had made up about the Good Samaritan. It was a story with strains of the Acts' 'more blessed to give …' and so forth, but with the humorous twist that Matthew, after his own death, became a saint within the Roman Catholic Church and had, ever since, been working as the patron saint of tax collectors and customs officials.

There was a lot to choose from in Proverbs, too. That things go poorly for he who is stingy, that he who gives his money to Pastor Anders instead will flourish like green leaves and a number of other things. Of course it didn't literally say 'Pastor Anders', but that would be a simple matter to twist around. But it was too bad that Proverbs was in the Old Testament. It meant she would have to bring that whole book into the package.

The priest had finished working on her plan. The Church of Anders would be a stronghold of generosity, with Jesus as a hostage and God the Father as an underlying threat for the very stingiest members of the congregation.

According to the receptionist's calculations, five per cent of the proceeds should go to Hitman Anders, five per cent to the security team, five per cent to general expenses, and five per cent to the needy. That left just eighty per cent for the priest and the receptionist, but they would have to settle for it. If they let greed get its claws into them, their venture might end poorly. Furthermore, of course, the hitman's share would be freed up in the instant he took a bullet between the eyes.

And, as Scripture so consolingly said, a generous person will be enriched.

* * *

As weeks went by, the interest in Sweden's, and perhaps Europe's, most interesting person died away. Initially, at least 150,000 kronor poured in each day via Facebook and the bank deposit account the receptionist had so hastily set up. But that amount was soon halved, and halved again a few days later. People forgot so damn fast.

Before all the pieces were in place, the number of donations to the glorified hitman had sunk to nearly zero. This made the receptionist, in charge of the budget, nervous. What if no one came, what if the priest and the receptionist had to sit there all by themselves and place their last few coins in the collection box while the hitman preached God knew what?

The priest was more relaxed. She smiled at her receptionist and said that faith could move mountains this way and that in the Bible and that now was not the time to lose their own. She was about to start a week-long course in preaching methods with the pastor. Meanwhile, it would be great if the receptionist made sure that Jerry the Knife and his recruits polished their procedures so that her work would not suddenly be in vain.

Speaking of which, Jerry the Knife had brought up a complaint. He wasn't happy that the church had no second way of egress in the event that the pastor was attacked as he stood in the pulpit. Any old burglar knew that you needed at least two escape routes in case of unexpected company. During a job. As a thief, that is. Or, in this case, as a pastor.

'Basically, Jerry's argument involves getting a tradesman to knock a hole in the wall to the sacristy. I said I'd take it up with you first, but … well, it's a holy room in a holy building, so I'm not sure how …'

'I'm sure a holy hole in the wall will fit in just fine,' said the priest. 'A sacristy with an emergency exit. The head of the fire brigade would love us if he knew about it.'

* * *

The priest grilled Hitman Anders endlessly for six days in a row.

'I think he's ready now,' she said on the seventh. 'As ready as he'll ever be …'

'And the security team is on the ball,' the receptionist replied. 'Jerry the Knife put together a great gang. I hardly dare to walk into the church without showing ID.'

Speaking of which, Per Persson reiterated his fear that their generous hitman was about to sink into oblivion just as they were finally prepared to act.

'But there is something we can do about that,' said the priest, looking all Mona Lisa-like again.

She'd had an idea.

Wrong. She'd had two ideas.

The receptionist smiled back without knowing what she had up her sleeve. At this point, he had the greatest faith imaginable in her creative abilities. He felt like an Excel spreadsheet in comparison.

'You're much more than that, my darling,' said the priest, with more sincerity in her voice than she'd thought she had in her.

The receptionist was so inspired by her loving words that he found himself suggesting a little hanky-panky out of sheer momentum.

'But where?' the priest wondered, without a note of hesitation.

Right, dammit. They couldn't live in a camper-van with Hitman Anders for the rest of their lives. They still had to sort out the housing situation. For hitmen and good honest people.

'Behind the organ?' he suggested.

CHAPTER 32

It was surprisingly easy to get Hitman Anders to understand what he was supposed to say to the journalist and why. What was more, he even said what he was supposed to, plus a little nonsense too, but that was just how it went with him. Every time he was about to start saying something truly crazy, Johanna Kjellander had time to interrupt and supply her own version of matters.

The Express had sent the same reporter and photographer as they had two and a half years earlier. They arrived just two hours after they were offered an exclusive interview with the hitman who had found Jesus and was now about to start a church. Neither of them looked anywhere near as nervous this time.

During the interview, Hitman Anders expounded upon the glory in giving rather than taking, even though he admitted that he and no one else had cheated parts of the underworld out of money. And that it had happened in the second most ghastly way possible.

'*Second* most?' the reporter wondered.

Well, in many cases the criminals had commissioned straight-out contract killings, and paid in advance. The only way this could be more ghastly was if the murders had actually been committed. But, of course, they never were. The money meant for that purpose had instead been handed out to the needy, while the murderer who had quit murdering hadn't kept a single öre for himself (except for a few comparatively minor expenditures in the form of communion wine and ... communion wine). Incidentally, more donations were pending!

As luck would have it, the reporter asked for the names of those who had contracted Hitman Anders for hits. That gave the him the chance to remember to say that he didn't want to say, because he prayed for them every night and would welcome them into the fold of his newly formed church, where he promised to introduce them to Jesus Christ, who, in turn, would take them into his arms.

'Hallelujah! Hosanna! Oh, me, oh, my,' Pastor Anders exclaimed, raising both hands to Heaven, upon which he received an elbow in the side from the priest.

This was no time to go off the rails: one crucial item remained. Hitman Anders seemed to have forgotten what it was. The priest had to remind him. 'And also you have taken certain measures,' she said.

'I have?' Hitman Anders asked, lowering his arms. 'Yes, I have! I have made sure that the names of all those who commissioned murders and broken limbs will be made public, along with evidence, in case I'm run over in the street or shot in the forehead or found hanged in an apparent suicide, or if I should happen to depart this life prematurely in any other way.'

'You mean if you die, the world will know who hired you as a hitman once upon a time and ... Will we also learn who the intended victims were?'

'Of course! In Heaven we have no secrets from one another.'

The priest thought that the hitman was expressing himself in such a nutty fashion that it almost sounded good. And *The Express*'s reporter continued to appear interested.

'So you're afraid that the underworld is out to get you?'

'Oh, no,' said Hitman Anders. 'I can sense inside me that they're all about to become converts. Jesus's love can reach everyone. There is enough for everyone! But if the devil is still riding any one of them, it is important for society … something. Hosanna!'

And with that, everything worth saying had been said. The priest thanked the newspaper for their time, but now Pastor Anders had to prepare for his first sermon. 'Which is coming up on Saturday, by the way. It will start at five p.m. Free parking and free coffee for all!'

The plan to meet the press again had been two-pronged. It was important, of course, to advertise the Church of Anders before the première. But in addition, the count, the countess, and the rest of the hooligans would learn just what they were in for if they harmed a hair of the priest and the receptionist's pastor.

It was a good plan.

But not good enough.

Because the count and the countess were even angrier than anyone would have thought.

CHAPTER 33

'He's a clever bastard, that one,' the countess muttered, tossing aside the following day's issue of *The Express*.

'No. I've known him for almost forty years,' said the count, 'and clever is the last thing he is. He has someone doing his thinking for him.'

'The priest?' said the countess.

'Yes. Johanna Kjellander, according to the paper. And that car thief at her side. Per Jansson, if I remember correctly. I ought to have cut off his dick after all. Although it's not too late yet.'

The count and the countess had more authority than anyone else in the darker circles of Greater Stockholm. If anyone were to call for a joint initiative among the more important hoodlums in the capital, it would be the two 'nobles' who did the inviting. And that was just what they did.

* * *

Sweden's first and largest general meeting of the criminal element was held in the count and countess's half-empty car dealership, the one in Haninge.

They'd had an extra good sales week at that location. Any illegally imported, collision-damaged vehicle can be made to look new with a few tricks of the trade. The count and countess did not feel obliged to report what any given vehicle had experienced earlier in its life, or how it was feeling deep down inside. And, after all, cars can't talk, except in the movies.

Ten units of this illegal sort had rolled out of the showroom in the past few days, all for just under sticker price. On none did the airbags work as advertised, but that didn't matter as long as their new owners had the good sense to stick to the road.

A good week, on the whole, if it hadn't been for the reason behind the general meeting they were about to hold.

Incidentally, putting together a relevant list of participants had also taken a few tricks of the trade. After all, there wasn't a master list of who had contracted to have his nearest and dearest maimed or murdered. The notice had to go out by word of mouth via four carefully chosen pubs.

The result was that seventeen men came to the car showroom at the prescribed time, in addition to the count and the countess, who were standing on a podium at the very front.

The podium was actually meant for the finest car in the showroom, but that car had just been sold to the tune of a kilo of top-shelf methamphetamine. It had left behind an excellent stage for the couple, who liked to emphasize that they were a cut above all the others.

The count was second-angriest; the countess was angriest. The latter called the meeting to order. 'As I see it, the question is not "Will Hitman Anders be allowed to live?" it's "How will we see to it that he dies?" The count and I have a few ideas.'

A number of the seventeen men at the foot of the podium squirmed. It was just that the contracts that had been made would become public knowledge if the killer who refused to kill got the treatment he deserved. One of the seventeen even dared to argue along those lines (as it happened, he had paid dearly to be rid of both the count and the countess). He took the floor and said that the elimination of Hitman Anders might lead to an out-and-out bloodbath in the capital city, and it would be better if they just kept to business as usual without too much infighting.

The count objected, saying it was not in his nature to allow himself to be blackmailed. What he *didn't* say was that he and the countess had succeeded – all on their own – in doing away with the two business competitors whom Hitman Anders and his sidekicks had not offed but had taken payment from, in the form of both money and camper-van.

But then another of the seventeen dared to agree with the first man. He hadn't been able to afford to off both the count and the countess; he'd settled for the countess, who in his opinion was the more destructive and unpredictable of the two. He, too, out of sheer survival instinct, had reason to wish Hitman Anders a long life.

A third had paid to have a cousin of the count fall victim to aggravated assault, and that was bad enough. Several other members of the group had taken out contracts of varying degrees against at least eight others in the same group. If any one of them could be called innocent, in a limited sense, it was only because he didn't have enough money to make himself guiltier than he was.

The count and the countess were feared by all. But seventeen strong men at the foot of the podium found the courage, at last, to resist. All of them insisted that it would be best for business to forget about it. Revenge stood in direct opposition to the current working environment. And the working environment was more important.

The countess swore at the seventeen men, calling them spineless insects and other unpleasant things, and making some of them long to be able to pay Hitman Anders once more, as long as he would finish the job this time.

One of the seventeen, however, was pondering whether it wasn't the case that all insects are *de facto* without spines, but he had enough sense not to bring up the matter just then.

The meeting was over in less than twenty minutes. All the big- and small-time scoundrels involved had had a representative on site. The only one who was missing was the man who'd paid 800,000 kronor to have his neighbour put to death because said neighbour had made a face at his wife. The vengeful and soon destitute man had taken his own life after his wife had left him for the far-too-alive neighbour, with whom she even travelled to the

Canary Islands, for the dubious face-making had in fact been a sophisticated form of flirtation.

End result: Hitman Anders would be allowed to remain alive, according to seventeen out of nineteen still-living defrauded defrauders. And he would die, preferably along with Johanna Kjellander and Per Jansson, or maybe Persson, according to the two others.

CHAPTER 34

Two days before the formal opening of the Church of Anders, it was time to launch the latest priestly idea – that is, another donation with national uproar as the intended consequence. Taxi Torsten behind the wheel, the priest, the receptionist, and Hitman Anders in a row in the back seat: In the lap of the latter, a carefully wrapped package containing 500,000 kronor and a personal greeting to the recipient.

The tourist season hadn't yet arrived but the area surrounding the palace in Stockholm is never completely deserted. Above all, the main guard is always standing there, and has been doing so uninterrupted since 1523 (it's not always the same guard, and one has to imagine that the guards were allowed a break when the palace burned down around the turn of the eighteenth century and wasn't rebuilt until fifty years later).

Taxi Torsten was a creative motorist. He veered off Slottsbacken, drove up onto the cobblestones, and slowly cruised up to the soldier who was standing at attention in his dapper dress uniform, a gleaming bayonet on his rifle.

Hitman Anders stepped out and held up his parcel. 'Good day,' he said solemnly. 'I am Hitman Anders and I am here to hand over half a million glorious kronor to Her Majesty the Queen and her World Child … something … Foundation. I've forgotten the name even though we recited it all the way here in the car from … Well, it doesn't matter where we came from. The long and the short of it is that …'

'Just hand over the parcel,' the receptionist shouted from the car.

But that was easier said than done. The soldier did not accept suspicious parcels. But he did press his panic button and start to recite a memorized statement: 'He who desires admittance to protected property or who loiters in the vicinity of protected property is bound by law to state his name, birthdate and place of residence upon the request of any guard who protects said property, and must submit to a bodily search from which letters or other private documents are exempt, and must submit to a search of any vehicle, ship or aircraft.'

Hitman Anders stood there with his parcel and stared wide-eyed at the soldier. 'Are you feeling okay?' he said. 'Can't you just accept this damn thing in the name of Jesus so we can get out of here?'

The soldier at the sentry box took another breath. 'In order to ensure that his task is properly executed, the guard of a protected property may also, to the extent necessary, refuse entry, remove or, if these are not sufficient, temporarily detain a person within or in the vicinity of the protected property …'

'Well, you can *try* to detain me, you fucking tin soldier,' Hitman Anders said angrily, as the terrified guard continued with his lesson: '... if the person in question infringes any prohibition that is in effect based on any decision according to this law, refuses to give information upon request, or gives information that can reasonably be assumed to be false, refuses to submit to a bodily search, or ...'

That was about when Hitman Anders shoved the silly soldier aside and placed his parcel in the sentry box. 'Now you make sure that this gets to the Queen,' he said to the soldier, who had tumbled onto his bottom. 'You're welcome to give it a body-search if you must, but don't you touch the money, or else!'

Then Hitman Anders returned to the priest, the receptionist, and Taxi Torsten, who managed to disappear into the traffic along Skeppsbron just seconds before the fallen soldier's backup arrived from the other direction.

* * *

At first it was said that Hitman Anders had 'attacked the palace', but only until the Queen held a press conference in which she thanked him for the fantastic (and X-rayed) gift of 494,000 kronor for children in need by way of the World Childhood Foundation.

'When are you planning to learn to count to five hundred?' the receptionist asked Hitman Anders, who chose to look surly instead of responding.

The publicity had been unparalleled, with a first wave of references to a potentially threatening situation, a second wave in which the Queen herself cleared up the matter, and a third wave in the form of a complete recap of the unique life story of Johan Andersson, a.k.a. Hitman Anders, a.k.a. Pastor Anders. 'Or should I call myself Reverend?' he wondered.

'No,' said the priest.

'Why not?'

'Because I said so.'

'How about Dean?'

CHAPTER 35

It certainly was a tall order for Jerry the Knife to convince his team of bodyguards that they should not resemble the country's most dangerous motorcycle gang, bearing leather jackets, brass knuckles, and fully visible thirty-five-thousand-krona Soviet Avtomat Kalashnikova model 47s obtained via what was easily the nation's least trustworthy weapons dealer.

Instead, chinos and jackets were the order of the day – garments the majority of the bodyguards hadn't worn since the graduation none of them had actually had. Where appropriate, machine-guns should be kept hidden under a light overcoat and the American hand grenades tidily placed in each jacket pocket.

'We are here to take out the hostile element,' explained Jerry the Knife, 'not to scare off good, honest visitors.'

The most expensive investment had been a metal detector for the entrance. The biggest advantage in Jerry the Knife's opinion was that he could make sure no weapons were smuggled in. The priest and the receptionist realized that in time, with the help of the metal detector and hidden cameras, they would learn who had coins to put in the collection plate and who had notes. They had no intention of wasting church space on people who wanted spiritual care but weren't prepared to pay for it.

The cemetery had been transformed into a car park with space for five hundred vehicles. Under the asphalt lay an unknown number of the dead, dating from 1800 to 1950. No one inquired what these souls might think of the paving; the souls in question made no noise about it.

If the car park filled, that would surely mean a thousand visitors, but the church, while certainly ample in size, could seat no more than eight hundred. So the receptionist had a giant screen installed outside, with a sound system of such quality, for such a price, that he came down with stomach-ache. The screen arrived on the morning that the first sermon was to be preached. The installation was paid in cash. All that remained of what had once been a fortune was in the two suitcases.

'Don't worry!' said the priest. 'Remember that faith can move mountains, both in the Bible and outside it.'

'Outside it?'

Why, yes. During her theological studies, the priest had become engrossed in alternative theories, beyond Genesis, where God whips up both Heaven and Earth in just a few days. Another truth one could choose to believe in was what they called Pangaea, the supercontinent that broke itself apart and formed all the current-day continents, mountains, valleys, and so on. Maybe because someone believed in it hard enough – who was the priest to judge?

The priest's calm made the receptionist feel calmer as well. The state of affairs was such that soon the yellow and the red suitcases would likely be filled to the brim again with money. What did it matter if the priest's faith moved a mountain or two at the same time? And she could decide for herself whence she gathered that faith.

'Then I will go with the Bible just this once. Solely to save time. God took a week. Pangaea slid apart over thousands of millions of years, and I can't tolerate Hitman Anders, camper-vans, and all the rest of it for that long.'

'All the rest of it? Not even me?' wondered the receptionist.

'For a thousand million years? Well, maybe.'

* * *

There were just hours left until Hitman Anders's première. Jerry the Knife stood on a small rise in the north-western corner of the churchyard and swept his eyes left to right and back again. Everything seemed nice and calm.

But what was that on the gravel path? An old man with a rake! A threat? It looked like he was doing what people usually do with rakes.

He was raking.

Was he planning to do the entire path, all the way from the road to the church porch?

'We have a problem at the end of the gravel path,' he informed his staff, via the communication equipment, which hadn't exactly been free either.

'Should I waste him?' wondered the sniper in the bell tower.

'No, you idiot,' said Jerry the Knife. 'I'll go and find out who he is.'

The old man was still raking. Jerry clasped his favourite knife in his jacket pocket. He introduced himself as the head of security with the Church of Anders and asked who the man was and what he was doing.

'I'm raking the path,' said the old man.

'Yes, so I see,' said Jerry the Knife. 'But who asked you to do it?'

'Asked me? I've raked this path before each service for the last thirty years, once a week, except it's been less frequent for the past two years, ever since the ungodly decision to shut down this house of God.'

'Blast it all,' said Jerry the Knife, who had been practising for several days to avoid using swear words at his new job. 'My name is Jerry,' he said, letting go of the knife to shake hands with the old man.

'Börje Ekman,' said the raking man. 'Churchwarden Börje Ekman.'

CHAPTER 36

Churchwarden Börje Ekman did not believe in luck, good or bad. He didn't believe in anything beyond himself, God, Jesus, and rules and regulations. But an outsider, a not particularly religion-inclined observer, would likely say that his coming encounter with Hitman Anders was unlucky.

The man who had reason to wish for his life to take a different direction from the one it was about to take had, until the day before, been a civil servant in the Ministry of Labour. Forty years at the same workplace, although it had changed names a few times. He had undertaken the work as churchwarden for what had now become the Church of Anders on a voluntary basis, in the hopes of sitting well in the eyes of St Peter on Judgement Day.

For the past three decades, the ever more disillusioned man had merely been serving out his time at the ministry. Things had been different in his early years. Back then he'd worked for his salary. And that wasn't all. He'd waged an out-and-out war against the Wild West attitude that prevailed in at least one of the departments Börje Ekman's ministry was in charge of. Börje discovered that agents at the employment agency regularly left the office at irregular intervals to wander aimlessly about the city on the hunt for available jobs to be the agent of. This they called going out to 'meet employers', to 'make connections', to 'build trust'.

According to the young Börje Ekman, this roll-up-your-sleeves strategy was thoroughly vile. Just think of the risk: with no one sent out to check on him, an agent might visit an establishment to have a beer.

Alcohol. During working hours. My God!

Börje Ekman would have preferred the employment agency to be so perfectly structured that unemployment in the country could be described in detail: age, sex, trade, demography, education, almost down to the individual. Making that happen required clear organization; a hierarchical structure without internal tension or conflict. The employment agency would become the perfect workplace. In the long run, this would lead to a completely predictable result. For Börje Ekman, it had been a joy to think about.

But as long as the agents were running around looking for available jobs, it would be impossible to control the results. At one time an agent in Täby had become so friendly with an executive that he had managed to convince the man in question to add an extra shift to his business, which had created eighty new jobs in the community, a nightmare for any employment analyst. There were no columns to calculate the results that might be achieved between businessmen and employment agents in the sauna or after a round of golf (which the employment agent in question would lose on purpose, even if it sometimes took double strokes into the water hazard on the eighteenth hole).

Börje Ekman was not so stupid that he didn't understand that eighty jobs were eighty jobs, no matter how they had arisen. But there was always the bigger picture to consider. Because what the employment agent in question had done, besides play golf during working hours, was overlook the administrative side of things. Thanks to a single employment agent, that quarter's statistics ended up skewed and incomplete for the entire northern district of Greater Stockholm. What was more, the agent had refused to certify the activity reports of the eighty formerly unemployed persons.

'Grunt work,' he'd said to Börje Ekman. 'I can't spend weeks sorting through papers about people who already have jobs, can I?' And then he'd hung up, before going out to golf his way to seven new jobs in the plumbing and HVAC industries.

Those were, however, the last things he did before being fired for refusal to work and for a few other infractions that Börje Ekman had been forced to make up to get the guy off his back. In some ways it was too bad, because the man was fantastic at arranging new jobs. And he'd done so right up to the end, because the result of his dismissal was the opening of a new opportunity at the employment agency's Täby offices. Börje Ekman immediately pulled enough strings to make sure that the man's replacement had a different perspective. Above all, structure and statistics, so the politicians could clearly see what the employment market looked like. With madcaps like the man who had just been let go, the risk was close to one hundred per cent that the quarterly prognoses did not reflect reality. The political opposition *loved* prognostication errors, so they were the worst thing a civil servant could spend his time on.

Now, it goes without saying that a written prognosis cannot adapt itself to reality, for the simple reason that it has already been written down. Thus reality must adapt itself to the prognosis. For Börje Ekman, this was a truth that applied to all situations except the weather. That was something the Lord ruled with an extra-steady hand, to the presumed despair of the prognosticators at the weather service in Norrköping. Time and again the meteorologists predicted sun for the next day, upon which God called for rain. Börje Ekman shuddered at the thought of having to work at such a place, but he was simultaneously intrigued by the idea of being the one with a direct line to the Lord, with a bit of help from the weather stations and satellites. He would take meteorological accuracy to new heights.

Loosely translated, then, the important matter was the degree of predictability rather than the quality of the result. Even more loosely translated: from a strictly weather-related perspective, all citizens should be forced to relocate to the area just north of Gothenburg. Then it would be clear exactly how many meteorologists were needed: none. All anyone would have to do to be correct on 200 to 250 days out of 365 was predict rain the next day. Add to this Börje Ekman's contact with God, and the accuracy would rise to around eighty-five or ninety per cent, depending on the Lord's availability at any given moment.

When applied to the Ministry of Labour, Börje Ekman's logic dictated that nothing should happen from quarter to quarter. On those occasions when something happened anyway, a bunch of analysts within the department were forced to start their calculations again from scratch. While this certainly supported employment in that particular department, it was also the sort of thing that annoyed politicians and could even cause them to lose elections. And if there was anything civil servants had learned over the years, it was that no office or desk in the Ministry of Labour was so small or remotely placed that there wasn't another somewhere else that was even smaller and even further from all the action.

Börje Ekman was a living example of this principle. In forty years he had made so many missteps that by the time he retired he had been moved, moved again, and ultimately moved and forgotten by the organization he ought to have been part of. Börje didn't bother to remind any of his colleagues of his existence. Instead he slowly counted down to the day he turned sixty-five, when the head of the department, the minister herself, gave a short speech about what an extraordinary colleague Börje Ekman had been, but only after she had carefully looked up his name and what sort of work he might have been involved in.

For the last time, Börje Ekman left his office, which was not much bigger than a large pantry. He was not bitter in the least! He found that now, several decades after burning with enthusiasm, the Ministry of Labour had begun, step by step, to adopt his vision of statistics and supervision in place of the fumbling, ad hoc arranging of jobs. But the work of not arranging jobs as a primary task was done half-heartedly. The doomed politicians interfered, as did the doomed citizens in general. Every four years there was a democratic election, before which the political parties promised to combat unemployment in one way or another (or a third way). No matter how they did it, it made a muddle of the ministry. If only the voters would stop changing parties all the time. Now, after each election, the civil servants had to administer a new unsuccessful jobs policy instead of continuing with the old, equally unsuccessful one.

The civil servant, single all these years, would thus have had a relatively meaningless life if it hadn't been that he made sure to fulfil himself in other ways. He left unemployment behind, placing it in God's hands, to build himself a career in the divine.

And a good career it was. It consisted of constantly building up churchly structure in the congregation to which he belonged and of which he eventually controlled all aspects.

His religious existence brought Börje Ekman outright happiness. And he had intended to become even happier once he retired. He would get to spend all his waking hours as the congregation's unofficial shepherd. And the sheep all listened and obeyed, including the ram in the pulpit.

Until catastrophe struck. The church closed its doors, and the congregation – including eighteen of the nineteen active members – joined the neighbouring church. Instead of going with them, as the nineteenth and final member, Börje Ekman walked around lamenting his old church. Now and again he made sure to keep the gravel path free of weeds. Granlund, in the neighbouring church, was nothing but a conceited ass (that is, someone who wouldn't allow Börje Ekman to decide what he wanted and how he wanted it).

And then, a few weeks earlier, the former churchwarden's former parish was sold, church, cemetery, and all – to the newly saved former hitman the whole country seemed to be talking about. The thought of reporting to such a man was not inviting; it might even have caused him to reconsider the position he intended to occupy upon reaching the Pearly Gates. But this was his church, after all, and he would soon help the hitman to realize that fact (unlike Granlund, who understood nothing). Sweden's best churchwarden was back, although no one knew it yet.

Börje Ekman had already been over two or three times to rake before the fresh start, but no one discovered him until the grand opening day. Jerry, his name was. Head of security? Over what?

Between rakings, Börje had got through his last few days in his pantry at the ministry with a smile. In his mind, he was working full-time with his new congregation. Three days left, two days, one … a cakeless farewell – and now, on the first day after his last day, it was time for the grand opening of his beloved church.

He had purposely avoided making himself known. He'd been planning to wait until after the first sermon.

He would pop up like a pleasant surprise for the congregation leadership, who would surely be at a loss, and who had everything left to learn.

These were the sorts of thoughts that called up the very smile that, in the not-too-distant future, would stiffen.

CHAPTER 37

Sweden's second and next-largest general criminal meeting was held in the cellar of one of the preferred pubs of the clientele mentioned below.

Seventeen men, no count or countess. On the agenda: getting rid of the noble couple. And this must be accomplished before they had time to harm a hair on Hitman Anders's head. This matter was approved by a vote of 17–0.

But who would make it happen, and how? This was the topic of discussion over beer after beer delivered from the floor above.

Among all the hoodlums there was one unofficial leader: the man who had been first to dare defy the countess during the last general meeting. After two large beers, the leader hoodlum recalled what everyone already knew: that Olofsson and Olofsson had burned down the Sea Point Hotel.

'What does that have to do with anything?' wondered Olofsson.

'Yeah,' said his brother.

Well, the leader hooligan reasoned that if the building hadn't burned down, Hitman Anders would still be there today, and then all they would have had to do was go over there and hide him from the count and the countess.

Olofsson protested, saying that up to now Hitman Anders had been hiding himself pretty well, even without their help, and, anyway, it wasn't the hitman's hiding that had started the whole mess with the count in the first place but rather the opposite: he had stopped hiding. Instead he had reappeared, accompanied by Jesus, and drawn attention to himself in the newspapers by saying that unfortunate stuff about what would follow if anything happened to him.

'If not for all of that, it's unlikely that the seventeen of us in this cellar would have gone to the Hotel to have a chat with the hitman over a cup of tea, then politely asked him to move to some cabin in the mountains so nothing bad happens to him,' said Olofsson.

'Right?' said his brother.

Olofsson's reasoning was far too convoluted for the rest of them to follow it much further than halfway. Thus, by a vote of 15–2, the brothers were tasked with snuffing out the count and the countess before the noble pair snuffed out the man who ought to have been snuffed out at the start, but whose flame it was now in everyone's best interest to keep as well-lit as possible.

The hoodlums in the cellar weren't used to being in agreement when it came to money; it wasn't in their nature. It was even more surprising that the fifteen who weren't heading out into the field were able to agree that Olofsson and Olofsson's remuneration would consist of

400,000 kronor per nobleperson, plus a million more if they managed to get both of them at once.

Olofsson and Olofsson looked unhappy. But a million kronor was a million kronor, and that was what it would take for the brothers to get back on their financial feet again. At that moment, fifteen angry hoodlums were standing there staring at them, waiting for confirmation.

The brothers had two options: accept it …

Or accept it.

CHAPTER 38

Now there was only an hour left before Hitman Anders's preaching debut. The priest went through their plan and strategy one last time. She wasn't sure how it would go. He seemed to be halfway teachable and contemplative, but the other half was only slightly more gifted than a croquet ball. Which half would take over in the pulpit was impossible to predict.

The church was filling up. Furthermore, a considerable flock was gathering at the screen outside, and newcomers were arriving in a steady stream. There was a pair of snipers with telescopic sights in the bell tower, a guard at every possible entrance to the church, and the sole tolerably presentable half-gangster had been placed, in quiet protest, in a black suit alongside the electronic security monitoring station at the entrance. He had undergone a crash course in correct behaviour, taught by the priest (for the sake of time, the crash course was of the speediest variety).

'Why is there a security check at the entrance to a church?' asked a visitor, who didn't want to be there but had been dragged along by his wife.

'For security reasons, my dear sir,' said the suit-clad man.

'Security reasons?' the visitor repeated cheekily.

The priest had decided that visitors would be separated from the truth, which was that the pastor and they themselves were under threat.

'Yes, security reasons, my dear sir,' said the suit-clad man again.

'Whose security, and which reasons?' the cheeky man persisted.

'Can't we just go inside, Tage?' said his mildly annoyed wife.

'I must confess that I agree with your lovely wife,' said the suit-clad man, who was inwardly longing to deck the bastard with his right fist, the one he was clenching very tightly in his jacket pocket. He just had to remember to let go of the hand grenade first.

'But there's something fishy about this, Greta,' said Tage, who had spent the entire day trying to make sure they prioritized the hockey finals on TV.

The line grew longer and longer behind the intractable man, and the suit-clad bodyguard could no longer manage to act suit-clad.

'If you don't understand the phrase "security reasons," how will you understand what the pastor is about to say? Turn around, for Christ's sake, go home in your fucking Volvo to your fucking semi-detached house in your fucking suburb and sit down and rot on your fucking IKEA sofa, if you don't like the salvation we're offering.'

Fortunately, at that moment the priest happened to walk by and heard the end of the dialogue that had gone so thoroughly in the wrong direction. 'Forgive my intrusion,' she said. 'My name is Johanna Kjellander, and I am the assistant pastor to God's perhaps second-most prominent messenger here on Earth. The security officer with whom you have just been confronted is part of Pastor Anders's beginners group and he hasn't yet made it past Genesis.'

'So?' said the cheeky man.

'Well, that book doesn't say much about how to conduct oneself, aside from not eating forbidden fruit, although both Adam and Eve did so after encouragement from a talking snake. One might think that sounds a bit peculiar, but the Lord can do just about anything.'

'A talking snake?' said the now more confused than cheeky man (who, in contrast to his wife, had never opened a Bible).

'Yes. He could listen as well, that snake, and Heavens, what a scolding that devil got from God. That's why he crawls around in the dirt to this day. The snake, that is, not God.'

'What is all this? What are you getting at, Pastor?' wondered the ever less cheeky but increasingly confused man.

What the priest was trying to get at, above all, was an off-balance cheeky man – and so far, so good. Now she appeared to be considering her words for a second or two before continuing, in a slightly quieter voice, to say that the power in Pastor Anders's words might know no bounds. Perhaps it was too much to hope that Jesus Christ himself would appear during the sermon, but in case it did happen, it would be just terrible if someone were to attack him. It was also conceivable, of course, that he would send one of his apostles, perhaps not Judas Iscariot as a first choice, but there *were* eleven more to choose from. The long and the short of it was that no one could be certain which powers the pastor might unleash, starting today. Hence the security arrangements.

'But we would never force anyone to meet the pastor. We would never force anyone to meet Jesus Christ or his apostles. Everything that is about to happen will probably end up in the newspaper tomorrow anyway, so you won't miss anything. Would you like me to show you out?'

No, the formerly cheeky man supposed he would not, and his wife *certainly* wouldn't. She gripped his arm firmly and said: 'Come on, Tage, let's go inside before the seats fill up.'

Tage allowed himself to be led in, but he had the presence of mind to let the unpleasant security guard know that he and his wife had in fact been driving an Opel Corsa for the past two years.

Hitman Anders's task was to talk about generosity, generosity, and generosity. And on top of that, a dollop of Jesus and then some more generosity. Other catchphrases included this thing about how it was more blessed to give than to receive, that Heaven awaited he who emptied his wallet into the collection plate, and that this same Heaven could not be totally ruled out for he who opened his wallet just a crack (in line with the principle that 'every little helps').

'And try to keep a lid on your hallelujahs, Hosannas, and other things you don't understand,' said the priest.

But Hitman Anders was feeling nervous now that everything was coming to a head. If he were to keep a lid on everything he didn't quite understand, it was unlikely much would get said. He asked if an alternative might be to recite the scientific names of mushrooms, in case of emergency, because that might sound very religious to someone who wasn't totally in the know. And, as proof, he demonstrated: '*Cantharellus cibarius, Agaricus arvensis, Tuber magnatum* ... in the name of the Father, the Son, and the Holy Spirit, amen.'

'What is he saying?' wondered the receptionist, who had just entered the room.

'I'm not sure, but I think he just worshipped the chanterelle, the horse mushroom, and possibly the truffle,' the priest said, then turned back to the hitman and forbade him to go anywhere near what he'd just said, much less anywhere near the toadstool, whatever that might be called.

'*Amanita muscaria*,' Hitman Anders managed before he was interrupted.

The priest told him that this was no time to lose confidence (while simultaneously thinking that 'toadstool' in Latin actually sounded better than a misplaced Hosanna). 'Keep in mind that you're a national hero, the next Elvis,' she said, as she filled the communion vessel she had found the day before in an eighteenth-century cabinet, which might itself be worth more than the entire rest of the church.

The same cabinet, as it happened, also contained a box of wafers, which she guessed would taste rather dusty. The priest offered the body of Jesus to Hitman Anders to complement the wine, but the pastor, who was already in the process of emptying the vessel he'd just got his hands on, preferred a second round of blood instead. He had already hidden a bag of cinnamon rolls in the pulpit in case he should suddenly need some body during the sermon.

CHAPTER 39

An unparalleled cheer and thunderous applause greeted Hitman Anders when he made his entrance. He waved to the right, he waved to the left, and he waved straight ahead. And then he waved again with both arms until the audience had calmed down a bit.

'Hallelujah!' was the first thing he said.

Another cheer went up.

'Hosanna!' Hitman Anders continued, at which point the priest, in the wings, whispered into the receptionist's ear that soon the toadstools would be all he had left.

But the pastor moved on to a different track: 'Generosity, generosity, generosity!' he said.

'That's progress,' said the priest.

As two hired classes of students from Mälar Upper Secondary School dashed about with moneyboxes in and outside the church, Hitman Anders continued his sermon. 'The blood and body of Christ!' he said, and applause broke out again.

'"Body and blood" is the more formal order,' the priest whispered to her receptionist. 'But to each his own.'

'As long as he doesn't take out the cinnamon rolls,' the receptionist responded.

Thus far, the pastor had not offered a word about his own story, about his new purpose in life. Thus far, he hadn't uttered a single coherent sentence. But to the surprise of the priest and the receptionist, it seemed he didn't need to. They were treating Hitman Anders like he was ... well, Elvis.

Presently he fished out a Post-it and placed it in front of himself. He had found something of extraordinary value during his Bible studies in the camper-van. 'As Paul once wrote to Timothy: "No longer drink only water, but take a little wine for the sake of your stomach."'

The receptionist smacked his forehead. The priest was mortified. What else did the fool have on his list?

This time the cheering was mixed with laughter and smiling. But the reactions still seemed affectionate. The atmosphere in the church was only improving.

The priest and the receptionist were standing behind a curtained area just to the left of the pulpit, and from there they were able to study the congregation without being seen. The young people from Mälar Upper Secondary School were rushing along the rows of pews. Almost all of the visitors had a coin to give, but didn't it look like ...?

'Is it my imagination,' said the receptionist to his priest, 'or are those who are happiest also giving the most?'

The priest gazed out at the sea of people as Hitman Anders continued to speak with the aid of his very own notes: 'Even the prophet Habakkuk set his sights on wine. Funny name, isn't it? Anyway, as it says in Scripture, "Drink thou also, and let thy foreskin be uncovered. The cup of the Lord's right hand shall be turned unto thee.'"

This quotation was taken completely out of context, but it had the effect of making the mood even more festive. And the priest could see that the receptionist was right. The moneyboxes weren't big enough, so some of the students were walking around with buckets, and someone had even put his entire wallet into one!

The priest seldom cursed. In this, she took after her father the parish priest. He used foul language very occasionally, and on those occasions it was always aimed at his daughter. Except on Sunday, in the hours leading up to church services. Then the parish priest would awaken, sit up in bed, stick his feet into the slippers his wife always made sure to place in the perfect spot, realize that it was Sunday, and summarize the day even before it started: 'Well, shit.'

So it's noteworthy that the priest said what she did when she saw five-hundred-krona notes and entire wallets vanishing into moneyboxes and buckets. She felt that what she was seeing was best summed up with a short and sweet 'I'll be damned.' In her defence, she said it so quietly that she herself was the only one to hear it.

As the icing on the cake, Hitman Anders really pulled himself together during the remaining twenty minutes of his sermon. He thanked Jesus for allowing a wretched murderer to be reborn. He sent a greeting to his friend the Queen and thanked her for her support. And he tossed out another few quotes from his Post-it, but they were a bit more relevant this time: '"God so loved the world that he gave his only son, so that everyone who believes in him may not perish but may have eternal life."' And then he repeated, backed by such tremendous applause that it was almost impossible to hear what he was saying: 'Generosity, generosity, generosity. Hallelujah, hosanna, and amen!'

Several of the visitors interpreted the unplanned 'amen' to indicate that the pastor had finished (he himself didn't know whether he had or not), upon which they left the pews and rushed up to him. At least three hundred of the remaining congregation followed. Elvis is Elvis.

After that came two and a half hours of autograph-signing and people who wanted to capture a picture of themselves alongside Pastor Anders. Meanwhile, the priest and the receptionist gave the upper secondary students a hundred kronor each out of the collection and set to counting what was left over.

In one corner at the very back of the church stood a man who for once didn't have a rake in his hand (it would have set off the metal detector anyway).

'Thank you, Lord, for giving me the task of bringing order to this chaos,' said Börje Ekman.

The Lord did not respond.

CHAPTER 40

The grand opening had brought in 425,000 kronor after the wages paid to the teenagers from Mälar Upper Secondary School. In other words: 21,250 kronor each to the security team, Hitman Anders, the general expenses fund, and charitable purposes. The remaining 340,000 kronor was placed in the priest and the receptionist's yellow suitcase in the eighteenth-century cabinet in the sacristy. They didn't need the red one yet (the suitcases were probably not the safest deposit boxes in the world, but the receptionist insisted that all their assets should be kept there so that, in an emergency, it would take less than thirty seconds to flee).

That evening, as a reward for a job well done, Hitman Anders received an extra bottle of red and the promise that he wouldn't have to wait longer than about twenty weeks before he could hand out his next half-million to the recipient of his choice.

'Fantastic,' he said. 'But I would like a bite to eat. Can I borrow five hundred for some food?'

The receptionist realized they'd forgotten to inform the hitman that he would actually be drawing a salary, and since he wasn't asking for one, they could just as well leave that matter as it was. Forgotten.

'Of course you may borrow five hundred,' he said. 'Heck, you can have it! But don't waste it all at once, please. And take Jerry the Knife with you if you're going anywhere.'

Unlike Hitman Anders, Jerry the Knife could count: 21,250 kronor would not cover the costs for him and his staff.

'Then let's double it,' said the receptionist.

The guards received what the hitman didn't understand he should have had, so no budgetary harm was done.

But before Hitman Anders was able to leave with Jerry the Knife, yet another person entered the scene. 'What a wonderful evening in the service of the Lord,' lied the man who had been delegated the heavenly task of putting everything to rights.

'Who are you?' asked the priest.

'I'm Börje Ekman, churchwarden of this congregation for the past thirty years. Or thirty-one. Or twenty-nine, depending on how you count. The church lay fallow for some time.'

'Churchwarden?' said the receptionist.

Trouble, thought the priest.

'Dammit! That's right. I forgot to tell you about him,' said Jerry the Knife, who in his rush had also forgotten to watch his language.

'Welcome home,' said Hitman Anders, who was feeling blissful because he had received praise from two different sources in the span of one minute. He gave Börje Ekman a hug on his way out. 'Come on, Jerry, let's go. I'm thirsty. I mean hungry.'

CHAPTER 41

Börje Ekman didn't manage to get to a single one of the fourteen opinions he had jotted down about the evening's service. Instead he was led away by the receptionist and the priest, with the promise that they would talk more in the time to come. To this he responded that there wasn't much they needed to discuss, aside from a few important details about message, tone, service times, and a few other things: he knew how to build up the ideal congregation and had already established some contacts among the visitors.

'How much money did we bring in tonight, by the way?'

'We haven't counted yet, but definitely over five thousand,' the receptionist said quickly, hoping that he hadn't under-exaggerated by too much.

'Oh!' said Börje Ekman. 'A congregational record! Just imagine how much we can bring in once I've fixed up all the organization and contents and a little of most of the rest of it. Why, I'd bet a pretty penny that we'll break ten thousand kronor one day.'

Trouble, trouble, trouble, thought the priest.

With 'I'll be back on Monday to rake the path all nice and neat again. Maybe I'll see you then,' Börje Ekman finally left the room.

'Why can't I just be happy for once?' the receptionist said.

The priest felt the same, but they would have to wait until the next week to fire the man who had never been offered a job in the first place. Right now it was time to celebrate by eating a seven-course dinner and checking into a hotel. And, above all, it was time to discuss concept development, based on their experiences that evening.

* * *

Immediately following their first toast with a 2005 South African Anwilka, the priest presented her new idea.

'Communion,' she said.

'Ugh, right,' said the receptionist.

'No, not ugh!'

By communion she meant not what kept Hitman Anders going, or communion in the proper sense of the word, but communion in a new, free, Church-of-Anders sense.

'Please tell me more,' said the receptionist, taking another exquisite sip of the South African wine for which they would soon pay more than two thousand kronor, given that they hadn't ordered a second bottle.

Well, they had discovered the link between happy visitors and increased generosity. Hitman Anders made people happy (at least, he made everyone happy except the two of them and possibly that miserable church-warden): therefore he made them generous. Add wine, and people would be even happier, *ergo* even more generous! It was simple mathematics.

The priest concluded that if they managed to get anything from one glass to half a bottle down the hatch of each visitor, depending on said visitor's thirst and body size, they could very well double the Saturday proceeds. Not from five thousand to ten thousand, as the man with the rake had suggested, but from half a million to a whole.

'Unlimited amounts of communion for everyone?' said the receptionist.

'I think we should stop calling it communion, at least internally. "Financial stimulant" sounds better.'

'What about a licence to serve alcohol?'

'I don't think we need one. In this wonderful country, so full of prohibitions and regulations, you can more or less uncork whatever you like, as long as you keep it within the four walls of the church. But to be on the safe side, I'll check it first thing on Monday. Cheers, my darling. This is a good wine. Far too good for our church.'

CHAPTER 42

The following Monday, at 9:01 a.m., the priest made a call from the sacristy to the regional alcohol-and-tobacco authority, introduced herself as the assistant pastor of a newly formed congregation, and wondered if there was any situation in which a licence was required to serve communion during a service.

No, the strait-laced representative of the authority informed her. Communion could be freely served.

At this, the priest asked – to be on the safe side – if there was any limit on how much wine each member of the congregation was allowed to toss back.

The strait-laced man seemed to lace himself even straiter as he sensed something untoward about the question. As a result he chose to supplement his formal answer with a personal reflection. 'While the amount of communion wine served is not the sort of thing the licensing authority has any opinion on, becoming intoxicated is not, in the eyes of the law, the main purpose of communion. One might wonder, for example, if the religious message will get across if too much wine is served.'

The priest was about to say that, in this case, it would probably be just as well if the message fell by the wayside, at least parts of it, but she thanked him briskly and hung up. 'Green light!' she said to the receptionist. And then she turned to Jerry the Knife, who was present in the same sacristy. 'I want at least nine hundred litres of red wine delivered on Saturday. Can you make that happen?'

'Sure,' said Jerry the Knife, who had plenty of contacts and then some. 'Two hundred five-litre boxes of Merlot from Moldova, at one hundred kronor a box, will that do? It doesn't taste all that—'

'Bad,' was what he was about to say, but he was interrupted.

'Alcohol content?' said the priest.

'Enough,' said Jerry the Knife.

'Then let's do it. Wait, just get four hundred boxes all at once. There'll be more Saturdays after this next one.'

CHAPTER 43

Börje Ekman was raking his gravel path. It was truly his, and no one else's. Hitman Anders happened by with Jerry the Knife trailing him silently. The pastor admired the quality of the raking and received kind words about his debut sermon in return.

'Not much to complain about there,' said Börje Ekman, both smiling and lying.

This white lie was his intended beginning of his three-step plan to, in Phase A:

1. have opinions about the contents of the sermons
2. proceed to inform the pastor of the main points he must stick to, so that the churchwarden could
3. write the Sunday sermons himself, just like in the good old days.

And to think that they had chosen to hold Sunday services on an early Saturday evening. He would work on that in Phase B. Or C, depending on how difficult the priest, the pastor, and that other fellow might end up being.

The hitman's constant companion, Jerry the Knife, had enough sense to tell the priest and the receptionist about the incipient familiarity between the pastor and the self-designated churchwarden.

'Trouble, trouble, trouble, trouble, trouble,' said the priest.

The receptionist nodded. That Börje Ekman called himself the churchwarden without having been designated as such was a small problem in and of itself. But he seemed to be married to the very church and the area surrounding it, and he would keep coming back, no matter how far Jerry the Knife and his crew chased him off. He would come back and he would discover what he had missed the last time, namely what large amounts of money they were actually dealing with. What was more, there was a risk that he would twist the already twisted mind of the pastor and make a huge mess of everything.

'Next time you and Hitman Anders catch sight of Börje Ekman, try to lead that scatterbrain in the other direction,' said the receptionist.

'Which one? The hitman or the guy with the rake?' asked Jerry the Knife.

CHAPTER 44

The debut had gone better than one might have expected in the present circumstances. The newspapers had been there and delivered further free advertising in the form of reports on Pastor Anders's success, as well as speculation about who might receive the next half-million from the newly saved, altruistic former hitman. None of the journalists was overly impressed by the sermon itself, but there had certainly been nothing wrong with the pastor's and the congregation's enthusiasm.

A few days later, the matter was discussed again in the papers. According to an anonymous source, the free coffee would be replaced next Saturday by free wine. They had been notified that communion was a crucial part of the Anderssonian liturgy. High mass would take place each Saturday evening at five on the dot, year round, according to what the papers had learned. When Christmas Eve fell on a Saturday, the wine would be temporarily replaced by equally alcoholic *glögg*, but otherwise everything would remain the same.

'Thank the good Lord for anonymous hotlines,' said the receptionist, when he read the free publicity in the nationwide tabloids.

'Where in the Bible does it say that God created anonymous hotlines?' said the priest.

* * *

Then it was Saturday again, and once more tons of people came streaming in, but this time the place wasn't quite as crammed. The priest and the receptionist had been aware that this might happen; many people had already got their autograph or photo, and had no desire to pay for the same thing twice. But, still, there were two hundred more visitors than could fit into the church.

Last weekend, one carafe of coffee had been allowed for every twenty seats. This time, there was a wine glass at each seat and a Moldovan box of wine on the floor every sixteen feet.

No one dared to touch the wine before the pastor made his entrance, which he did as the clock struck five.

Standing in the same out-of-the-way corner of the building as the week before: Börje Ekman.

Already deeply bewildered.

'Hallelujah and Hosanna,' Pastor Anders began, before, for strictly personal reasons, he got straight to the point: 'Jesus – my friends – took the suffering of all humanity upon himself. Let us begin with a toast to that!'

He filled his glass from the communion vessel as the rows of pews descended into half a riot. After all, there are few things as embarrassing as returning a toast without anything in your glass.

However badly the pastor wanted to knock back what he held, he waited until a sufficient number of the congregation appeared ready. 'To Jesus!' he said at last, emptying the contents of his cup in one giant gulp. At least seven hundred of the eight hundred people in the building followed their pastor's lead. Even this was more than fifty of them could handle.

After an inappropriate 'That hits the spot,' Pastor Anders launched into his sermon by explaining that he was a simple servant of the Lord, who had formerly not understood that the path to Heaven was found by way of the blood and body of Christ. But he had seen the light. Above all, he was able to reveal to the congregation where the whole idea of communion had come from in the first place. It was best not to get into details, but the short version was that Jesus had felt hungry before he was crucified and invited his friends to one last hullabaloo. It was him and the apostles, but recent research, conducted by Pastor Anders himself, suggested that they had put away a great deal more wine than had previously been known. And the crucifixion had been delayed for some time, so there is a chance Jesus was dangling there on Calvary with a hangover on top of everything else. That might explain his anguished 'My God, my God, why have you done this to me?'

Hullabaloo? A hung-over Jesus on the cross? Had Börje Ekman heard correctly?

Pastor Anders had prepared another Post-it, so he was able to elegantly cite the most recent quotation as Mark 15:34. After that he made an unplanned digression into the curse of the hangover before he turned back to Jesus and the cross. For, according to Pastor Anders, the truly interesting thing Jesus said before sailing into eternity was 'I am thirsty' (John 19:28).

That was the blood of Christ. When it came to his body … No, wait, first it was time for yet another toast in the name of the Lord: no one must stand or sit there becoming hung-over himself, and the answer was to keep drinking.

It wasn't long before almost the entire congregation was tipsy. The pastor fitted in three toasts around his cobbled-together declaration of communion before arriving at the next planned item on the agenda.

'It is said that they also broke bread with their wine, but, hello, dry white bread with red wine, is that how we're supposed to honour the Lord and his son?'

Here and there, a few weak cries of 'No!'

'I can't hear you!' Hitman Anders said, in a louder voice. 'Is that how we're supposed to honour them?'

'No!' many more cried this time.

'Once more!' said Hitman Anders.

'No!' shouted the entire church and half the car park outside.

'Now I can hear you!' said Hitman Anders. 'And I take your word as law.'

At a prearranged signal, the classes from Mälar Upper Secondary School began their task. Each student carried, in one hand, a bucket to fill with banknotes and, in the worst case, a coin or two. In the other hand was a tray with various sorts of crackers, seedless grapes, butter and cheese. The trays passed from visitor to visitor, and when one was about to empty, the students immediately refilled it.

The pastor, at the front of the room, had his own plate. He nibbled at what was offered and chewed with relish.

'Fit for a bishop,' he said.

After having subsisted on the blood of Christ alone for several weeks, plus the occasional hamburger or cinnamon roll, Hitman Anders had seen fit to read up a little on what communion actually was (a *little*, mind, not a lot). In this he was cheered on by the priest: if only foolishness came out of Hitman Anders's trap week after week, the consequence would be a pastor who couldn't arouse enough enthusiasm for the masses to give enough money to get closer to Heaven. And this would soon turn out to be as profitable as running a business in the assault trade without having any assault to offer.

But there was another way, besides communion, to stimulate the flat-out boozing that was now taking place within and immediately outside God's house. This time the priest had inspected Hitman Anders's Post-it ahead of time and added an item or two she thought might influence the mood and thus the generosity.

That was why the pastor was currently telling the story of Noah, the man who built the world's first vineyard, and as a result was the first to get raging drunk. Afterwards he passed out naked in his tent, all according to Genesis 9:21, but then he came to again, scolded one of his sons while hung-over ('That bloody hangover again!') and lived another three hundred and fifty years on top of the six hundred he already had behind him.

'Now let's raise our glasses one last time,' Pastor Anders concluded. 'We drink of the blood of Christ. The wine gave Noah nine hundred and fifty years of life. Without the wine he would have been dead long before that.'

The receptionist was thinking that Noah had probably already been dead long enough, but the pastor seemed able to get away with just about anything.

'Cheers and welcome back on Saturday!' said Pastor Anders, draining his vessel, not bothering with a glass.

The receptionist snapped his fingers to tell the students to make another collection, which brought in another ten thousand or so kronor in addition to what had already been given, along with the unfortunate offering of an older woman, with a feather boa around her neck, who had the poor taste to throw up into one of the buckets.

As people staggered out of the church, full of bliss and wine, the priest and the receptionist summed up the evening's developments. A very rough estimate indicated that they had made over a million kronor this time, which meant that their investments in the Moldovan wine and the snacks had paid for themselves many times over.

* * *

The suitcases of money were already closed when Churchwarden Börje Ekman entered the sacristy from which the business was run. He was red in the face; he didn't look happy.

'For one thing!' he began.

'For one thing, you should probably learn to say hello politely,' the receptionist snapped.

'Hello there, Börje,' said the oblivious hitman. 'What did you think about this evening's sermon? As good as last time?'

Börje Ekman had lost his train of thought so he started again. 'Good evening to all of you,' he said. 'I have a few things to say. For one thing, it is total chaos outside the church. At least four cars have backed into each other, people are dragging their feet as they walk down the gravel path, which will make it twice as hard to rake on Monday ...'

'Maybe it would be best to pave it, then, so it will match the car park better,' said the receptionist, who was in a fighting mood.

Pave the gravel path? To Börje Ekman, this was tantamount to swearing in church. As he tried to recover from what he'd just heard, Hitman Anders, who was more intoxicated than his body actually needed to be, said: 'Hey, listen, tell me what you thought of my fucking sermon.'

Swearing in church was definitely tantamount to swearing in church, according to Börje Ekman.

'What on earth is going on here?' he said, looking down into the only bucket that hadn't yet been emptied and hidden in the closest suitcase. It was the one that contained vomit, on top of what had to be several thousand kronor! 'The sermon?' he went on. 'That was a booze-fest!'

'Speaking of which,' said Hitman Anders, 'wouldn't you like a few drops yourself? I can't guarantee it'll make you live to nine hundred and fifty, but I'm sure it'll put you in a better mood than you seem to be right now.'

'A booze-fest!' Börje Ekman repeated. 'In God's house! Have you no shame?'

Somewhere around that point, the priest had had enough. Mr Blasted Ekman was the one who had no shame. Here they were, fighting to bring in a few measly kronor for the poorest people on our Earth, all while Ekman was grumbling about a gravel path. How much had *he* put in the collection plate, hmm?

The self-designated churchwarden had not put in a single krona, which troubled him for a second or two before he collected himself. 'You are twisting the word of God, you are turning the service and mass into a circus, you, you … How much money have you brought in? And where did it all go?'

'That's none of your business,' the receptionist said angrily. 'And, anyway, isn't the important thing that each krona goes to the needy?'

On the topic of 'needy,' the priest and the receptionist had, a week before, exchanged the camper-van for the Riddarholm Suite at the Hilton, and that wasn't exactly free.

But instead of saying so to the self-designated church-warden, the priest suggested that 'Mr Jerry here' could show him the way out if, perchance, he was unable to find it himself. She also suggested, in a milder tone, that they meet again once emotions had settled a bit. Like this coming Monday, for example, might that work?

By taking action, she intended to do away with the unrest in the room but without spurring him to run to the police or do something equally horrid.

'I can find it myself,' said Churchwarden Börje Ekman. 'But I'll be back on Monday to rake the path, clear up the pieces of glass from all the collisions and, I'm sure, wipe up a patch of vomit or two that I haven't found yet. And for next Saturday I demand more order than we had today. Do you understand? We will meet to discuss it at two o'clock!'

'Two thirty,' said the priest, because she didn't want to let Börje Ekman decide.

CHAPTER 45

One of the few who didn't drink a drop during the second Saturday service was a middle-aged woman who wore a blonde wig and glasses she didn't need. She sat in the eighteenth row of pews and placed twenty kronor in the bucket every time it went by, no matter how much it pained her soul to do so. It was important not to stick out. She was there for reconnaissance.

No one in the building knew her name. Not many people outside it did either, as it happens. In the circles where she spent her time, she was simply called 'the countess'.

Another seven rows back sat two men who emptied one of the Moldovan boxes all on their own. In contrast to the above-named, they did not put a single krona into the collection plate. Anyone in their immediate vicinity who happened to share an opinion about this was offered a thrashing.

The men were there on the same errand. One was named Olofsson. The other was too. And no matter how much they wished to cut the pastor into ribbons, their assignment was the opposite: to analyse his chances of survival up there in the pulpit. To put it simply, Hitman

Anders must not die. Especially not before the count and countess happened to do so.

The first thing that Olofsson and Olofsson encountered was a metal detector at the entrance, which led them to make an extra circuit around the car park to hide two revolvers in a bush they were unable to find later because they were too drunk.

While their eyes were still sharp enough, they had time to take note of a considerable security team. Olofsson was the first to discover the two snipers in the bell tower. He asked his brother discreetly to confirm his discovery, so Olofsson did.

Later that evening, the brothers made a report to the other fifteen members of the group, who had unanimously decided that the count and the countess must be taken out. The fact that the informants were drunk made the meeting a muddle, but the others at least succeeded in getting out of Olofsson and Olofsson that Hitman Anders seemed reasonably safe for the time being. It would take a good deal of cogitation and initiative for anyone to get near him.

Unfortunately, cogitation followed by initiative perfectly described the count and the countess. The latter informed her count that, luckily, it would not be as simple as stepping into the church and blasting Hitman Anders's skull to pieces: security was too tight for that. By 'luckily,' she meant that such a procedure would not cause the hitman as much suffering as he deserved.

So, Saturdays were not the best time to strike. But, unfortunately, Hitman Anders existed on the other six days of the week as well, and it seemed he always had one bodyguard at his side.

'*One* bodyguard?' said the count, with a smile. 'You mean that with one well-aimed shot from a distance, he would be standing there alone, a headless bodyguard at his feet?'

'More or less,' said the countess. 'I saw at least one sniper up in the bell tower as well, but I can't imagine he sits there all week long.'

'That's it?'

'We should probably count on more of them, spread out around the church. It has at least four entrances. One was recently built, and I would guess that all four are under guard.'

'So five or six security guards, one of whom never leaves Hitman Anders's side?'

'Yes. I can't be more precise than that. Not yet.'

'Then I suggest that, for our first step, you keep your wig on and stick around the area to see if our soon-to-be-dead killer dares to stick his nose out of the church. When we know a little more about his daily patterns, I'll take out first the bodyguard, if necessary, from five hundred feet away, and put the next bullet square in the middle of Hitman Anders's stomach. We can't be too particular when it comes to how painful it has to be. Bleeding out internally with your intestines in shreds isn't as awful as we'd hoped but, given the circumstances, it's awful enough.'

The countess gave a disappointed nod. But it would have to do. Anyway, 'intestines in shreds' sounded lovely.

The count was the same as ever, she thought, feeling a rare warmth inside.

CHAPTER 46

So Olofsson and Olofsson had been involuntarily saddled with the task of taking out the count and the countess. By pooling their resources, the other fifteen had managed to produce the money that had been promised to the intended perpetrators. However, it was 'look but don't touch' until such time as results were achieved.

So, the unholy alliance of seventeen had money. Ideas were not as forthcoming. The head hoodlum was just as confounded as the Olofsson brothers. But then it occurred to thief number nine in the group that he had cleared out the electronics chain Teknikmagasinet's central warehouse in Järfälla just a few nights ago, and for the second time. It had housed every sort of electronic equipment one could imagine, and all he'd had to do to kill the company's alarm system was snip one yellow and one green wire in an electrical box. Was that the cobbler's son going barefoot or what? There were at least five hundred surveillance cameras in the building, all neatly packed in boxes on a pallet, just waiting to be rolled out to the thieves' amply sized van without ending up in a single shot.

In addition, thief number nine had come into possession of more than two hundred sets of bathroom scales (a bit of a disappointment), a large number of mobile phones (smash success!), various GPS units, forty pairs of binoculars, and approximately twice as many bubble-gum dispensing machines, which in the dim light of the warehouse had looked like amplifiers.

'If anyone wants a bubble-gum machine, just let me know.'

No one did. With that, number nine turned the conversation to the GPS units that had come in with everything else. 'If I've understood correctly, we can attach something to the count and countess's car, for example. Then you can watch where the car goes on your very own mobile phone. I'm thinking it isn't such a bad idea for the people who wish them harm to know where they are.'

'And who were you thinking would just crawl up and attach that "something" to the count and countess's car?' Olofsson wondered, immediately regretting his question.

'How about you or your brother?' said the head hoodlum. 'Considering our agreement and all the money that you've only been allowed to look at so far.'

'We don't even know what kind of car they drive around in,' his brother Olofsson attempted.

'A white Audi Q7,' said well-informed hoodlum number nine. 'They park it outside their house at night. Bang next to an identical car. They each have one. Doesn't that make things nice and fair? Each of you can crawl up to one. Would you like the address? And another GPS to show you the way?'

Number nine might have been the star pupil, right up there with the head hoodlum. Olofsson and Olofsson could object no further. Which frightened them. Meeting the count and the countess in the manner they had just been tasked with might be the same as meeting their maker. Or his opposite.

And yet: a million kronor was a million kronor.

CHAPTER 47

The count had an impressive arsenal of weapons. He never stole them himself, but he had bought one thing and another throughout the years. And he had spent quite a bit of time practising out at the country home the countess had nagged her way to ten years previously. Target practice had been both fun and useful. You never knew when all-out war might break out in the world of car dealerships.

The most unusual item in the collection, in an ironic twist of Fate, came from the gun safe of a legitimate count, who resided north of the capital. It was a so-called double rifle, of 9.3 x 62mm calibre. And it had a telescopic sight. The weapon was most useful when one encountered an elephant, and that was a rare occurrence in the Stockholm area. And even if it did happen, the telescopic sight wouldn't be much help unless the robbed count was almost blind, thought the fake count.

Be that as it may, the weapon was about to be put to use. A quick trip to the countryside and back to zero in on the target. The plan was to load one barrel with a half-jacketed bullet and the other with a full metal jacket in preparation for the critical moment. This would allow the option of two shots fired in a single second. The first between the eyes of Hitman Anders's bodyguard. The half-jacket would take the whole skull with it.

And then a rapid shift in aim, just a few millimetres, before the second shot was fired to end up somewhere in the vicinity of Hitman Anders's navel. The full metal jacket would go right through his body and out the other side, causing irreparable damage in between. The hitman, however, would not kick the bucket immediately: first, he would experience terrible pain plus a good dose of mortal fear. Then he would slowly fall unconscious, bleed out, and die. A bit too quickly, but as slowly as the circumstances would allow.

'If we can just find the perfect spot to shoot from, we can reload in peace and quiet and fire another round in case he lies there floundering a little too long.'

In all his masculinity, the count had previously happened to toss out a shooting distance of five hundred feet, but presently he admitted that it wouldn't be a big deal if the firing spot were a bit closer.

A powerful weapon that could discharge two shots in one second, from two different barrels with two different targets. With a telescopic sight and everything. The count thanked his presumably half-blind elephant-hunting colleague for not having the good sense to lock his gun safe.

CHAPTER 48

One million, one hundred and twenty-four thousand three hundred kronor. Plus the contents of the puked-upon bucket, but the priest and the receptionist never got an exact amount from that one. After a visual inspection, on his knees, as he held his nose, the student representative from Mälar Upper Secondary School estimated that the bucket contained more money than the group otherwise would have been given, and thus he chose said bucket over the agreed-upon hundred-krona note per person.

'Great,' said the priest. 'Stand up, take your bucket, and go.'

'See you on Saturday,' the student responded, picked up the bucket and left.

The priest opened the newly installed double door of the sacristy to air the room (Jerry the Knife had gone all out to make sure that the extra escape route in case of war could be used as a loading dock in peacetime). She was a bit wary of exposing herself, the receptionist, and the pastor to the outside world simultaneously, but in this case she assessed the risks as low. There was a guard at the door, and Jerry the Knife was in the room, as always in Hitman Anders's immediate vicinity. Furthermore, there was only grass and open space in the hundred metres between the church and the road that passed it, and on the other side of that road a small patch of forest. Even if there were someone there, it would take a sniper with a telescopic sight to have time to shoot even one of them.

* * *

The Sunday follow-up meeting began with finances, quite simply because Hitman Anders apparently hadn't woken up yet. Otherwise they would have postponed that item.

This time, they had grossed about 625 kronor per visitor; the net was just under 600.

'I think we found a good balance between degree of intoxication and generosity,' the priest said, pleased.

At that moment, the hitman stumbled in. He'd heard the priest's last comment and said he'd been wondering if they should put sick buckets beside the pews to be safe. The advantage would be that they could dial up the communion mood a notch or two.

The priest and the receptionist weren't as enthusiastic about this idea as Hitman Anders had expected. Sick buckets might detract from the spiritual atmosphere. However you look at it, there's nothing heavenly about a sick bucket. No matter how passed out Noah might have been in that tent of his.

'And naked,' Hitman Anders added, to emphasize the degree of how very badly things had probably gone for him.

245

The hitman vanished again. The pub and relaxation awaited, since his weekly five hundred kronor hadn't been completely used up on Saturday evening. Plus, follow-up meetings were so boring. Or, really, meetings in general. If it weren't for the fact that he'd wanted to share his bucket idea, he would probably have been enjoying his first glass.

The priest and the receptionist were perfectly happy to do without the pastor in any meeting, no matter the type. When they were alone once more, they began to discuss the wretched churchwarden, a threat to their entire operation. Their conversation with him the next day would be crucial. As the priest saw it, they had two options. Either scare the pants off him, and surely Jerry the Knife could manage that. Or get him on board …

'By "get him on board" you mean bribe him?' the receptionist wondered.

'Something along those lines. We can praise him for his beautiful raking and offer him twenty thousand a week to continue.'

'What if he doesn't accept?'

The priest sighed. 'Then I suppose we'll have to bring the head of security in on the conversation. With his knife and everything.'

The priest and the receptionist were perfectly justified in being concerned about the churchwarden. Börje Ekman felt that the archbishop needed to know what was going on. But she was both a woman and a foreigner. To be sure, she was German, and the Germans liked order even if they might sometimes devote themselves to alcohol-related excesses. But they didn't do it in the name of the Church, and that was an important difference. But she was still a foreigner. And a woman. What was more, the Church of Anders was probably not under the control of the archbishop; it was a schism of the most vulgar sort.

But, still, he had to do something. Call the police? To what end? Or the Tax Authority? Yes, an anonymous tip about financial irregularities might be just the ticket.

Oh, well, it was almost Monday – time for raking followed by a meeting with the godless priest and her crew. He would put his foot down. If that didn't help, the Tax Authority would be the next step. And plans B and C. He just had to think them up.

CHAPTER 49

While the priest and the receptionist spent Sunday afternoon on worrying thoughts about Börje Ekman, Hitman Anders made another appearance, this time in excellent spirits. He'd been down to town and back again. At Stureplan there was a pub and a bathhouse next door to each other; together, they comprised chicken soup for a hitman's body and soul.

'Heigh-ho,' he said. 'I see we're grumpy today.'

He was freshly showered, freshly shaven, and was wearing a new short-sleeved shirt. Both arms were covered with tattoos, including knives, a skull, and two winding snakes. The priest realized she must remember never to allow him to preach without a jacket on.

'I *said*, I see we're grumpy today,' Hitman Anders repeated. 'Shouldn't we go through next Saturday's sermon soon? I have some ideas.'

'We're thinking, so it would be nice if you didn't bother us too much at the moment,' said the receptionist.

'All this thinking,' said Hitman Anders. 'What if you just stopped now and then to enjoy life for a second? Or, as it says in Psalm Thirty-seven: "The meek shall inherit the land and delight in abundant prosperity."'

How much must he browse through that confounded book? thought the priest. But she didn't say it. Instead she looked him up and down and said: 'And according to Leviticus nineteen, you're not supposed to shave or tattoo your arms, so shut your trap, if you please.'

'Nice one.' The receptionist smiled as Hitman Anders slunk off, freshly shaved, with his skulls, winding snakes, and all the rest.

Sunday became Monday, but no solution to the Börje Ekman problem presented itself. That was, no solution other than the either/or version they had already reasoned their way to: either Börje Ekman would voluntarily get on board or he would be *forced* on board by Jerry and his knife. May the two-thirty meeting go well: they didn't need any complications right now.

* * *

On Monday morning the churchwarden began his work before the clock had struck nine. There was a lot to be done. First the gravel path, of course. Then wash selected areas of the car park and clear up all the loose parts left by the cars that had backed into each other as a result of what had to have been Sweden's record-breaking drunk-driving event two days earlier. As the Stockholm police prioritized sobriety checks during the times of day and week when everyone was sober (including the police themselves), no one suffered any consequences.

At eleven o'clock or thereabouts, Börje Ekman took a short break. He sat on one of the benches along the path to the church, and took out his sausage sandwich and a small bottle of milk. He gazed emptily straight ahead, sighing for the umpteenth time when he caught sight of something in the rosebushes, which otherwise quite serviceably blocked the view of the car park west of the church. Was there no limit to how much litter those drunkards could leave?

But what *was* that thing? Börje put aside his sandwich and milk and went over for a closer look.

A ... revolver? *Two* revolvers!

His mind boggled. Had he found himself in the midst of some criminal matter?

And then he remembered the response when he'd asked how much the collection brought in. Five thousand? God in Heaven, how naïve he had been! *That* was why they plied the churchgoers with alcohol! So that they would put more and then more in the buckets, and, where appropriate, top it all with a pile of vomit under which, one might suspect, rested more money than they claimed made up their entire takings for the week before.

A former hitman, a priest who apparently didn't believe in God, and a ... well, whatever the other fellow was. The one who said his name was Per Persson. A made-up name, clearly.

What else? He'd heard the name only once. It was probably the pastor himself who'd said it, who called the head of 'security,' the man who never left his side, 'Jerry the Knife'! *They aren't thinking of the Lord, they aren't thinking of any starving children, they're only thinking of themselves!* thought Börje Ekman, who had essentially spent his entire life doing the very same thing.

In that exact moment, the Lord spoke to him for the first time, after Börje Ekman had spent his entire earthly life in his service. 'It is you, Börje, and no one else, who can save this, my house. It is only you who have seen the madness that is going on. You are the only one who understands. It is you who must do what you must do. Do it, Börje. Do it!'

'Yes, Lord,' answered Börje Ekman. 'Just tell me: what is it I must do? Tell me and I will do it. Lead me on the right path, Lord.'

But God was just like Jesus: he spoke only when he had the time or the inclination. He did not answer his subject, not then and not later. The fact is, God would never reveal himself again as long as Börje Ekman lived.

CHAPTER 50

The churchwarden cancelled the two-thirty meeting, citing a migraine and adding that it wasn't very urgent after all to sort out what needed to be sorted out. The priest was surprised to hear that the bushes were no longer burning, but she had plenty of other matters to worry about. She was satisfied to think that what had been about to be either/or might land somewhere in between.

Oh, how she did deceive herself.

The churchwarden just needed to gather his thoughts. He rode his bicycle home to his studio apartment. 'Sodom and Gomorrah,' he said to himself. Biblical cities where sin had reigned beyond all limits, but only until the Lord had put a stop to it. 'Sodom, Gomorrah, and the Church of Anders,' said Börje Ekman.

Maybe the situation had to get worse before it could get better.

That had been President Nixon's analysis of the situation in Vietnam, which had ended up getting worse before it had got even more worse. In the end, Nixon's career had perished (albeit for reasons other than Vietnam).

History does tend to have the unfortunate habit of repeating itself. A plan began to form in the mind of the churchwarden. Plus there was always the Tax Authority: he could count that as a plan in and of itself. First worse, then better (was his plan, anyway).

The end result? First worse, then even more worse. At which point Börje Ekman perished too.

* * *

The countess was currently crouching, deep in meticulous reconnaissance, in a patch of forest with a view of the newly constructed double side doors, which were opened and closed now and again. The doors were no more than four hundred feet away, although they were on the other side of the road. It was Wednesday and wine was being delivered; a truck had backed in, the doors were wide open, and box after box was carried into the church. Between the car and the door stood a guard armed with a poorly concealed machine-gun.

Just inside, the countess could see people who must be Johanna Kjellander and Per ... something ... Jansson? And beside them: Hitman Anders and his bloody bodyguard.

The countess had binoculars, and when she used them she found she didn't recognize the guard – it was some hoodlum from outside her circle of acquaintances. It didn't much matter what his name was. If she and the count grew curious later on, they could always find his grave and see what it said on the headstone.

What *was* important was that if they had been ready there and then, they could have taken out both Hitman

Anders and his bodyguard. The only remaining problem would have been the man with the machine-gun outside the door. If the worst came to the worst, he would come for them, and they would need time to reload. On the plus side: the road between the church and the woods.

With this positive thinking, she could dispense with her recce for now. There was no rush: the most important thing was to get it right.

The countess returned to her white Audi and took off.

'Let her go,' said Olofsson. 'She's just going home to report back to the fucking count.'

'Mm-hm,' Olofsson responded. 'We'd better go up to those trees and find out what she was looking at.'

* * *

The mood was once again merry among the leadership of the Church of Anders. A fresh delivery of wine had arrived, along with crackers, grapes, and the ripe pastor cheese.

'We'll do the same snacks again,' said the priest. 'They went down well. But maybe we should branch out for next week. We mustn't get stuck in a rut.'

'Burgers and fries?' Hitman Anders suggested.

'Or something else,' said the priest, adding that they had a sermon to prepare.

But the hitman was still coming up with ideas. Wine could be a bit harsh for some people's taste. He recalled his early teenage years, when he and his best friend (who later drugged himself to death; that was stupid) mixed rot-gut with Coca-Cola so they could get the decoction down themselves. When they learned, later on, to put Alka-Seltzer into the mix, it was even more fun.

'Sounds tasty,' said the priest. 'Like I said, we'll look over the menu in the time to come and I promise we'll take your views into account. Can we focus on the sermon now?'

The Bible was a cornucopia of homage to wine as a gift from God. The priest jotted down something from memory about wine to make the human heart glad, oil to make the face shine, and bread to give the heart strength (taken from Psalms). And she added another slightly less verbatim quote from Ecclesiastes that said life without a real bender now and then is meaningless, utterly meaningless.

'Does it really say "bender"?' wondered Hitman Anders.

'No, but let's not quibble,' the priest said, as she wrote down the prophecy according to Isaiah that on the Day of Judgement there would be a feast of rich food and strong wine, a feast of rich food filled with marrow and well-aged wines strained clear.

'I'm telling you,' said Hitman Anders. 'Rich food. Burgers and fries. We can skip the Coke and Alka-Seltzer.'

'Shall we take a little break?' said the priest.

CHAPTER 51

After the third Saturday it felt like things were starting to settle down a bit. For the second week in a row, the party had brought in a net sum of close to nine hundred thousand to the two needy people. The giant screen wasn't serving much purpose anymore, but the pews were still just as loaded as the people sitting in them.

Churchwarden Ekman had returned after a few days' absence, but he mostly seemed to slink around; thus far he hadn't asked for another meeting with the priest or the receptionist. He seemed like a ticking time-bomb, but at the same time there was so much more to think about. Sitting down to chat with him would, at best, lead to bribing him into membership of the club (that is, peace and quiet); at worst, they would be hastening a problem that seemed to have been put on the shelf.

'I'm far from certain that no news is good news in this case, but I still think we should avoid bothering him for the time being,' said the receptionist. 'As long as he's not bothering us.'

The priest agreed, even if she felt that things were going a little too well on all fronts. After a life in which everything goes wrong, it's easy to become suspicious when the opposite ensues.

There had, for example, been no incidents in the form of activity from the almost certainly frustrated underworld. Hitman Anders's threat that the list of contracts taken out would become public upon his demise seemed to have done the trick.

The deliveries of wine and treats each Wednesday at one p.m. were also flowing smoothly. The receptionist realized that this sort of routine was just the type of thing that potential attackers would love, but he trusted Jerry the Knife and his army. One of Jerry's soldiers, incidentally, had been dismissed when it was discovered that he had neglected his duties. He had been caught red-handed, snoring in the bell tower, hugging an empty Moldovan-wine box.

Since Jerry had acted so quickly, the incident inspired confidence more than anything. At the moment the group was one man short, but Jerry was holding job interviews and expected the team to be at full strength again within a month at most.

Aside from the nearly one million kronor they received each week in cash, the receptionist's superb handling of social media brought another couple of hundred thousand straight into the congregation's bank account. That money needed a great deal of attention from a purely administrative standpoint: in Sweden, it is automatically assumed that anyone holding more than ten thousand kronor in hand is either a criminal, a tax-dodger, or both. Thus there are rules about how much one may deposit or withdraw from one's own accounts without first meekly petitioning to do so several days in advance. But in keeping with the theme of 'going like clockwork,' it just so happened that the receptionist had met and charmed a woman at the bank who doubled as one of the most devoted and thirstiest of their congregation. So, he was able to visit the woman daily and withdraw a reasonable amount, without risking a call to the financial supervisory authority for suspected money laundering. She knew that the capital was being used in the service of the Lord (plus it bankrolled her weekend raves). Allowing the money to remain in the account was not an option the receptionist considered even for a second. After all, in case of trouble, they needed to be able to take off within half a minute; withdrawing hundreds of thousands of kronor from a Swedish bank took more like half a year.

'Now that the sun is shining down on us, it's probably not the time to be too greedy,' he mused. 'Should we let the fool loose on another half-million?'

'That might be advisable,' the priest agreed. 'But this time we'll count the money for him.'

* * *

Hitman Anders was overjoyed when he learned that the congregation had brought in 480,000 kronor in just a few weeks and that they would be able to hand out half a million once again, since the priest, in all her generosity, had donated the missing twenty thousand out of her own pocket.

'You will be given a place at the right hand of the Lord in Heaven,' he said to her.

The priest didn't bother to tell him how unlikely that was. Furthermore, David was already sitting there, according to the Psalms, in Jesus's lap, one had to presume, since according to the Gospel of Mark, Jesus had bagged the same spot.

The pastor began to consider where the money could go. Perhaps some non-profit association. But then he happened to recall something he had overheard once: 'All this talk about the rainforest, what's that all about? It sounds lovely to save a forest and, what's more, the forests were created by God. Or maybe it would be better to find one where it doesn't rain so much.'

The priest was no longer startled by anything that came out of the pastor's mouth, even if *Boletus edulis* – the porcini mushroom – was still a mystery. 'I suppose I was thinking along the lines of saving a few more sick or starving children,' she said.

Hitman Anders was not a pretentious man. Rainforest or starving children, it didn't matter: it was the act of giving in Jesus's name that was important. He did, however, allow himself to reflect that the combination of starving children *in* a rainforest sounded extra special. But would it be possible to find such a thing in Sweden?

CHAPTER 52

The dejected churchwarden was not at all dejected. He was biding his time, sneaking about in and around the church to gather evidence for his theory that all was not quite as it should be. If even one thing was.

A week passed, then three. Börje Ekman had previously seen with his very own eyes approximately how many thousands of kronor had been in the bucket of puke; all he had to do was multiply that amount by the number of buckets present to estimate the quantities they were dealing with.

At this point, the fake priest and the other fellow ought to have four or even five million kronor hidden somewhere. At least!

* * *

The latest donation had not been given to a forest, with or without rain. Instead the priest had come up with the idea of travelling to Astrid Lindgren Children's Hospital along with two newspapers, a radio station, and a TV channel to let Hitman Anders unexpectedly present a backpack of 500,000 kronor with 'Jesus lives' on it to the gravely ill children so that they might, as far as possible, continue to do the same.

The head of department, also a doctor and pediatric specialist, was not on hand for the occasion but was quick to issue a press release praising the Church of Anders and its head pastor for the 'enormous generosity he has shown the children and their parents, who are undergoing the most difficult of times'.

For one second, Börje Ekman wavered in his conviction that the pastor's generosity was backed merely by greed and cynicism. But when that second was over, he saw the situation with clear, sharp eyes. Perhaps there was nothing wrong with the pastor (other than that he was a murderer and unevenly gifted); the problem was that the priest and the fellow whose name was practically the same forwards and backwards were pulling his strings.

Börje Ekman sat in his studio apartment, thinking that that last half-million would have been most beneficial had he been the one to receive it. The Lord's foremost servant needed solid financial ground on which to stand if he were going to perform his duties in accordance with the Lord's will. That was why he had done such things as keep a tenth of the weekly collection for himself for all those years, without finding it necessary to inform the congregation. It was an agreement between the church-warden and God, and had nothing to do with anyone else.

CHAPTER 53

The countess had done the spade work, and now it was the count's turn. He was on the fence about what to do. On the one hand, he might want to outfit himself with enough weapons to be prepared for any contingency; on the other, he might want to avoid being too heavily armed in case he needed to vanish rapidly after fulfilling his duty.

The latter was still the most likely scenario. According to the countess, the double side doors had been opened pretty much precisely at one o'clock on each of the five Wednesdays she'd had the church under surveillance. The last time, the guard stationed outside was replaced by the man who was otherwise never further than two feet away from Hitman Anders; it seemed they were one man short and, for a limited time each week, the geographical distance between Hitman Anders and his bodyguard increased.

That both simplified and complicated the situation.

On the Wednesdays in question, Hitman Anders had been fully visible just inside the doors, along with Johanna Kjellander and Per Something. One might make the not unreasonable assumption that the same would apply for that day as well, the day of Operation Thank You and

Good Night. If that was the case, the plan was to take out Hitman Anders first, with the jacketed bullet, then have the half-jacketed bullet ready in case the bodyguard started towards them. That is to say, from jacketed to half-jacketed, instead of the other way around.

They could not be sure, though, that a single shot would fell the bodyguard. For one thing, there was a chance that he was reasonably professional, and would not remain standing there after report number one, waiting to depart this life. And for another, circumstances were now such that the aim would have to be adjusted more than a few millimetres and a few tenths of a second; now that the intended victims were not standing side by side it would take much longer.

Thus they needed a Plan B, and once that was settled, everything seemed relatively obvious. After all, they would be lying hidden in a grove of trees above a man who might potentially be stupid enough to counter-attack. If the count were to toss a hand grenade at just the right moment, it would have a one hundred per cent chance of causing the enemy to lose his train of thought.

'A hand grenade,' the countess commented, relishing the phrase as well as the thought of the effect it would have on the bodyguard.

The count smiled lovingly. His countess truly was the cream of the crop.

* * *

At ten to one, it was time to prepare to receive the weekly delivery of the blood of Christ, et cetera. The priest and the receptionist went to the sacristy that had become a storeroom, warehouse, office, receiving room, and more … only to find the self-appointed churchwarden with his nose deep in the yellow and the red suitcases, full of their millions.

'What the holy hell are you doing here?' said the receptionist, who was as surprised as he was angry.

'Hell indeed,' said the churchwarden, his voice calm but intense. 'Because that is where you two are going. Hitmen, fraudsters, embezzlers … what else? I'm speechless.'

'But you found our suitcases, you parasite,' said the priest, closing both receptacles. 'What right do you have to look through our accounts?'

'Accounts? You should know that I have taken measures. Soon you will no longer be of any account in the eyes of the Lord. Shame on you! Shame on you! Shame, shame, shame!'

The priest had time to reflect that they had attracted an unusually uncommunicative parasite, if 'shame on you' was his only response to their actions. But before she could counter with anything cleverer, Pastor Anders appeared. 'Hi there, Börje, it's been a while. How are things?' he said, as incapable as ever of reading a situation.

*

A few minutes earlier, Börje Ekman had been standing, rake in hand, about to finish the gravel path, when it had struck him: the suitcases!

Of course! *That* was where they kept the profits from the devil's work they were pursuing. In the red one and the yellow one. All he had to do was gather proof, and then he could call the police, the government offices, the children's ombudsman ... anyone who wanted to, ought to, and would listen.

It wasn't quite clear how the children's ombudsman would react, but the point was that everyone, absolutely *everyone*, ought to be made to understand. The newspapers, the National Food Administration, the Reverend Mr Granlund, the Swedish Football Association ...

One might, with good reason, suspect that a person who feels he must inform both the children's ombudsman and the Swedish Football Association about ongoing ecclesiastical crime is no longer thinking clearly. That was the case with Börje Ekman. In his mind, there was just one thing left to do before he made sure that the whole world found out. If he acted quickly enough, he would have time to gather up the tenth of the contents of the two suitcases that rightly belonged to him.

Perhaps it would have been preferable to hold caution above all else, considering what was about to happen, but both churchwarden and rake soon found themselves in the very sacristy where the suitcases were kept, without giving any consideration to the time or to the present location of all criminal elements.

Thus the current situation. Börje was caught with his

hand in the till, surrounded by a certain percentage of the nearby criminals. They included the man who never strayed from the pastor's side and whose name so fitted such a blasphemous situation.

Meanwhile, the pastor's cheerful greeting had caused Börje Ekman to suspect that the hitman was no more than a useful idiot in the ungodly game. 'Don't you realize they're exploiting you?' he said, as he took four steps toward the pastor, rake still in hand.

'Who? What?' Pastor Anders responded.

At that instant, there were two honks outside the double doors. The weekly delivery of financial stimulants had arrived.

Jerry the Knife made the rapid assessment that the clown beside the pastor was less of a threat than what might await them outside. He went to open the door, saying to the receptionist and the pastor, with a glance at Börje Ekman: 'If you keep an eye on the pest with the rake, I'll deal with whatever's out there.'

The oh-so-meticulous head of security began by checking the driver, the same man who had appeared the week before and the weeks before that. He checked the contents of the truck, then stood to attention outside the doors, his back to the wall and his eyes sweeping left to right and back again. The priest and the receptionist had to carry the boxes of wine themselves.

*

266

The count lay where he was, next to his countess, in the grove about four hundred feet away. With his proficiency and the telescopic sight, it would be a simple matter to take out the pastor's bodyguard first, according to the original plan. But, given the new circumstances, this would mean he risked allowing the currently fully visible Hitman Anders time to move before shot number two, thus giving him a chance of survival.

No matter how much the count would like to waste the bodyguard as a bonus, the main target was still Hitman Anders.

Thus the change in plan. The count placed Jerry the Knife in second place on his kill list and focused directly on the principal victim. (Neither Johanna Kjellander nor Per Jansson had any future ahead of them, but there were limits to how much one count could accomplish in a single day.)

While the priest and the receptionist finished their carrying, and while the man whose goal was an immediate murder took aim at Hitman Anders, a dispute had arisen between the pastor and Börje Ekman.

'They're just fooling you! They're keeping all the money for themselves! Can't you see that? Or are you blind?'

But Hitman Anders remembered, of course, his very recent success at Astrid Lindgren Children's Hospital. 'Dear, kind Börje,' he said. 'Have you been raking too long in the sun? What is the matter? Didn't you know that the Church has already given away its first half-million, before we'd even scraped it together? The priest donated the last of her own money so that we could make our first proper donation in the name of Jesus, earlier than our finances actually allowed.'

Börje Ekman tried again. The priest and the receptionist let him get on with it. So far Hitman Anders was doing well enough as their spokesman.

'How stupid can a person be?' said Börje Ekman. 'Don't you have any idea how much money you bring in every Saturday?'

Hitman Anders lost his cool after the bit about how stupid one could be. Partly because he didn't know the answer, and partly because he sensed an implicit criticism of his own personal intelligence. Thus he rebuffed Börje Ekman: 'You take care of your raking, and I'll take care of bringing in money for those in need.'

At this, Börje Ekman lost *his* cool. 'Fine. If you're that frightfully naïve [those were the rudest words he knew], you can just stay like that. You can tend the path yourself in your spare time,' he said, shoving the rake into the hand of his pastor. 'After all, I've taken certain measures,' Börje Ekman concluded. 'All I have to say is – Sodom and Gomorrah!' And he smiled a superior smile, just before the situation deteriorated for him.

Permanently.

*

The count in the grove had his sights set. There were no obstacles in his way. The shot would strike that bastard Hitman Anders just below his chest and go straight through his body. 'See you in Hell,' he said, and fired.

Sure enough, the loud report caused Jerry the Knife to go from a state of general readiness to one of immediate action. He threw himself to the ground, crawled straight to the double doors and made sure they closed. He remained outside (he was truly no coward), in the questionable shelter of the truck, which stayed where it was. Where had the shot come from?

The bodyguard had moved at lightning speed. All the same, the count had been able to see that his task was accomplished, in that Hitman Anders had keeled over backwards. By now the bodyguard was behind the truck, out of the count's field of vision. This prompted the latter to say to his countess that it would be best for them to leave. One bodyguard more or less didn't matter, as long as he didn't pose a threat, but that would only be the case if they continued to lie low in the bushes up on the rise. In order to inspire the bodyguard to stay put rather than take off on a suicide mission, he fired off the half-jacketed bullet as well, for no reason other than to hit the side window of the truck (the driver was lying on the floor, among the accelerator, the brake, and the clutch, and remained unharmed by a margin of eight inches or so).

Börje Ekman, as previously mentioned, did not believe in luck, good or bad. He believed first and foremost in himself and his own excellent qualities. God took second place; rules and regulations came third. But one must, from an objective perspective, call it bad luck for Börje Ekman that Hitman Anders and the crew had settled at his church in particular. And it was bad luck that he had just handed his rake to Hitman Anders when the shot was fired. It was also bad luck that the recipient happened to be holding it in such a way that the count's jacketed bullet struck the metal part of the rake instead of landing just north of the hitman's navel and travelling onward through his body. The force of the bullet caused the rake to fly up into Hitman Anders's face; he plopped onto his hindquarters, his nose bleeding.

'Ouch, dammit!' he said as he sat there.

Meanwhile, Börje Ekman said nothing. A person seldom does when he has just had a jacketed bullet ricochet into his left eye and burrow a good deal further into his brain. The former churchwarden was more former than ever. He collapsed onto the floor. Dead.

'I'm bleeding!' Hitman Anders complained, as he stood up slowly.

'So's the churchwarden,' said the priest. 'But, in contrast to you, he's not whining about it. With all due respect, your bloody nose is the least of our problems right now.'

The priest looked at her former tormentor on the floor. Blood flowed from the hole in the churchwarden's head that had once been the location of his eye. 'The wages of sin is death, Romans six, verse twenty-three,' she said, without reflecting upon why, if this were the case, she herself was still alive.

* * *

As the count plucked the hand grenade from his pocket – one last security measure before it was time to retreat – Olofsson and Olofsson finally arrived on the scene. They had taken the wrong exit out of a roundabout and lost the white Audi, despite all the electronic equipment they had at their disposal. On the way up to the rise, they'd heard one shot, then another. They were currently standing twenty yards from the count and the countess, who were crouching on all fours in a sparse but considerable lilac bush. The rifle in the count's hand was clearly double-barrelled. This, along with his surprised and slightly desperate expression when he caught sight of Olofsson and Olofsson, led the brothers to realize that he had finished shooting for the moment, unless he were to reload, and where would he find time for that?

'Finish them off,' said Olofsson to his brother. 'Start with the count.'

But Olofsson had never killed before, and it was no minor task even for a hoodlum like him. 'Since when am I your servant? Do it yourself, if you're so damn smart,' said Olofsson. 'And you should start with the countess. She's the nastier of the two.'

Meanwhile, the count was fumbling with his hand grenade, and he did so to such an extent that, all in the same second, he managed to show it to the brothers, remove the pin – and drop the grenade among the lilac branches.

'What are you doing, you idiot?' the countess said, her last words in this life.

For his part, the count had already spoken his last.

The brothers Olofsson had time to throw themselves behind a rock, and survived unscathed the shrapnel that tore the count and the countess, plus the bush, to bits.

CHAPTER 54

Jerry the Knife stood up cautiously from his position behind the car. He no longer had to wonder where the attack with its double shots had come from, since it had immediately been followed by an explosion in the grove on the other side of the road. He would find out later what damage the shots had wrought inside the room. His first task was to make his way to the grove and neutralize any opposition that remained.

Since Jerry had to move in a wide curve to avoid making an obvious, easy target of himself, he heard police sirens approaching before he arrived at the spot. It was impossible to work out exactly what had happened, but miscellaneous body parts suggested that the attackers, a woman and a man, had been blasted into such small pieces that he wouldn't have been able to say for certain how many people had been involved, if not for the happy coincidence that three feet in shoes lay in a neat row among the rest of the mess. Jerry guessed the first two were a man's size ten and a half, while the third was more like a woman's six, with a high heel. As long as the attacker hadn't been three-legged and bi-gendered, with two different shoe sizes, this meant a woman had been at the man's side. The count and the countess, perhaps? Presumably. But who had blown them up? Were they in luck – might there be differing opinions, among the hoodlums, about how best to deal with Hitman Anders? Two wanted him dead, and of those two all that remained were three feet that wouldn't be walking away, unlike Jerry the Knife, who left the scene before the police arrived.

On his way back to the church, Jerry had to repeat this theory to himself to dare even to believe it. Were things really so felicitous that some people who wanted to get rid of the people who wanted to get rid of Hitman Anders had been there to blast the count and countess to bits?

A second later, he realized that the explosion had come after the shots. The second shot had hit the truck, but what about the first? Hitman Anders, one had to presume.

All in all, this meant that the threat scenario against Pastor Anders had massively improved.

And that he was dead.

A minute or so later, Jerry the Knife found that the target he had failed to protect had been luckier than should have been possible.

'Our situation is now such,' he said before the priest, the receptionist, and the hitman with a nosebleed, 'that we have a crime-scene investigation taking place hardly five hundred feet away and a corpse on the floor at our feet. Police officers will be knocking at the church door as soon as they put two and two together.'

'Four,' said Hitman Anders, with paper towel stuck in one nostril.

Jerry the Knife wondered if it would be possible to stuff the churchwarden into one of the suitcases, but the body would have to be cut in half to fit, and there was no time for that. Plus, this was in no way a pleasant thought.

The receptionist said that the bullet seemed still to be somewhere inside the skull of what used to be Börje Ekman, and that, if this was so, it was in a good place, probably somewhere in the vicinity of the screw that had been loose in there.

The priest was annoyed that the churchwarden had made such a terrible mess on the floor, though the puddle of blood could be mopped up, of course. She volunteered, and suggested at the same time that Jerry should take the corpse under his arm and load it into the truck, after which he should make corpse and truck disappear. After all, the truck would have plenty to gossip about to any police officer, what with its broken side window.

That was all they could do. So they did it. Jerry the Knife got behind the wheel after managing to convince the driver on the floor to shift a few feet to the right so he could reach the pedals to drive. What was more, in his new position the terrified driver found the spent bullet: the last remaining evidence that a shot had been fired in a churchly direction.

Wine, grapes, cheese and crackers had already been unloaded, so there was plenty of room for a dead church-warden in the back. The fact was, there would have been room for an average-sized congregation to keep him company, had it been necessary.

It was not immediately obvious to the police that the hand grenade that had taken two lives had any ties to the religious building on the other side of the road. It took several hours for one inspector to make the potential connection to the Church of Anders. And the resultant visit from the police wasn't undertaken until the next day.

The priest received the officers, saying she had read in the paper about the terrible thing that had apparently happened just a stone's throw away, that they had heard a loud bang as they were receiving goods the day before, and police sirens immediately afterwards, which had felt reassuring 'because we knew the authorities were on their way to deal with whatever might be going on. It's really nice to know the force is so alert. May we offer you a little church coffee? I'm guessing you don't have time for a game of pick up sticks.'

Approximately ten hours earlier, Jerry the Knife had thrown a triple-bagged bundle containing 175 pounds of churchwarden and 33 pounds of rocks into the Baltic. After this he had conscientiously set fire to the truck on a remote gravel road with the help of ten gallons of petrol. To be on the safe side, he had done it on the other side of the Västmanland county boundary so that the investigation one had to assume would result from the fire would land on a different desk in a different district from that of the mysterious explosion north of Stockholm.

CHAPTER 55

The former churchwarden, who now lay in the Baltic Sea at a depth of sixty feet, would come back to haunt the group one last time, several days after his death.

'Sodom and Gomorrah,' Börje Ekman had said, time and again, the previous Tuesday, as he had sat in his studio apartment, porridge simmering on the stove. He had taken a bite of his crispbread with margarine and tried to decide what to do. To start with. 'Do I have the right idea, Lord?' said Börje Ekman, who received silence in response.

So he changed tack. 'If I have the wrong idea, Lord, tell me so! You know I will not leave your side.'

The Lord still said nothing.

'Thank you, Lord,' said Börje Ekman, who had received the confirmation he needed.

Thus, on Wednesday morning, the self-appointed church-warden of the Church of Anders took his bicycle and rode from Systembolaget outlet to Systembolaget outlet to speak to the men and women on the park benches outside. Some of them already suspected that the state-controlled drinks outlet would ban them for the day, but they were hanging out there anyway. Others were still sober enough to have a good chance of being allowed in when the doors were unlocked at ten on the dot. Systembolaget had the complicated task of, on the one hand, selling as much alcohol as possible to the people of Sweden, thereby maximizing the amount of tax payable to the nation, and, on the other, preaching to the same people that in the name of sobriety they should not drink the alcohol they had just paid for so dearly.

In their ambition to do the responsible thing, they found reason each day to send packing not only ten but up to twenty potential customers, chosen from among those who most needed their visit.

To the joy of this clientele, Börje Ekman biked around with the news that there would be free wine at the Church of Anders north of the city that coming Saturday. The generosity of the Almighty knew no bounds. It was all free, if you arrived on time. Snacks were included. No, you didn't *have* to eat; that was optional. No, no one was shown the door before it even opened; this was all arranged by the Lord, not by Systembolaget.

Börje Ekman knew that the students from Mälar Upper Secondary School began their duties at one o'clock. The boxes of wine would presumably be in place half an hour later. 'Anyone who arrives before two o'clock is unlikely to come too late,' he said, then bicycled on.

And he smiled as he pedalled onward into the chilly headwind. To the next Systembolaget. And the next. And the next. Just hours before his own death.

* * *

When Saturday arrived, Churchwarden Börje Ekman lay silent at the bottom of the Baltic Sea, while the most wretched examples of humanity he had previously spurred into action took seats in the pews of his church at just after eleven that morning.

Three hours later, the church was full. Another twenty minutes after that, everyone in the church was full. Of wine. In contrast to the boxes from Moldova.

The students had been given their instructions. An empty box must be immediately exchanged for a fresh one. The rule was in place in case an exchange or two became necessary towards the end of the service; no one expected every single box to have been replaced by another long before Hitman Anders had even changed his clothes.

The first fight broke out around four thirty. It began with an argument about who had ownership of the nearest box of wine and ended when no one could remember what they had been arguing about since there was always a refill at hand. Around the same time, visitors who were used to finding spots in the church began to arrive, their pockets full of money, but once they reached the door they turned to go home again.

At twenty minutes to five, the priest saw what was going on. The students had made an initial round with their buckets and collected twenty-two Swedish kronor and a West German Deutschmark from 1982. This averaged out to just over 2.7 öre per visitor. Plus the German mark, which was potentially worth a similar amount, but only if melted down.

At ten to five, the students' spokesperson informed her that the week's rations of wine were gone. Did that mean they should dip into next week's or switch to the trays of goodies?

Neither. It meant that the week's sermon was cancelled and that Jerry the Knife and his men must empty the church before a real drunken brawl broke out.

'It's probably a bit late for that,' said Jerry the Knife, as he gazed out through the curtains at the congregation.

People were sitting in and standing among the pews; someone had lain down to sleep; at least four different groups were arguing with each other; a shoving match was going on; and bickering was breaking out. A filthy woman and an even filthier man had lain down under a fresco of the baby Jesus in the manger and appeared to be trying to demonstrate how it had not gone down, according to the Bible, when the Virgin Mary became with child.

Apparently someone had called the police (Börje Ekman was, in this respect, not a suspect), because by now they could hear sirens outside. The metal detectors started beeping with each new officer that passed through them, which in turn made the two police dogs nervous. One barking dog in a church sounds like an entire kennel. Two barking dogs create chaos.

By the time the smoke cleared, forty-six people had been arrested for drunkenness, violently resisting an officer or both. Two more were taken into custody for disorderly conduct.

In addition, the priest in charge, Johanna Kjellander, was called in for questioning, under suspicion of ... well, it wasn't quite possible to decide what.

According to the Law of Public Order, chapter three, paragraph eighteen, an individual municipality may impose further prohibitions in addition to those already in existence, for the purpose of maintaining the general order.

Following the articles in the Sunday newspapers, the municipality in question passed a resolution the very next day concerning 'a ban on the consumption of alcoholic beverages in the private religious gathering place known as "the Church of Anders", where the aim of said consumption appears to deviate from that in the given rules and regulations.' The municipality's decision was not complicated by the Church's vague links to what was presumed to be a double homicide a few days previously, in which two members of the criminal element had been blasted to bits.

CHAPTER 56

After a business strategy based on the assault of people who were, in the best case, not entirely innocent, the priest and the receptionist had steered onto the new track of swindling money out of those whose hearts were full of faith, hope, love and generosity, and whose circulatory systems, just to be safe, had been filled with wine.

If it hadn't been for a dead count and countess – as well as the final action of a self-important former, now equally dead, churchwarden – this line of business might have continued even today. But first it turned out that the newspapers could not be trusted as free distributors of publicity. Instead, the journalists drew murky connections between the presumed double homicide of two of the underworld's central figures and the Church of Anders on the other side of the road. A few even broached the possibility that Hitman Anders had reverted to his old self and was behind it all. It was taken for granted that the so-called count and his countess were among those whom Hitman Anders had cheated out of their money a few months previously.

'Bloody journalists.' The receptionist summarized the situation he and the priest now found themselves in.

The priest agreed. It would have been so much simpler if the media hadn't bothered to do their jobs.

As if these articles weren't bad enough, on their heels came the hastily approved local ordinance forbidding the Church of Anders to base its operations on *wine* (as opposed to a windmill in north-western Värmland) as the source of all that is good, which meant that both priest and receptionist saw a never-ending uphill battle ahead of them.

The long and the short of it was that the eight hundred-strong congregation, plus two hundred in the car park, had decreased to seven in a matter of a few weeks.

Seven visitors.

Who generated barely a single one hundred-krona note, gross.

Jointly.

That hundred had to suffice for a priest, a receptionist, a team of bodyguards, and a number of upper-secondary students. Even Hitman Anders realized they were in financial trouble. But he said that the strength of his religious message remained intact. The priest and the receptionist should be patient. 'We know that suffering produces endurance, endurance character, and character hope,' said Hitman Anders.

'Huh?' said the receptionist.

'Romans five,' the priest said automatically, in surprise.

Oblivious to the impression he had just made on those around him, Pastor Anders said he had first thought it was a pity that Börje Ekman had departed this life, but he had got over it in the thirty-plus seconds it had taken him to realize that the alternative would have been a hole in his own stomach and out the other side. In light of this, Hitman Anders had to agree with the receptionist that the nosebleed he had suffered was bearable.

The aforementioned nosebleed, incidentally, had ceased after around fifteen minutes, and despite the relative flop the following Saturday, the pastor was still determined to continue his work in Jesus's name. He didn't think it mattered that they could no longer serve wine to the churchgoers as long as he himself could continue to warm up with a tankard. The seven people in the pews would soon become fourteen. And before the priest, the pastor and the receptionist knew it, there would be fourteen hundred of them once again.

'It's a bit of an understatement to call what happened when the police and the dogs arrived a "relative flop",' said the receptionist.

'Let's call it a giant flop. But faith can move mountains,' said Hitman Anders, citing Leviticus.

'Has that devil memorized the Bible?' the receptionist asked, as soon as Hitman Anders had left the room.

'Not really,' said the priest. 'I think we discussed how faith moved mountains both inside the Bible and out, but not in Leviticus. In that one they sacrifice animals and some other stuff.'

The receptionist could not imagine a future in which Hitman Anders's faith would move them towards anything but trouble. The priest agreed.

The Church of Anders had been run into the ground. All they could do was liquidate the enterprise as best they could, while making sure the pastor didn't understand what was going on.

'I actually thought it was too good to be true when things were too good to be true for a brief time there,' said the priest.

The receptionist absorbed what she'd said. 'I suppose that was around the same time I was thinking *things have finally turned around, after all these years*. I vow never to think that again, my darling.'

CHAPTER 57

The priest and the receptionist had 6.9 million kronor in cash in a yellow suitcase (freshly counted). They also had an empty red one; it was available to be filled with their belongings.

Beyond that, they had a pastor who, thanks to various and sundry circumstances, had lost all his commercial value and from whom they ought, therefore, to part. In some sense, one could say that they were back in the vicinity of Chapter 16 of this story. Back then it was all about closing a hotel and vanishing with two suitcases full of money. And shaking off Hitman Anders. This time it was a church that was about to close, with the same Hitman Anders to shake off. They just had to make a slightly better job of it this time.

Just how they would accomplish this, they didn't know, but they would be able to work it out in peace and quiet, since the pastor had no idea how screwed up everything was.

'Seven visitors last Saturday,' said the receptionist. 'I'm guessing there'll be between four and five this week.'

'What I'll miss most are the Bible quotes in the praise of wine,' said the priest. 'We have to hand it to Pastor Anders, he worked the crowd in the pews. We didn't even have time to make it to my absolute favourite before it was all over.'

'Your favourite?'

'"I have become like a drunkard, like one overcome by wine, because of the Lord, and because of his holy words."'

'Wow. Who said that?'

'Isaiah. He liked to hit the bottle. Doesn't it sound nice? God speaks, and anyone who listens gets a free buzz to boot.'

She said these words in a rather disrespectful tone. This caused the receptionist to imagine that it would probably take her another hundred years to forgive the Lord for allowing family tradition to place her in his service against her will. With a minimal amount of effort on God's part, he could have given her failing grades at college by fiddling with her impeccable exam papers. Alternatively, if that was too much trouble, he could have made sure that she was never accepted for the final semester at the Pastoral Institute. After all, without that there would never have been any priesting for the priest, no matter how many plates her father the parish priest broke when he was in a rage.

Though, of course, you could turn this on its head, just like anything else. Perhaps her dad would have started throwing the plates at his daughter instead, which meant that God had been saving her life by humouring her father. In which case one might wonder to what extent God was currently regretting his actions.

The receptionist had long been aware of his own short-comings when it came to theological musings. He felt more at home with solid figures, like 6.9 million kronor, two blown-up gangsters, one slightly infelicitously, but on the whole felicitously, shot-to-death churchwarden and, previously, all those fractured arms and legs with occasional faces thrown in. What he and the priest ought to hope above anything else, the receptionist thought, was that Heaven didn't exist. Otherwise the two of them would find themselves in deep shit.

'Hello and good morning!' Hitman Anders sailed into the sacristy in what bordered on a stupidly good mood. 'I have a couple of alcohol-free beginnings to the week's sermon that I want to test out on the priest, now that everything has turned out as it has. Just have to pee first!'

He vanished as quickly as he'd come, out through the double doors Jerry the Knife had installed as an extra escape route. Not because he was on the run, but to do his business on God's green earth.

Neither the priest nor the receptionist had had time to comment upon the hitman's appearance and disappearance before they heard another voice, this time from the doorstep of the sacristy.

'Good day,' said a little man in a suit. 'My name is Olof Klarinder. I am from the Tax Authority and I would like to go through your accounts, if you don't mind.'

In Tax Authority language, this meant that Olof Klarinder intended to go through the accounts whether the potential delinquent minded or not.

The receptionist and the priest looked at the man.

Neither of them knew how they should respond but, as always, the priest was the quickest to improvise. 'I'm sure that will be fine,' she said. 'But you've turned up rather abruptly, Mr Klarinder. Pastor Anders isn't here today, and we are merely his humble servants. What would you say to coming back tomorrow at ten o'clock and I will inform the pastor that he should be here? With all his binders, of course. Will that be okay?'

The woman in the clerical collar had spoken with authority and in such an innocent voice that it crossed Olof Klarinder's mind that perhaps there were no tax-related inconsistencies in this congregation, after all. The disadvantage of anonymous tips was that they often had a basis in acrimony rather than truth.

That there were binders to page through was good news. Nothing was more satisfying to Olof Klarinder than paging through a binder. 'Well, the whole point of this sort of visit is that it's meant to happen unannounced,' he said. 'At the same time, it is not the aim of the Authority to be rigidly inflexible. Ten o'clock tomorrow will do, given that the pastor responsible for the finances is present at that time, with his … Did you say binders?'

Civil servant Klarinder had barely left before Hitman Anders came lumbering back from the other direction, still fumbling with his flies. 'You two look weird,' he said. 'Did something happen?'

'No,' the priest hastened to say. 'Nothing. Nothing at all. How was peeing?'

* * *

Time for a meeting with the only bodyguard who had not yet been dismissed: Jerry the Knife. And without the pastor.

Jerry was the man who had, with advance notice of mere days, arranged a weekly delivery of Moldovan red wine in boxes for hardly any money at all. He had contacts, whereas the priest had had a sudden idea. The idea in question was no more moral than others she had entertained during recent years, or in all her adult life, depending on how you looked at it. But it was still an idea.

'Rohypnol,' she said to Jerry the Knife. 'Or something along those lines. How long would it take you to get your hands on some?'

'Is it urgent?' said Jerry the Knife.

'You might say so,' said the priest.

'What is this all about?' said the receptionist, who in the rush had not been properly informed of the plan.

'Since Rohypnol is no longer sold in Sweden, I'm afraid I need some time.'

'How much?' said the priest.

'What is this all about?' the receptionist said again.

'Three hours,' said Jerry the Knife. 'Two and a half if traffic isn't too bad.'

'*What is this all about?*'

CHAPTER 58

The receptionist was soon brought up to speed, and after a certain amount of hesitation had given his blessing, so to speak.

Thus: when Hitman Anders was at his happiest, around four thirty in the afternoon, the priest and the receptionist delivered the news that it was about time he take over leadership for real. Among other things, this meant they would sign over to him formal ownership and responsibility straight away; there was no reason to wait. It also meant that the pastor would allocate the future earnings of the congregation as he pleased. The priest and the receptionist would take a step back but would remain at his side for moral support.

Pastor Anders was extremely touched. Not only had they always given him five hundred kronor per week to spend as he pleased (except towards the end, when the income from the collection had temporarily reached only three digits at best), now they were about to hand over the whole lot to him.

'Many, many thanks, dear friends,' he said. 'I confess that I misjudged you at first, but I understand now that you are good people through and through. Hallelujah and Hosanna!'

Upon which he signed all the necessary papers, without even coming close to learning what they said.

When the administrative stuff was out of the way, the priest suggested that the pastor lead the meeting with the legal representative who was expected to drop in for a routine inspection the next morning, but she supposed it was best if he were to tell it like it was, and that would be the end of that.

'How much do we have in the donation account?' Hitman Anders wondered.

'Thirty-two kronor,' said the receptionist.

* * *

They planned to meet again in the sacristy the next morning at nine o'clock. The priest and the receptionist offered to have breakfast with Hitman Anders and, no, there would be nothing newfangled about it. The morning vino was the same sacrament as ever; it couldn't be replaced with coffee just because they were expecting company. There would, however, be freshly baked bread, the priest promised.

Hitman Anders understood. That is, he didn't understand the word 'sacrament', but he understood that the standing tradition of communion was under no threat. 'See you tomorrow morning,' he said. 'Is it okay if I take a box of the Moldovan stuff with me now? I'm frugal when it comes to myself, but I have a friend or two and we were planning to come together in the camper-van this evening for some Bible study. I suppose you two are still living in your aunt's cellar?' he asked, looking at the receptionist, who by now had bargained his way to a discount for the Riddarholm suite at the Hilton.

'Yes, free of charge, God bless her,' said the receptionist, who had never had any aunt. 'Do take a box for your friends. Or two. But at nine o'clock tomorrow morning, on the dot, we want you here, awake and sober. Or something along those lines.' At this, the receptionist smiled, all in accordance with their aims, and received an aimless smile in return.

* * *

Hitman Anders was not present at nine o'clock the next day. Neither was he there at a quarter past. But just before nine thirty he tumbled in. 'I'm sorry I'm late,' he said. 'My morning toilet took longer than expected.'

'Morning toilet?' said the priest. 'The camper-van is just seventy yards from here, and it hasn't had a working toilet for at least a week.'

'I know,' said Hitman Anders. 'Isn't that terrible?'

Anyway, there was no time to lose. The hitman was served a glass of wine, spiked with just the right amount of vodka, then a second glass. To complement the wine he was given three sandwiches with cheese and carefully powdered Rohypnol in the margarine. A milligram per sandwich ought to be just right. If a little extra got in, it wouldn't matter.

The hitman, who for several years had lived by the motto 'alcohol and pills, never again,' said that the wine seemed extra delicious today, that perhaps the Lord wanted to prepare him in the best way possible for his meeting with the representative from the Tax Authority. 'Although don't you imagine the worst that can happen is that he could demand twenty per cent tax on those thirty-two kronor?' He didn't comment on the sandwiches, other than to ask for one more, which the priest, to be safe, spiked with another milligram of the substance chemically known as $C_{16}H_{12}FN_3O_3$.

The priest and the receptionist found an excuse to leave at five minutes to ten; they handed over three binders they had filled with hole-punched comic books to lend them a certain weightiness (you make do with what you have to hand; and in this case what they had was a bundle of comics that for some inexplicable reason had been lying in a wardrobe in the sacristy; what they did not have was any documentation concerning anything other than the ownership that had so recently changed hands). And then they told Hitman Anders to call one of them if he needed help. With this, they went on their way, turning off their phones as they left.

'As far as I can tell, that amount of booze and pills ought to be enough to knock out a horse,' the receptionist said to his priest, once they had reached a safe distance from whatever events might ensue.

'Yes, but it's an ass we're dealing with at the moment. And this ass has a previous habit. I think we can rest assured that the meeting between the ass and the tax man will be tragic enough.'

The civil servant from the Tax Authority introduced himself to Pastor Anders, who was starting to feel odd as they shook hands. There was something superior about the man's handshake. And he had said, 'Nice to meet you!'

What did he mean, *nice to meet you*? And what was with that tie? Did he think he was better than everyone else?

What was more, the tie character started asking provocative questions about cash registers, control units, models, serial numbers, record-keeping, and other stuff the pastor didn't understand. Plus, he was ugly.

'What the fuck is your problem?' Hitman Anders said, as his insides began to roil.

'What's my problem?' said Olof Klarinder, a bit anxiously. 'Nothing. I'm a civil servant just trying to do my job. A sound taxpayer morale is a cornerstone of any democratic nation. Don't you agree, pastor?'

The only thing that the pastor could agree with while he was undergoing a personality change was that the Tax Authority could take twenty per cent of the collected assets of thirty-two kronor. Exactly how much this would amount to, the pastor couldn't say, but surely it wouldn't be more than a fifty-krona note, would it?

Olof Klarinder had the feeling something was not quite right, yet he couldn't resist the urge to open the first and second of the three binders. Luckily, he survived the abuse he was subjected to by the pastor, who completed his transformation back into a murderer after the civil servant offered the opinion that seventeen copies of the

Phantom from 1979 to 1980 could not be considered a substitute for the information concerning the congregation's enterprise that the representative of the Tax Authority had requested. He survived, but was thoroughly battered when Hitman Anders tried to bash into him the bookkeeping he wanted to have a look at, with the help of the third, not-yet-delivered, binder.

Afterwards the pastor didn't remember what had transpired, but based on experience he admitted his guilt and was, in accordance with the third chapter, seventh paragraph of the Criminal Code, sentenced to sixteen months in prison. He received another nine months in accordance with the fourth paragraph in the Tax Offences Act. Twenty-five months in all, which, he was happy to say, was the shortest amount of time he'd ever been locked up for. Everything truly was moving in the right direction.

Immediately after the trial, he was given the opportunity to have a short talk with the priest and the receptionist. He delivered a sincere apology; he had no idea what had got into him. The priest gave him a long hug and said he shouldn't blame himself too much.

'We'll visit you,' she said, with a smile.

'We will?' said the receptionist, as they left the future prisoner behind.

'No,' said the priest.

* * *

After a thanks-for-everything dinner in honour of Jerry the Knife, all that remained was the priest, the receptionist, their suite at the Hilton, and a yellow suitcase containing nearly seven million kronor (which included the money that had been regularly withdrawn from the bank account). These days, the church and the camper-van were registered in Hitman Anders's name, so they were seized by Olof Klarinder's colleagues at the Enforcement Agency, while Klarinder gave himself time to heal at Karolinska Hospital, with fractures here and there. It wasn't too boring for him, since he'd happened to bring with him two of the three accounting binders from the Church of Anders. The *Phantom* had always secretly been a Klarinderian favourite.

PART THREE

YET ANOTHER UNUSUAL BUSINESS STRATEGY

CHAPTER 59

The receptionist lay in bed next to his priest, under the duvet, unable to fall asleep. He was thinking about how things had gone for them; how things had gone for him. He thought about his devil of a grandfather, who had frittered away all of the family's money and indirectly caused his grandchild to become recreational director of a whorehouse.

And now he and the priest had a respectable number of millions in a yellow suitcase. They were almost as rich as Grandfather had once been. They lived in a suite at a luxury hotel and frequently indulged in *foie gras* and champagne. Partly because it tasted good, but mostly because Per Persson insisted that everything they ate and drank should be expensive.

Per Persson had taken his economic revenge. And he was left with a strange feeling of … something. Or maybe it was the lack of … something else.

If Grandfather's financial ruin had finally been put to rights just over fifty years later, why, then, was he not completely satisfied? Or at least considerably satisfied?

Did he have a guilty conscience because he and the priest had made sure that Hitman Anders ended up where he belonged?

No, why would he?

In general, man and beast had all got more or less what they deserved. Except maybe the churchwarden, who had first started to grasp far too much and later ended up being more dead than was necessary, given the circumstances. An unfortunate factor, certainly. But, on the whole, it had been just a peripheral event.

This might be a good time for a minor digression in defence of the receptionist. One might find it an understatement to call manslaughter resulting from a failed homicide a 'peripheral event'. But anyone who took Per Persson's genetic heritage into account could find, if not an excuse, at least an explanation.

He had inherited his moral compass from his father, the drunkard (who had abandoned his son for a bottle of cognac when the boy was two years old), and from his grandfather, the horse dealer, a man who had dosed his foals with precise amounts of arsenic from birth onwards so that they would grow used to the poison and be in tip-top shape not only on the day of sale but, in slowly declining degrees, on the days, weeks and months after that.

A person who sold animals at a Saturday market only to be faced with complaints on Sunday that the animal had died would find that his reputation quickly went downhill. But Per Persson's grandfather's horses stood steady on all fours all night long, and their eyes blinked alertly even the next day. They didn't die until months later, of chronic stomach problems; cancer, lung or otherwise; liver or kidney failure; and other ailments that were difficult to connect to the ever-richer respected dealer. Since he always weighed and measured correctly, his horses' coats never turned greenish just before their death. This was a common side effect of a sloppy arsenic overdose hours before a sale. After all, horses are not green by nature (in contrast to nature itself, and some types of tractor). What's more, working horses should preferably not be dead before they have been put to use. Imagine a farmer who spent a Saturday afternoon purchasing first a hardworking draught animal, then enjoying a weekend bender to celebrate the deal, and awoke the next day with a headache, in contrast to his newly bought horse, which didn't wake up at all. Such a man had at least two reasons to skip church, take up a pitchfork and track down the seller, who had managed to put a considerable number of parishes between them.

Per Persson's grandfather had been too cunning for that, until he became too stupid to realize that the tractor's infringement on the market was many times worse than any pitchfork tines in the backside.

Since the apple didn't fall all that far from the family tree, it is possible to understand the receptionist's thoughts on the present matter. A skilfully poisoned horse and a felicitously departed churchwarden: what difference could there be, from a purely ethical standpoint?

When Per Persson had tossed and turned in mind and body for long enough, he sought help from the woman who lay sleeping by his side. 'Darling? Are you awake?'

No response.

'Darling?'

The priest moved. Not much, but a little. 'No, I'm not awake,' she said. 'What's the matter?'

Ugh, how the receptionist regretted this, dragging her into his speculation in the middle of the night … idiot, idiot, idiot. 'I'm sorry if I woke you up. Go back to sleep and we'll talk in the morning.'

But the priest fluffed her pillow and sat up halfway in the bed. 'Tell me what you wanted, or I'll stay up all night and read to you from the Gideon Bible.'

The receptionist knew this was an empty threat. The priest had thrown out of the window, on their very first night, the Gideon Bible that littered practically every hotel room in the entire country. And yet he realized he had to say something. But he didn't know what to say, or how to say it.

'Well, darling,' he tried, 'we've actually been pretty clever on the whole, don't you think?'

'You mean that everyone who got in our way is now dead, super-dead, or locked up, while we enjoy champagne?'

Hmm, no, that wasn't exactly what he'd meant, at least not formulated in such a straightforward manner. Per Persson pointed out that they had done a pretty good job of cleaning up after life's historic injustices. This grandson had exchanged his grandfather's financial ruin for a luxury suite, *foie gras*, and bubbly. And they had the money for it because Per and Johanna had pooled their strength to distort the meaning of the Bible her father and forefathers had forced upon her.

'I suppose what I might be saying is that we've kind of reached our goal. And that it would be … annoying if that woman, the poet, whatever her name was, the one who wrote that the path is worth the pain … if she had …'

'The path?' said the drowsy priest, starting to suspect that the conversation would not be over for quite some time.

'Yes, the path. If our goal was a luxury suite with the Gideon Bible thrown out of the window, then why isn't our life a walk in the park now? Or maybe you think it is.'

'Is what?'

'A walk in the park?'

'What is?'

'Life.'

'What time is it?'

'Ten past one,' said the receptionist.

CHAPTER 60

Was life a walk in the park?

Well, one thing was for sure: if it was, this was a new phenomenon for Johanna Kjellander. Up to now life had mostly just jerked her around.

It was all because of that stuff with her dad. And his dad. And his dad. And his dad. In some collective fashion, they had decreed that she should be a he, and that he should be a priest.

In the first instance, it hadn't worked out as they'd desired, and Johanna was forced to hear throughout her childhood that it was her own fault she wasn't man enough to be a man.

But become a priest she had. And if she were to stop and think instead of falling asleep again, perhaps this had less to do with her lack of belief and more to do with not believing as a matter of principle. After all, the Bible could be read from so many different viewpoints. The priest chose her own – and in so doing affirmed her bitterness towards her father, grandfather, great-grandfather, and so on, all the way back to somewhere beyond Gustav III (who had, incidentally, certain similarities to the church-warden, the difference being that the King, in his day, had taken his shot in the back rather than in the eye).

'So you do believe in that book a little bit after all?' said the receptionist.

'Let's not go overboard. There's no bloody way Noah lived to the age of nine hundred.'

'Nine hundred and fifty.'

'Or that. Remember, I just woke up.'

'I'm not sure I've ever heard you swear before.'

'Oh, it's happened. But mostly after one in the morning.'

They smiled at each other. Not that it was visible in the darkness, but they could feel it.

The receptionist kept talking, confessing that the question he'd just posed might be silly, but the priest had thus far avoided answering it.

Johanna Kjellander yawned and confessed that this was because she had forgotten the question. 'But feel free to ask it again. The night is ruined anyway.'

Right, it was about the point of everything. And whether things were going as well for them as they should. Whether life was a walk in the park.

The priest was silent for a moment, then decided to take the conversation seriously. She did enjoy eating *foie gras* at the Hilton with her receptionist. Much more than standing in a pulpit and lying to a flock of sheep once a week.

But Per was right, of course, that each day verged on being the same as the one before, and it was not a given that they should remain in the suite until they ran out of money. Which they probably would rather quickly at this place, wouldn't they?

'If we're conservative with the *foie gras* and champagne, the contents of the suitcase will last for about three and a half years,' the receptionist said, allowing for some miscalculation.

'And then what?' said the priest.

'That's what I'm saying.'

The priest had registered Per Persson's flirtation with one of the country's most famous poems, the one that began 'A day of plenty is never blessed; a day of thirst is always best.'

What spurred her into an extra round of pondering their existence was not the poem *per se*, but that the poet had committed suicide just a few years later. This could not reasonably be considered the meaning of life.

When Johanna thought back to the moments she had actually found pleasurable since meeting the receptionist (aside from their sexual relations and the accompanying quality time on a mattress, in a camper-van, behind an organ, or wherever else was available), it was the times when they had handed out money left and right. The hullabaloo in the Red Cross store in Växjö had perhaps not been a high point, but seeing a Salvationist stagger backwards outside Systembolaget in Hässleholm was the sort of thing you could smile about afterwards. And that time with the camper-van parked willy-nilly outside the headquarters of Save the Children. And the time Hitman Anders had told off the tin soldier who didn't want to accept a suspicious package meant for his queen ...

The receptionist nodded in recollection, but he was also growing nervous. Was the priest trying to say they should give the contents of the yellow suitcase to needy people other than themselves? Was *that* the way …?

'Like hell it is!' said the priest, sitting up even straighter in bed.

'You just swore again.'

'Well, stop talking such goddamn rubbish!'

At last they came to an agreement that their life had been a walk in the park for a while because they had given with one hand while no one could see that they were taking many times more with the other. That it was more blessed to take than to give, but that giving did have its advantages.

The receptionist tried to summarize and look to the future. 'What if the meaning of life is to make other people happy as long as we have the financial means to make ourselves just a little happier? Like the Church project, but without God, Jesus, or snipers in the bell tower.'

'Or Noah,' said the priest.

'What?'

'Without God, Jesus, snipers in the bell tower or *Noah*. I can't stand him.'

The receptionist promised to think up a new equation on the theme of goodness versus neediness in which no one had occasion to know that they considered themselves to be the neediest of all. And the equation – whatever it would turn out to be – would under no circumstances include Noah or his ark.

'Is it okay if I go back to sleep while you work out the details?' asked the priest, preparing herself for the 'yes' she had reason to expect.

The receptionist thought she was a worthy conversational partner even when she was half asleep. And she might as well stay that way a little while longer. For he had just had a micro-idea on the theme of the Meaning of Life. So he said she was welcome to fall asleep again, unless she could be persuaded to respond positively to the fact that he had suddenly started coveting his neighbour. Per Persson wriggled closer.

'It's almost one thirty,' said Johanna Kjellander. And wriggled in to meet him.

CHAPTER 61

Sweden's third and third-largest general criminal meeting was held in the same cellar as meeting number two. Fifteen men; since last time, two had been captured by the law after they had committed, while far too high on drugs, an armoured-car robbery in which the armoured car had turned out to be a bread van.

Even though their spoils were no more than a ten-pack of sandwich buns from Eskelund's Bakery (one of the robbers was hungry), loaded weapons had been involved and their punishment was handed down accordingly. Eskelund's Bakery was mentioned in every newspaper imaginable, which led the manager of the bakery to send two lovely potted geraniums to the jail where the two robbers sat awaiting trial. The staff at the jail suspected attempted smuggling of narcotics: never before had recent arrivals been sent (or, for that matter, wanted to be sent) flowers as a thank-you for a crime poorly committed. Thus, the geraniums were plucked to bits before they could safely be handed over to the recipients, which didn't happen because there was no longer any point.

The current situation for the rest of them was that the count and the countess had departed this life after an intense battle with the brave brothers Olofsson, who

311

were not exactly raring to give any more details about how it had all gone down.

'Trade secret,' Olofsson had said, while his brother nodded in agreement.

What was more, Hitman Anders was locked up and his peculiar church project abandoned.

The question that remained for the fifteen men was what they should do with Hitman Anders's two sidekicks. All reasonable logic dictated that they were sitting on many millions of kronor. Since the hitman was safe and sound in prison, and thus alive, it shouldn't be dangerous to have a not-altogether-friendly conversation with the sidekicks on the topic of 'handing over all the money'. There were, however, fifteen different, absolutely un-voiced opinions on how the cash should then be divided among them.

The man called Ox argued that the sidekicks ought to meet the same fate as Mr and Mrs Count, like, for example, being forced to swallow a hand grenade each, and he also felt that the Olofsson brothers might as well take care of this since they were on a roll.

After a certain amount of arguing, it was decided by a vote of 14–1 that it was not possible to swallow a hand grenade, no matter how hard a third party might push (and this was not even considering the security risk for whoever took on the pushing), plus that two blown-up sidekicks might provoke Hitman Anders to reveal things he shouldn't.

So, no more killing for the time being. The consensus was still strong that the information about who had ordered what from Hitman Anders in regard to contract killing and general limb-breaking must not get out. Even if the count and the countess were now spending their days in Hell (they would likely all wander that path one day), there were still plenty of revelations to be had about who had wished to harm a hair on whose head. Allowing the priest and the other guy to go free after they'd paid their debts would simply be a security measure.

A decision was made by a vote of 13–2 to assign Olofsson and Olofsson the task of bringing in the two sidekicks. The brothers managed to whine their way to a fee of fifty thousand kronor for the job; more was out of the question now that the ending of lives was off the table.

* * *

The unhappy brothers Olofsson had no idea where to start looking for the priest and the other guy. They began by hanging around the church for a few days and then a few days more. But the only difference from one day to the next was that weeds sprouted in the gravel path that led up to the porch. Beyond that, nothing was going on.

After almost a week, one of the brothers realized they could try the handle on the door at the top of the gravel path to see if it was unlocked. It was.

Inside, the church still looked like a battlefield; no one from the Enforcement Agency had prioritized the cleaning of the seized property.

But they were unable to find any clues about where the priest and the other guy might be.

In the sacristy, however, they found what had to be a thousand litres of wine in boxes, and that was worth a try. It didn't taste bad, but neither did it lead to anything, other than making their unpleasant existence slightly pleasanter.

There was also a collection of comics in a wardrobe. Judging by the dates, they had been lying there for thirty years or more.

'Comics in a church?' said Olofsson.

His brother didn't respond. Instead he sat down to read *Agent X9*.

Olofsson moved on to a wastepaper basket alongside the sacristy's desk. He turned it upside down and skimmed through various crumpled notes. They all turned out to be of the same sort – receipts for cash payments for a room at the Hilton near Slussen in Stockholm. First one night, then another night, then one more night … Had they been staying at the Hilton, those pigs, and paying for it with the money that belonged to the Olofssons and the others? One night at a time. Always ready to take off.

'Come on!' said Olofsson, who had just reached what was, without question, the most gifted conclusion of his entire life.

'Hold on a minute,' said Olofsson, who was now in the middle of an issue of *Modesty Blaise*.

CHAPTER 62

The priest and – above all – the receptionist continued to search for the meaning of life. After six days, they were more in agreement than ever that it was not to be found in the Riddarholm Suite at the Hilton.

It wasn't until they decided to find somewhere to live that it occurred to them how expensive housing was. A three-room apartment in Stockholm would mean using the entire contents of the suitcase, and what would be the point in having fun without bankrupting themselves if they started off by bankrupting themselves? And it was pretty senseless to enter the housing queue for a reasonable rental property unless you aimed to live to 950, as we know only one person, so far, has managed to do.

Neither the receptionist nor the priest had any experience of how the housing market worked. Per Persson had spent his entire adult life sleeping behind a hotel lobby or in a camper-van. Johanna Kjellander's knowledge of the same matter encompassed little more than her dad's parsonage, a student-housing corridor in Uppsala, and her dad's parsonage again (as a new graduate she'd had to commute between her childhood bedroom and her job, twelve miles away; this was the most freedom her dad would allow).

But now they knew, and they made a joint decision that they were far too enamoured of the contents of the yellow suitcase to use it just for living.

The most economically sustainable option they discovered was a fishing shack on an island in the middle of the Baltic Sea. They had discovered this pearl of Gotland online and were attracted to the price (slightly more than free), in conjunction with the distance (just over a hundred nautical miles) from those Stockholm criminals who had not yet blown one another up.

There were reasons for the low price. One was not allowed to live in the shack on a permanent basis, one was not allowed to insulate the walls or roof, and one was not allowed to install a toilet.

'I'm sure we can make uninsulated work if we just build a big enough fire in the stove,' said the priest, 'but I'm not keen on the prospect of sitting in a snowbank in freezing temperatures to do you-know-what.'

'I think we should take it, then start a test fire in the stove first thing, using the authorities' rulebook as kindling. After that, we can insulate the walls and build a bathroom in all our ignorance.'

'What if someone catches us?' The priest still had a fear of authority after all those years under her father's thumb.

'If someone catches us? Who would catch us? The special toilet inspector of the Gotland region? The man or woman who goes from door to door to make sure that people poo where they're supposed to?'

In addition to the aforementioned rules, it was hardly

permitted to walk around outside, or that was how the shack's seller made it sound as he prattled on, over the phone, about protected beaches, protected waters, protected animals, protected biotopes, and a handful of other protections that not even the priest, in the end, could tolerate listening to. But at last he got to the point, which was that he couldn't imagine handing his cultural treasure to just anyone. But now he felt confident: a servant of the Lord wished to take over its care.

'Glad to hear it,' said the priest. 'If you could send us the documents straight away, I'm quite eager to do the taking over.'

The seller preferred that they meet in person: they could seal the deal over a bowl of seaweed soup. But the eavesdropping receptionist heard this, decided enough was enough, took the receiver, introduced himself as the assistant of parish priest Kjellander, and said that he and the priest were currently at a conference at the Hilton in Stockholm but that in just two days they were to leave for Sierra Leone to take part in a humanitarian project aiding leper colonies; it would be best for the seller to sign the documents and forward them to the hotel. They would be countersigned and sent back by return.

'Wow,' said the man who had wanted to give them soup, then promised that he would do as he'd been asked immediately.

When the phone call was over, the priest informed her receptionist that leper colonies didn't really exist nowadays, and the illness was treated with antibiotics rather than by the laying on of hands of former parish priests.

'But in general, well done,' she praised him. 'Sierra Leone – what made you think of that?'

'I don't know,' said the receptionist. 'But if they don't have leprosy there, I'm sure they have something else.'

* * *

Time to pack their bag. Singular. Thanks to the cost of the Hilton, their store of money had dwindled enough to allow their negligible personal belongings to fit with the remaining millions.

The couple and the yellow suitcase checked out one last time. The red one remained in the room, empty. Their aim was to walk to Central Station and continue their journey by bus to Nynäshamn, where the ferry to Gotland awaited them.

But none of that came to be.

CHAPTER 63

Olofsson and Olofsson had not exactly run into bad luck when they had encountered the count and the countess some time before. Neither were they faced with it now. Altogether, their wait in the car outside the entrance to the Hilton lasted about ten minutes.

'Well, Hell's bells!' said Olofsson to his brother, who still had a comic in hand. 'There they are!'

'Where?' Olofsson said, disoriented.

'There! With a yellow suitcase! They've checked out. They're heading somewhere!'

'Yeah, to our cellar,' Olofsson's brother spat, tossing the comic into the back seat. 'Follow them, and I'll grab them as soon as I get the chance.'

The chance in question occurred just over fifty metres later, at Södermalmstorg. Olofsson dashed out of the passenger side and forced the priest and the receptionist into the back seat with the help of a revolver that was double the size of the one he had previously boozed away outside the Church of Anders (his thinking was, the larger the revolver, the less likely he would be to repeat the mistake). With an impressive Smith & Wesson pointed at them, neither the priest nor the receptionist hesitated to follow the advice they had just received from the strange man.

That left the suitcase. Olofsson considered leaving it on the street, but in the end he decided to throw it onto the laps of the abductees. After all, it might contain clues leading in one direction or another, if the two people he had seized were stupid enough to keep their mouths shut about where all the money was.

* * *

The priest, the receptionist and the yellow suitcase stood in a row in the gathering place of Greater Stockholm's underworld: the cellar beneath one of the city's pubs that was least inclined to pay taxes. To the priest's surprise, no one in the group took any immediate notice of the suitcase.

'Welcome,' said the unofficial leader of the fifteen hoodlums. 'We promise you'll get out of here. In body bags, or some other way.' Then he stated that the priest and the other guy owed the group at least thirteen million kronor.

'Well, that probably depends on how you count it,' the priest said bravely. 'Thirteen sounds like a rather high amount to start with.'

'To start with?' said the head hoodlum.

'*Per Persson*,' said the receptionist, who didn't like being called 'the other guy'.

'I don't give a shit what your name is,' said the head hoodlum, turning back to the priest. 'What do you mean, "to start with" and "how you count it"?'

The priest was not sure where and how this had started and how one should count it, but the ball was rolling. And it was important to keep her eyes on it. Talk first and think later was her style in this type of situation. 'Well, as a rough estimate, I think just over ten million would be plenty,' she said, as she realized she had just been stupid enough to name an amount that far exceeded what they actually had to buy their way to freedom.

The head hoodlum countered with a question of his own: 'Hypothetically, if we decided to settle for the priest's rough estimate, where might that ten million kronor be?'

Per Persson was definitely not the best at improvising in situations such as this. He searched for a thought that could be transformed to words that might turn things around to their advantage, but the priest beat him to it. 'First and foremost, I would like to discuss the amount,' she said.

'The amount?' said the head hoodlum. 'Didn't you just fucking say ten million?'

'There there, no need to swear,' said the priest. 'The man upstairs sees and hears everything.'

She's on a roll now, thought the receptionist.

'I said that, by a rough estimate, ten million was a more reasonable amount. But, without being too indiscreet, I must point out that at least three of those ten millions can be traced back either to what the count and countess ordered from us to get several of you out of the way, or to what several of you ordered from us to do just the opposite, and a few other minor bits of mischief.'

An anxious murmur rose among the hoodlums in the cellar. She wasn't about to say more about who had ordered what, was she?

'If I may continue,' the priest continued, 'I'll allow myself the opinion that it would be immoral of you to take money from Hitman Anders just because he didn't murder any of you.'

The receptionist was barely following the priest's reckoning. No one else in the cellar was even close. She had lost most of them at the word 'immoral'.

'What's more, I think that further rebates might be in order, considering the final results in the case of the count and the countess. If they hadn't been aiming a gun at the man who had been paid to kill them, they would never have died. Isn't that right?'

Further murmuring.

'What are you getting at?' the head hoodlum asked peevishly.

'That we have a red suitcase,' said the priest, placing her hand on the yellow one beside her.

'A *red* suitcase?'

'Containing exactly six million kronor. Our combined assets. I imagine that at least a few of you were confirmed into the Church once upon a time. Perhaps one or two of you still believe that there is a life after this one and that it doesn't necessarily have to end in meeting the count and countess again. Mightn't six million kronor be a fairly good substitute to avoid having to kill a priest?'

'And a Per Persson,' the receptionist rushed to say.

'And a Per Persson, of course,' the priest added.

The head hoodlum repeated that he was not interested in Per Persson's name. Meanwhile, another round of murmurs rose among the rest of the hoodlums. The priest attempted to interpret the tones. There seemed to be differing opinions. So she added a bit more: 'The suitcase is hidden in a secure place. Only I know where it is, and I can imagine that I would readily tell you, but only if I were subjected to torture. And again – torturing a priest! Could that really be the best way to appease the Lord? Plus there's the fact that, as far as I know, Hitman Anders' being locked up doesn't mean he has lost the ability to speak.'

That made several people in the group shudder.

'Thus my suggestion is that this man here, whose name you don't want to know, and I will hand over six million kronor to you in the very near future and in return you will swear on your honour as thieves that you will allow us to live in good health.'

'Or three million,' said the receptionist, who was relatively heartbroken at the thought of becoming a pauper once again. 'And then maybe we'll all end up in Heaven together when the time comes.'

But Per Persson's relationship with the hoodlums had definitely gone awry.

'Not only do I not give a shit what your name is, I also don't care where you'd end up in the event that I cut you open from navel to chin,' said the head hoodlum, and it appeared that he wished to launch into a second tirade when he was interrupted by the priest.

'Or six million, like I said,' said the priest, who'd had time to perform an analysis and found that they wouldn't get away with sacrificing any less.

Even more murmuring. In the end, the hoodlums agreed that six million kronor would be an acceptable payoff to be spared the trouble of killing the goddamned priest and the man who insisted that he had a name. Sure, it would have been simpler just to kill them, but murder was murder and the police were the police. Plus there was that nuisance Hitman Anders and his big trap.

'Okay,' said the head hoodlum. 'You lead us to your red suitcase with the six million, we'll count it down here in the cellar to double-check the contents, and if it contains the correct amount you can leave and we won't bother you again. After that, as far as we're concerned, you'll no longer exist.'

'But we'll exist as far as *we*'re concerned?' the receptionist wished to clarify.

'It's up to you whether or not you want to jump off the Väster Bridge, but you won't be on our list any longer. Assuming you hand over the red suitcase and it contains what you say it does.'

The priest lowered her gaze a notch and said that the Lord had always been understanding of lies as long as they were white as snow.

'What do you mean?'

'The red suitcase … is actually yellow.'

'The one you're leaning against?'

'Speedy delivery, right?' The priest smiled. 'Is it okay if my friend and I take with us a couple of toothbrushes, some underwear, and a few other things that are in there with the money when we go?'

And she made sure to open the suitcase to show off its magnificent contents before the head hoodlum and his under-hoodlums could change their minds.

CHAPTER 64

As the collective personification of greed stuck nose and hands into the suitcase full of money, the priest grabbed underwear, a toothbrush, a dress, a pair of trousers, and something else, then whispered to her receptionist that their best opportunity to disappear happened to be this very second.

Not even the head hoodlum noticed when the prisoners vanished, for he was no less greedy than anyone else in the room. He did, however, roar that everyone must stop snatching money. They had to divide it among themselves in an organized fashion.

His roar resulted in most, but not all, of the banknotes being returned to the suitcase. Hoodlum number two had clearly seen hoodlum number four shove a whole bundle of cash into his left front pocket, and now number two was in the process of proving it.

But hoodlum number four was not the sort who let people grope him, especially not so close to his personal machinery and definitely not while others were watching. Thus, to retain his place in the hierarchy, he struck number two with a fist. Number two collapsed to the floor and, happily enough, passed out when his head hit the concrete, or the whole situation would have gone off the rails then and there. Instead it held off for four more minutes.

The head hoodlum was temporarily able to restore order in his classroom. The task they were faced with was to divide six million kronor among fifteen people, or maybe fourteen, depending on whether the guy on the floor was planning to wake up or not.

But how did you divide six by fifteen? Even this was too much for any of them to work out. When, in addition, voices rose to say that the Olofsson brothers should be given a smaller share, since they'd already received payment, plus their share should count as one – not two – because they had the same name, the angrier of the brothers became angrier than usual. So angry that he happened to inform hoodlum number seven (the one who went by the name Ox) that he regretted Hitman Anders hadn't cut his throat as agreed.

'Aha, you bastard,' said Ox, 'you had a contract out on me!' And he took out a knife to do to Olofsson what Olofsson had wanted Hitman Anders to do to Ox.

This, in turn, caused the other Olofsson to attempt a half-panicked diversionary measure. All he could think to do in his haste was fire a shot from his enormous Smith & Wesson 500, straight into the suitcase of money, at point-blank range. But, of course, he was handling one of the world's largest revolvers, the sort that could take down a real ox if necessary, so it was no wonder that the fireworks sparked a small fire among the banknotes.

This achieved the intended effect, in so far as Ox and the rest (except the guy on the floor) first lost their hearing for a few seconds, thanks to the report, then immediately redirected their attention. As many feet as could fit stamped simultaneously on the burning five-hundred-krona notes and, sure enough, the fire was just about to give up the ghost when hoodlum number eight came up with the bright idea of sacrificing a bottle of 90 per cent home-brew to put out what few flames remained.

Both Olofsson and Olofsson had, for survival purposes, left the cellar just seconds before it started burning in earnest. The rest of the hoodlums soon had to do the same (except for the guy still lying on the floor, who, if he hadn't already done so when the back of his head struck the floor, died): 90 per cent home-brew does not have – nor has it ever had – any sort of mitigating effect on fire.

The next night, four men paid Olofsson and Olofsson at visit at home. They didn't ring the doorbell; they didn't even knock at the door. Instead they chopped their way through with an axe until the door was in splinters and all they had to do was step inside. But, no matter how hard they looked, they found neither Olofsson nor his brother, just a frightened hamster named Clark, after a famous bank robber from the past. Olofsson had forced his brother to leave Clark in the apartment to which they would never return. Instead, immediately following the debacle in the pub cellar, they had taken a train to Malmö, 370 miles away from what might have been the angriest clientele anywhere in the world at that particular moment.

Malmö was a nice city; in fact, it was even one of Sweden's most encumbered by criminals. No one would notice another crime or two per week in the statistics, as

Olofsson philosophized while he and his brother robbed a petrol station of all its money, plus four Kexchoklad bars, then helped themselves to the manager's car by force.

CHAPTER 65

There was just one thing the receptionist didn't get. How there could have been exactly six million kronor in the suitcase? Shouldn't there have been at least six hundred thousand more?

Yes, but the priest had secured some cash on her person as she packed. The toothbrushes, underwear, and so on might have fitted anyway, but she'd thought it would be a pain to have to open the suitcase every time they wanted to pay for a measly little bus ticket.

'Or for a measly little fishing shack on Gotland?' said the receptionist.

'Exactly.'

So life could have been worse, after all. To be more precise, they had 646,000 kronor once they'd paid for the shack. And just under six hundred thousand once it was furnished and clearly in violation of an unknown number of statutes, which they had begun by burning, in accordance with the plan. To be on the safe side, they did not call to ask if it was okay to kill an annoying colony of beach-dwelling, endangered sand wasps with bleach.

It ought to be possible to grow even just half a million if they could find sufficient Toms, Dicks and Harrys to exploit, thought the pastor.

The receptionist agreed, screwed the cap back onto the bottle of bleach, and reminded her of the crucial point: that Tom must not be awarded a single öre more than Dick and Harry would immediately give back in return.

CHAPTER 66

The medieval city of Visby and its shops were preparing for the approaching Christmas season. Interest rates were down to 0.0, which encouraged people to spend money they didn't have so that Christmas sales would break records once again. As a consequence, people were generally able to keep their jobs, which meant they could afford to pay off their new loans. Economics is its own special kind of science.

For several months, the receptionist had contemplated how the principle of 'more blessed to take than to give' could (while appearing to be the other way around) be converted into a practical methodology. Thus far he had not got much further than various forms of the giving half of the equation. After all, it was easy to donate a coin or two. And it was fun. And it was exceptionally stupid unless you got at least as much back in return.

Once upon a time it had worked well, in the form of a generous former murderer on the one hand and a large number of collection buckets on the other. But now they had neither murderer, buckets, nor a congregation. The only one of those things that could be reacquired was probably the buckets, but what would be the point?

And then, during a walk along Hästgatsbacken, it so happened that the priest and the receptionist encountered an old man dressed in red with a fake white beard; he had likely been hired by the town association. He walked up the hill and down the hill saying 'Merry Christmas' to everyone he met as he handed out gingerbread to the children. People big and small were delighted to see the man in red. Perhaps he spurred them on to do more shopping in the local outlets, but it seemed doubtful.

At any rate, the priest mentioned that perhaps everything would have worked out differently if she had only talked Hitman Anders into believing in the existence of Santa Claus rather than Jesus.

The receptionist smiled at the mental image of Hitman Anders in a pulpit, calling upon the almighty Santa Claus, with *glögg* and gingerbread for the congregation instead of wine and cheese.

'*Glögg* made with strong wine,' the priest mused. 'Details are crucial.'

That gave her receptionist reason to continue smiling, until he suddenly grew serious. The difference between God in Heaven and Santa Claus (wherever he lived) was not, in fact, all that great.

'Are you thinking first and foremost of their non-existence or of beards?' the priest wondered.

'Neither. Both of them have the reputation for being good, right? We might have the germ of an idea here.'

Calling God 'good' in front of the priest was not the sort of thing a person got away with scot-free. She said she could come up with a hundred examples of reasons that the Lord, according to all the stories of the Bible, was surely diagnosable. She didn't know how things stood with Santa in that respect, but it really didn't seem healthy to pop in and out of chimneys as one's primary occupation.

The receptionist countered cheerfully, pointing out that neither of them was one of Santa's or God's most beloved children. A rough calculation indicated that they routinely broke nine out of the Ten Commandments. Adultery was pretty much the only one they hadn't managed yet.

'Speaking of which,' said the priest, 'shouldn't we get married as we're hanging around together like this? Assuming it's a secular marriage and that you buy the rings.'

The receptionist immediately said yes and promised rings of gold, but to go back to the Commandments for a second, he wanted to make a correction. They had not, in fact, killed anyone of their own accord.

This was true, which meant their Commandment score was not 9–1 but 8–2. Not that this was a terrific score either.

Per Persson didn't respond: it was unnecessary. But back to the Commandments. How did it go again – were you at least allowed to covet your future wife? And your joint pile of five-hundred-krona banknotes?

The priest said this was a matter of interpretation, but also that she wanted to put the Bible behind her once and for all. The Pearly Gates did not exist, and if they did there was really no point in queuing to go through them.

The thought of being told off by God on the threshold to his kingdom was not one she could tolerate. Instead she wanted to know whether Santa Claus had just become the receptionist's main channel into the theme of 'generosity that one could simultaneously cash in on'.

Per Persson gave an honest answer: there was still no main channel at hand, unless the priest – unlike Per himself – would be satisfied to give while skipping the act of taking. 'And I have no reason to believe that is the case.'

'Correct,' said the priest. 'And, anyway, what will we do afterwards, once the money is gone?'

'Get married?'

'We've already decided on that. And it's not going to make us any richer, is it?'

'Don't say that. There's always the children's allowance. With six or seven kids, maybe that would be enough.'

'Idiot,' the priest said, with a smile.

At that moment, she caught sight of a jeweller's. 'Come on, let's go in there and get engaged.'

CHAPTER 67

Winter became spring; spring became early summer. At last, the sinning would be over in at least one respect. It was time for the priest and the receptionist to become a lawfully wedded couple.

The most secular person they could find to do the job was the county governor of Gotland, who agreed to marry them by the fishing shack at the edge of the water.

'Do you live here?' she had happened to inquire.

'As if!' said the priest.

'Then where do you live?'

'Somewhere else,' said the receptionist. 'Can we get cracking now?'

The young couple had desired the version that was over in forty-five seconds, but the celebrant made an argument for the three-minute alternative. After all, she would have to travel quite some distance, and it would be a waste just to toss out a 'Do you take this …' once per client, then go straight back to her office. Furthermore, she had prepared a few (in her own opinion) lovely remarks on the theme of 'We must take good care of each other just as we do our fragile ecology in Gotland.'

When it dawned on the receptionist, after a certain amount of arguing over the telephone, that the county governor's participation would be free of charge, no matter the length of the ceremony, he agreed to allow her to confuse love with biodiversity if she absolutely must. So he thanked her for calling, hung up, and made sure to hide all the bottles of bleach that might otherwise put the celebrant of their marriage in an unnecessarily bad mood. To be safe, he purchased ten Little Trees air fresheners and shoved them into the seaweed so that the county governor's precious Nature would smell like it wasn't: alive.

* * *

They had a marriage licence and proof of marriageability, and for this the bride and groom received praise from the county governor.

'But where are your witnesses?'

'Witnesses?' said the receptionist.

'Oh, hell,' said the priest, who had married enough people in her day to realize straight away that this was something they had overlooked. 'One moment,' she added, and ran towards an older couple who were walking along the beach some distance away.

As the county governor made note of the fact that she was just about to perform a secular marriage with a swearing priest for a bride, the priest in question argued with the couple, who turned out to be from Japan and did not understand Swedish, English, German, French, or any other of the many languages that involved some form of logic. They did, however, understand that the priest wanted them to come with her and, as the obedient Japanese people they were, they did as she asked.

'Are you the bridal couple's witnesses?' the county governor asked the Japanese couple, who just looked at the woman who had said something they didn't comprehend.

'Say *hai*,' the receptionist told them (that was the only Japanese he knew).

'はい,' said one witness. He didn't dare to do otherwise.

'はい,' said his wife, for the same reason.

'We've known each other for a long time,' said the priest.

It took a little extra administration and a certain amount of creativity on the county governor's part to make the marriage valid. But she was the sort of person who preferred solving problems to creating them, and after some time the priest and the receptionist were in possession of written confirmation that they had become one.

* * *

Summer passed; autumn took hold. The priest was already four months pregnant.

'Our first child allowance payment is on the way!' the receptionist hollered when he found out. 'Four or five more and we'll be in business. If we space them out right, we'll only need *one* set of clothing for all of them. One will get the second's hand-me-downs, who will get the third's, who will get the fourth's, who—'

'Can we start by getting the first one to the finish line, please?' said the priest. 'We'll deal with number two later. And the rest as they happen.'

With that, the priest changed the subject. These days they were living a peaceful life in a two-hundred-square-foot fishing-shack-plus-loft in which they had no legal right to live. Their cost of living was minimal. Noodles and tap water were not as luxurious as the *foie gras* and champagne they had once enjoyed, but now they had an ocean view and each other. Furthermore, thanks to the bleach, they had long been rid of not only sand wasps but also ants, sweat bees, emerald wasps, velvet ants, tachina flies, and almost everything else that was responsible for guaranteeing biodiversity.

Of the millions in the suitcase, not even the suitcase was left. So, honestly, how were the receptionist's give-but-take-a-little-more plans going?

The priest had her doubts, under the circumstances. Given their current financial situation, perhaps take-and-only-take would be a better starting point.

The receptionist admitted that progress was slow. He came back to Santa Claus time and again, but that bastard never took anything in return.

The priest, who was starting to get bored with the fact that life involved little more than an expanding stomach and the approach of yet another Gotland winter, suggested they divert themselves with a trip to the mainland.

'What would we do there?' the receptionist wondered. 'Aside from potentially running into a hoodlum who doesn't like us. Or two.'

The priest didn't quite know. But one idea might be to entertain themselves at various establishments where they could be reasonably sure no hoodlums would appear. Like the National Library, the Maritime Museum … As she said it, she could hear just how much fun that sounded. 'Or we could try doing something nice, as long as it doesn't cost money,' she continued. 'If it doesn't make us happy, maybe we're on the wrong track. This could be an important piece in your never-ending future puzzle.'

'*Our* future puzzle, if you please,' said the receptionist. 'Something nice? Help old ladies cross the street?'

'Well, why not? Or we could pay a visit to the mushroom-picking hitman, whom we so handily managed to send back to prison. If I remember correctly, I did happen to promise him a visit, in our hurry to leave.'

'But that was just a lie, wasn't it?' said the receptionist.

'I know it was. But I read somewhere that you're not supposed to bear false witness against your neighbour.' His priest smiled.

A little visit to Hitman Anders would bring the score to 7–3, in the Commandments game they would never win. But it was always nice to boost their numbers.

The receptionist gazed sceptically at the priest, who admitted that the idea of meeting the man they had finally got rid of could have something to do with raging hormones. She had read about pregnant women who lived on tuna fish in oil or ate twenty oranges per day or chewed chalk, so it was probably something like that. But still. At the moment, their lives were standing as still as the biological activity in the washed-up seaweed. There was not a single sand wasp left to annoy them. Perhaps a short ferry trip followed by an even shorter prison visit might make a difference in one direction or another. And at a price that would hardly register, given the context.

The receptionist realized now more than ever that there was something about pregnancy. His beloved priest was apparently pining for murderers and sand wasps. As dad-to-be, he had to take responsibility. And it would probably not be sufficient to go out for a box of oranges. 'I suggest we go early next week,' he said. 'If you check with the prison about visiting times, I'll book the ferry tickets.'

Johanna Kjellander nodded, pleased, as Per Persson barely maintained a happy expression. Seeing Hitman Anders again could not possibly be the meaning of life. But if his wife had raging hormones, then that was it. Also, neither the National Library nor the Maritime Museum seemed much more tempting.

'For better or for worse,' he mumbled. 'I think we can chalk this one up in the "worse" column.'

CHAPTER 68

'Dear friends! God's peace be upon you, hallelujah and Hosanna.' Hitman Anders initiated the meeting in the prison visiting room.

They hardly recognized him. He looked hale and hearty and his entire face was practically overgrown. The explanation for this last bit was that the priest had once taught him that, according to the Old Testament, one must not shave one's face. He did not remember exactly how those words had gone, and he hadn't been able to find them on his own, even though he'd looked, but he trusted his dear friend.

'Leviticus nineteen,' the priest said automatically. '"You shall not eat anything with its blood. You shall not practise augury or witchcraft. You shall not round off the hair on your temples or mar the edges of your beard. You shall not make any gashes in your flesh for the dead or tattoo any marks upon you: I am the Lord."'

'Oh, right, that was it,' said the former pastor, scratching his beard. 'It's tough to do anything about the tattoos, but Jesus and I have worked through that and put it behind us.'

Hitman Anders was thriving like a fish in water. He held Bible study groups three times a week and had snared at least three disciples, plus just as many who were wavering. His efforts had gone awry only once, and that was when he had tried to start everyone saying grace in the cafeteria, at which the cook, who was in for life, was struck by a fit of rage and started a brawl. The man who had happened to be standing closest to him in the food line when it all began was a small foreigner whom everyone called 'Chatterbox' because he never said anything (mainly because he didn't have anything to say in any language other than the one he and no one else understood). The cook thrust a broken bottle into the neck of Chatterbox, who actually said, 'Ouch!' in Swedish, the last word he uttered in this life.

'The guy with the bottle got his sentence extended by another lifetime for that. And he was downgraded to dishwasher.'

One or double life sentences, it was all the same to Hitman Anders (although it might have been a fate worse than death to stand there washing plates for two whole lives in a row). Instead he was eager to tell them that, although he had weaned himself off communion in the time he'd been locked up, his relationship with Jesus had suffered no ill effects. Now, the priest and the receptionist must not be offended, but Hitman Anders had discovered, during his Bible studies, that the two of them might have misunderstood a thing or two about communion. Just because a person turned to Jesus didn't mean that he had to down one or several bottles of wine each day. If they liked, he could explain in greater detail?

343

'No, thanks,' said the priest. 'On the whole, I think I understand.'

Well, they could always come back to it at a later date. The long and the short of it was that the cook, who would now have to wash plates every day until he'd died twice, served only milk and lingonberry juice, in accordance with the current prison regulations. Since none of the prisoners really got going on either milk or lingonberry juice, a smuggling operation brought in large amounts of the kind of stuff Hitman Anders hadn't downed in several years and would never go back to.

'Like what?' the priest wondered.

'Rohypnol and terrible stuff like that,' said Hitman Anders. 'Nothing used to make me as crazy as Rohypnol did with a little alcohol. That was a long time ago now, thank the Lord.'

The only cloud in his bright blue sky was that the Prison Service had discovered what a shining example of a good prisoner he was, and they had forged a plan behind his back to give him early release.

'Early release?' said the receptionist.

'In two months,' said Hitman Anders. 'And barely even that. What will happen to all my Bible students then? And to me? I'm absolutely beside myself with worry.'

'But that's fantastic news,' said the receptionist, in a tone so genuine that the priest was shocked. 'Let us come and pick you up on the day you're freed. I think I have a job for you,' he said, to the priest's double shock.

'God be with us!' said Hitman Anders.

The priest said nothing. She had lost the ability to speak.

* * *

Per Persson had, during the present meeting, noticed something that had not occurred to the priest. Thanks to Leviticus 19:27–28, Hitman Anders had transformed himself into an exact copy of Santa Claus. All they would have to do was groom his tousled hair and put a more Santa-like pair of glasses on him. The beard was real, of course, and it was just the perfect shade of white.

The receptionist took this as a sign from … someone … and one instant later, the Santa Concept came to him. It was as though a higher power had been involved, if only he hadn't known beyond all shadow of a doubt that *no* higher power, no matter how high, would ever lift a finger to help either himself or his priest.

CHAPTER 69

As soon as the receptionist and the priest were alone again, one explained to the other what had been revealed to him in the visiting room at the prison. Once they got home, they sat down to page through some old issues of the local *Gotlands Allehanda* and more or less immediately found reason to believe that the receptionist's idea would hold water. It was an article about a man who could not continue to live in his rental apartment because the walls were full of bedbugs. The landlord refused to consider the bedbugs his problem, and now the man had nowhere to live, yet he was forced to keep paying rent.

'All I have to live on is my retirement pension,' said the old man to the newspaper, feeling sorry for himself with good reason.

The old man's miserable situation didn't much interest the receptionist or the priest. He was far too wrinkled and stooping to have any sort of commercial value. He and his bedbugs, therefore, would have to manage as best they could, although the receptionist spent a second or two considering whether he should phone the old man and tell him about bleach, which seemed to kill just about anything.

But the fact that the old man had told his sob story to a local newspaper and that another unfortunate soul of a different sort had done the same in the competitor paper, *Gotlands Tidning*, just a few issues later, gave the priest and the receptionist all the confirmation they needed.

The number of distressing stories in daily publications across the country ought to be nearly infinite. Even if they didn't count old men with bedbugs, millionaires with Spanish slug infestations in their gardens, and injured rats tossed into a dustbin by an emotionally disturbed teenager with an airgun, there would still be an infinite number.

The receptionist took out one of the two tablets he had purchased a few years earlier with money from the collection buckets and got to work.

* * *

'How's it going?' the priest asked, as she rubbed her belly and watched her husband, who had his nose in an iPad and a notebook at his side.

'Good, thanks,' said the receptionist, telling her that the final order of an electronic copy of a Swedish daily paper was done and dusted.

'*Ljusdalsposten*,' he said. 'One hundred and ninety-nine kronor per month.'

Well, why not? the priest wondered. Ljusdal was lovely, but that didn't mean there weren't people there for whom one might feel sorry. And then she made the mistake of asking to which other newspapers they had electronic access (because the answer almost never ended).

'I've got the list here,' said the receptionist. 'Let's see …
Okay, Östersundsposten, Dala-Demokraten, Gefle
Dagblad, Upsala Nya Tidning, Nerikes Allehanda,
Sydsvenskan, Svenska Dagbla—'

'Stop! That's enough,' said the priest.

'No, it's not, if we're going to build up the infrastructure we need to represent every little corner of the nation.
I've got more here and just as many again on the other
side of this piece of paper. There must be around fifty
altogether. And it's not free, although a few have introductory offers. Hats off to *Blekinge Läns Tidning*, by the
way. One krona for a month-long trial period.'

'We could practically afford two of those,' said the
priest. 'Too bad it would probably say the same thing in
both.'

The receptionist smiled and called up his internal Excel
spreadsheet. In the long run, their subscription budget
would cost around a hundred thousand kronor for the
whole year, but introductory pricing, short-term subscriptions and trial periods had brought their initial investment down to an amount their available funds would
allow. This would probably end well for both giver and
(above all) taker. Other people's generosity was generally
a bit greater than their own, which guaranteed a positive
number on the bottom line. Maybe not from the start,
but within a time frame short enough that they could feel
good about it.

'Aside from the fact that I think other people's generosity is generally *much* greater than our own, I am in
complete agreement, my dear,' said the priest.

The greatest threat to their success, she thought, was Santa Claus himself. Hitman Anders was and remained a security risk. But if their plan went to Hell for one reason or another, they'd just have to accept it. The receptionist's idea was far too attractive not to try out on a full scale immediately.

'So let tomorrow bring worries of its own. Today's trouble is enough for today. Matthew six, verse thirty-four.'

'Did you just voluntarily quote the Bible?' asked the receptionist.

'Yes. Imagine that.'

* * *

Humanity, in general, is a potpourri of many traits. For example: stingy, self-involved, jealous, ignorant, stupid, and frightened. But also: kind, clever, friendly, forgiving, considerate – and generous. Not all of these traits find room in every soul, as the priest and the receptionist knew, not least from personal experience. It is possible that philosopher Immanuel Kant hypothesized that each person bears a functional moral compass within himself only because he never had occasion to meet our priest or our receptionist.

The new take-and-(by all means)-give plan, which had vague origins in a fake commercial Santa in Visby whose sole gift was gingerbread for children, was now fully cobbled together, polished, and ready.

First the receptionist had opened an investigation, led

and implemented by himself. He needed to gather know-ledge of what the market and any potential competitors looked like.

There were several competitors out there to consider. For example, it turned out that the Swedish postal service accepted more than a hundred thousand letters to Santa Claus each year, addressed to 'Tomten' (Santa's Swedish name) at '17300 Tomteboda, Sweden'. The postal repre-sentative proudly told the receptionist, over the phone, that everyone who wrote received an answer – along with a small present.

The receptionist said, 'Thank you for the information,' hung up, and mumbled that the value of that 'present' must surely be less than the cost of the postage. Which meant that it entailed a combination of extremely limited goodness and extremely limited profitability. Not such a bad idea, at the heart of it, but it wouldn't quite do. Taking into account administrative costs, such an enter-prise would likely result in zero profit at best. And the only numbers the priest and the receptionist disliked more than zero were those that began with a minus sign.

Beyond the postal service, there was Santa Land in Dalarna. Because the receptionist read what he wanted to read into what Santa Land had to offer, he came to the conclusion that it was an amusement park in which a person who paid the entry fee, ate and drank at the cost of a few hundred kronor, and stayed overnight for a few thousand, was allowed to hand over a wish list to a fake Santa, who in turn could use said lists as kindling later that evening.

This idea wasn't so bad either, but it was clearly biased towards taking rather than giving. *Balance* was crucial in this matter!

Another Santa Claus, with a polyester beard, lived in Rovaniemi, Finland. The concept seemed similar to that in Dalarna. With the same problems and shortcomings.

Incidentally, it turned out the Danes were of the opinion that Santa lived in Greenland. The Americans bet on the North Pole, the Turks on Turkey, and the Russians on Russia. Out of all of these, only the Americans made a proper industry out of their Santa, partly in the way he seemed to prefer Coca-Cola over all other beverages, and partly in the form of at least one annual Christmas film in which Santa first screwed everything up and then, at the last minute, made all the children in the entire world happy. Or at least one of them. For pretend. For twelve dollars per movie ticket.

And then there was also Santa's cousin, Sinterklaas, or St Nicholas. According to what the receptionist learned, he had begun as the patron saint of all former thieves, and that was certainly a lovely thought. But, still, he didn't really count because he brought children presents too early – on 6 December.

'Though doesn't it depend on how global we want to go with this?' said the priest.

'One country at a time,' said the receptionist. 'Just take Germany, with ten times as many citizens as Sweden has. That would probably require ten Santas of a Hitman Anders nature, and all would need the ability to say at least "Frohe Weihnachten" without going totally off the rails.'

Two words in foreignese. That was two more than Hitman Anders would be capable of dealing with, as both the priest and the receptionist were aware (unless they were talking about the Latin names of mushrooms). There was also the risk that 'Hosanna' was German for 'Hosanna' as well.

* * *

So, for a Santa who gave out presents for real, without being paid ahead of time, competition was limited if not non-existent.

The profitability of this business venture would depend on how many sob stories they could find in the papers. Preferably involving single mothers, sick children, or abandoned pets of every adorable ilk. Ugly old men with bedbugs would not set quite as many hearts afire; neither would tortured rats in a dustbin. When it came to multi-millionaires with Spanish slugs in their gardens, Swedish tradition would seem to hold that the millionaires deserved it.

The plan to proceed, based on carefully selected stories in the local paper, was truly brilliant in that the recipient in question had by definition already spoken to the media once, and thus ought to be willing to do it again, following a surprising encounter with Santa Claus.

This, in turn, would generate traffic to the website where one would discover Santa – with a beard that could withstand tugging.

And if God was adequately good (the receptionist was

about to say), this, in turn, would lead to a donation or two. Or a hundred. Or why not a thousand?

All that remained before the plan could be set in motion was for the Prison Service to follow through with its own plan – as crazy as it was splendid – to set Hitman Anders free.

CHAPTER 70

The basic idea of Project Santa Claus, of course, was that the only thing that could possibly be more fun than giving was taking. A person who managed to do both, as the priest and the receptionist saw it, should have every chance of living a long and happy life. After all, it wasn't exactly their goal to starve to death along with their as-yet-unborn child. Not even Hitman Anders deserved that sort of fate.

With that in the back of his mind, the receptionist created a Facebook page with the slogan 'The real Santa Claus – spreads joy year-round.'

The page was full of messages of love in varying tenors (none of which was of a religious nature). In the space that was left, a message ran that everyone was free to open his heart (that is, his wallet) to help Santa in his mission. This could occur via bank transfer, credit card, direct transfer, smartphone, or one of a few other methods. No matter which it was, the money ended up in an account at Handelsbanken in Visby. The account belonged to the Swedish firm Real Santa Claus AB, which was held by an anonymous Swiss foundation. Under no circumstances could they allow word to get out of who was spreading joy in people's lives; the Hitman Anders brand had been run into the ground. Meanwhile, Santa Claus's own brand had been way up there for ages, along with Nelson Mandela, Mother Teresa, and the guy who would remain nameless.

Thus far, the plan was remarkably similar to the internet-based division of Hitman Anders's previous donation site. (These days, that site was full of comments from people demanding their money back.)

To be on the safe side, the receptionist had also ordered the taxpayer's directory, all of Sweden's twenty-three editions of it, for 271 kronor a pop. This had cost more than 6,200 kronor, but it was worth it. In doing so, he gained access to names, addresses and taxable employment income, plus capital income, for every taxpayer in the country. That was how Sweden worked. Nothing was a secret. Aside from the identity of Santa Claus. It would never do to donate money to someone the newspaper felt sorry for, then discover that this person was sitting on an annual income of two million kronor in a yellow turn-of-the-century thirteen-room manor house in Djursholm. With or without Spanish slugs.

Santa Claus's very first mission would instead come to involve a young woman with an address that spoke of apartment living. Further investigation revealed that the apartment was rented and her taxable income was 99,000 kronor per year.

CHAPTER 71

Thirty-two-year-old Maria Johansson lived in a cramped two-room apartment in Ystad, as far south as you can get in Sweden, with her five-year-old daughter Gisela. The dad was not at home; he hadn't been for over a year. Mama Maria was unemployed and someone, according to *Ystads Allehanda*, had thrown a stone through her bedroom window. There was a problem in getting the insurance money to repair it because the insurer considered it proven that Gisela's father had thrown that stone one Saturday night. The main point of evidence was that he had confessed during a police inquiry, in which he admitted that after visiting a restaurant he had gone to the home of his former girlfriend, screamed at her, and accused her of being a prostitute when she refused to open the door and allow him to have sex with her, even if he gave her money. He had rounded off his visit with that stone through the window.

The problem, from an insurance perspective, was that Gisela's father was still listed as living at the address in question. One who knowingly breaks items in his own home cannot expect reimbursement from the insurance company. Thus Maria and little Gisela would be forced to celebrate Christmas with a sheet of hardboard covering the bedroom window, or spend the last of Maria's savings on a new window and cancel Gisela's Christmas. Since winter was cold even way down south, Gisela would end up with neither presents nor tree. That was how it all stood when there came a knock at the door of Maria and her daughter's home. Mama Maria opened it cautiously, in case it was …

But it wasn't. It was Santa Claus. The real Santa Claus, it appeared. He bowed and gave Gisela an interactive doll, one she could talk to! The doll was given the name 'Nanne' and became Gisela's most cherished possession, even though Nanne's programming had been rather sketchy.

'I love you, Nanne,' Gisela might say.

'I don't know. I can't tell the time,' Nanne replied.

With the doll, Santa handed over an envelope containing twenty thousand kronor to Gisela's mom. And then he said, 'Merry Christmas!' because that's what Santa says. After that, he happened to add, 'Hosanna!' in violation of his instructions, because this Santa was one reindeer short of an airborne sleigh.

He vanished as quickly as he'd come, in a taxi driven by a man called Taxi Torsten. In the back seat sat two happy elves, neither in elf clothing, one eight months pregnant.

Operation Santa Claus had begun in Ystad. After this, the journey continued northward. Next stop, Sjöbo. Followed by Hörby, Höör, Hässleholm, and on up through the country. On average, another gift of between ten and thirty thousand kronor was given each day, for four weeks in a row. Sometimes in the form of money, sometimes Christmas presents, sometimes both.

Single mothers were good. Orphaned refugee children were almost better, though girls were preferable, and the younger they were, the more financial potential there was. The sick and the handicapped worked well, too. Cute little boys and girls with cancer – bingo.

As it happened, Santa Claus had been to Hässleholm in a former life. Taxi Torsten drove to a particular address, Santa entered the stairwell and rang the bell at the home of the elderly Salvationist he had rained money over once before.

The Salvationist opened the door, accepted a fat envelope containing a hundred thousand kronor, looked inside, and said: 'God bless you. But haven't we met before?'

At this, Santa hurried off to his taxi and was gone before the Salvationist could say, 'May I offer you some mashed turnips?'

According to the budget, the first month's expenses ought to come very close to the five hundred thousand kronor they had left. And that would mean their adventures and their money would be gone by February – assuming they received nothing in return.

But for the period from 20 December to 20 January, the overall expenses were no higher than 460,000 kronor, despite the extraordinary outlay in Hässleholm and that they had worked non-stop for those first four weeks. Beyond this, the plan for the future was to spend three weeks of each month on the Swedish roads and the fourth week resting at home on Gotland. Assuming – again – that they didn't go bankrupt. In which case their only recourse would be to produce children as rapidly as possible.

'Better than we budgeted for!' said the priest, becoming so excited that her waters broke. 'Ow! Whoa! We have to go to the hospital now.'

'Hold on! I'm not ready yet,' said the receptionist.

'Hosanna!' said Santa Claus.

'I'll bring the car around,' said Taxi Torsten.

* * *

It was a girl, six pounds, nine ounces.

'There we go!' said the receptionist, to his exhausted priest. 'Our first child allowance! When do you think you'll be ready for the production of number two?'

'Not today, thanks,' said the priest, as the midwife stitched her up in the necessary area.

A few hours later, as the little baby lay sleeping, full and content on her mother's belly, the priest found the strength to ask what it was the receptionist had not had time to finish saying when they were interrupted by other matters.

Just think, the receptionist had totally forgotten about that when the contractions had started for real. But there was no time like the present. 'Oh, I was going to say that it's great our costs topped out at four hundred and sixty thousand. But we've brought in a small amount via our internet campaign as well.'

'Oh, have we?' said Mama Priest. 'How much?'

'In our first month?'

'The first month is fine.'

'An approximate number?'

'An approximate number is fine.'

'Well, with the caveat that I might be misremembering a little, because I didn't have time to write down the exact number, and with the caveat that another krona or two might have trickled in while we were having a baby, and with the caveat that—'

'Could you get to the point?' the priest said, while simultaneously thinking that, really, she had done more of the baby-having than he had.

'Right, sorry. With all those caveats in mind, I would say about two million three hundred and forty-five thousand seven hundred and ninety kronor.'

The priest's waters would probably have broken again, if only it had been technically possible.

CHAPTER 72

The more visits Santa had time to make in one day, the more happiness he spread, and the better the business seemed to pay its way. Thousands in small donations came in each day, from around Sweden and, in fact, the world. Single mothers cried for joy; cute little girls did the same; puppies whined in gratitude. The daily papers wrote articles, the weekly magazines produced whole spreads, radio and TV did follow-ups. Santa Claus brought true happiness around Christmas, but he didn't stop when winter turned to spring and spring turned to summer. It seemed it would never end.

The Santa Lands in Mora and Rovaniemi were forced to rethink their concepts. It was no longer enough to have an old man with a polyester beard who nodded sympathetically when little Lisa wanted a pony of her own. Either the polyester Santa had to give her what she wished for (but this would never turn a profit), or he had to say, as pedagogically as he could, that what he had to offer was a small packet of Lego® in cooperation with the Lego Group, Billund, Denmark. No ponies, not even hamsters. The small cost of the present (which would never satisfy little Lisa anyway) was offset by a slightly higher entry fee.

Investigative journalists tried to find out who Santa was and how much he or she might conceivably be bringing in in the form of donations. But none got any further than Handelsbanken in Visby, where no one saw any reason to report how much was transferred, in accordance with Swedish law, to the anonymous foundation in Switzerland. And since each giver gave so little (after all, it was the large number of givers that had led to the millions), not a single journalist was able to poke holes in the image of the anonymous Santa as genuinely benevolent.

On one occasion, someone managed to capture Santa in a photograph, but he was so dolled up in his long beard and everything that no one made the connection to the former murderer/pastor of the Church of Anders. To play it safe, Taxi Torsten had stolen a pair of new licence plates while running an errand to Stockholm. What was more, he had used a bit of paint to transform an F into an E, so now his taxi appeared at first glance to belong to no one or, at second glance, to an electrician in Hässelby.

Speculation abounded and rumours flew. Could it be the *King*, running around spreading joy among his people? After all, the Queen was well known for her devotion to children and the weak. This notion took hold in various threads of speculation on the internet up until the day His Majesty happened to bag a four-pointer in a Sörmland forest at exactly the same moment that Santa was blessing an orphaned twelve-year-old refugee girl in Härnösand.

The priest, the receptionist, Santa Claus and Taxi Torsten jointly shared eight per cent of the profits, which allowed them all to live and be happy on the island in the Baltic Sea that had become their home. The rest was reinvested in glorious giving. The receptionist had also begun to work on the priest's original plan to expand their activities into Germany. The Germans had money and heart. And they played good soccer. Plus there were so many of them that it was almost impossible to calculate how much Project Santa Claus would earn by giving away money there. The only issue was finding ten German Santas, understanding what they said, and making them understand what they were supposed to say. And getting them to keep their mouths shut about what they were up to.

* * *

And then there was all this stuff about the ways of the Lord and so on. Because at approximately the same time, the receptionist's mom – the woman who had nearly become a German teacher – got tired of all the eruptions from husband and volcano in Iceland. During one of their rare visits to civilization for provisions, she simply called the police and told them where her embezzling husband could be found and, with that, she was rid of him.

The next step was to contact her son via Facebook, and by the time all was said and done she had her own fishing shack on Gotland, not far from her son and his family, as well as a job as head of development for the coming launch in Germany. Meanwhile, the Icelandic courts decided that her husband would spend six years and four months in prison for economically relevant moral rehabilitation.

Hitman Anders, for his part, met a certain Stina, whom he soon moved in with. She had fallen in love with him when he happened to know what cauliflower fungus was called in Latin (this, in turn, could be explained by the fact that the hitman, before he had become a hitman, had bought a book in the hope of learning how to make mushrooms magical in various drug-related ways, only to realize after his twelfth read-through that he knew the names of every mushroom in existence but nothing about how to make them any more entertaining than they already were).

Together they failed to find truffles (*Tuber melano-sporum*) with the help of their tame but slightly dense pig, then started again and eventually attained the same level of success in growing asparagus (not least because the pig was a real scoundrel when it came to rooting in the garden).

Stina was simple-minded enough; she never did work out what her beloved Johan was doing when he spent three weeks in a row on the mainland. The important thing was that he came home when he said he would, with a larger amount of pay each time. And that they could go to church on the fourth Sunday and thank the Lord for everything except their luck with truffles and asparagus.

When he wasn't acting as Santa's private chauffeur, Taxi Torsten took the opportunity to drive his taxi on the island. Not because he needed the money, but because he liked driving. He never worked outside noon till four, on Monday through Thursday of every fourth week. He spent the rest of his time at the pub or sleeping in. He had a permanent room at an apartment hotel in central Visby, within staggering distance of every imaginable thirst-quenching establishment.

The priest and the receptionist chose to remain in the simple fishing shack by the sea, with their little baby; Grandma acted as babysitter in a pinch.

They no longer needed four or five more kids to scrounge food money via the paltry child allowance. But one or two more would probably be nice. Out of sheer love. There was no reason why they couldn't harbour ill will towards the rest of the world or stop doing so, as the receptionist accidentally suggested one night just before bedtime.

'Stop?' said the priest. 'Why?'

Oh, it was just something he'd happened to say. It was probably because their list of exceptions was becoming cumbersome. The baby was on it, of course. And maybe the hitman. He was actually pretty nice, if only he weren't so stupid. And that lady, whatsername, the county governor, who allowed them to get married even though she might have suspected that the witnesses had no idea what they were witnessing.

The priest nodded. They could probably even make a few more additions to the list. The baby's grandma, the hitman's new girlfriend, and if not Taxi Torsten, at least his taxi.

'By the way, I saw a sand wasp buzzing around the seaweed today. We're out of bleach. We either have to buy some more or count sand wasps among hitmen, county governors, and the rest of them.'

'Let's do it. Add the sand wasps, I mean. There'll be quite a few, but I suppose there's always room for more. Should we draw the line at that for now? And keep hating everything else?'

Yes, that was a good compromise.

'But not tonight. I seem to be a little too tired for hating. It's been a long day. Good, but long. Good night, my dear former receptionist,' said the equally former parish priest, and she fell asleep.

EPILOGUE

The priest was standing down the slope from the family's fishing shack one beautiful evening and gazing across the sea. It was almost as smooth as a mirror. Far in the distance, the Oskarshamn ferry glided silently through the water. A lone oystercatcher was strutting across the washed-up seaweed nearby. To her surprise, he found a bug to put in his stomach: that hadn't happened for a long time around there. Otherwise everything was quiet as the sun slowly went down, changing colour from yellow to orange.

And then the silence was broken.

'You're not a bad person, Johanna. I want you to know that. No one is bad through and through.'

Was someone there?

No. It was coming from inside her.

'Who's there? Who's speaking?' she said anyway.

'You know who I am, and you know that Our Father is always ready to forgive.'

The priest was astounded. Was it *him*? After all these years? She felt dizzy at the thought of his existence. And irritated. If he did exist, against all odds, couldn't he have put down his foot earlier and stopped Papa Kjellander from terrorizing his family while there was still time?

'*My* father forgave nothing, and I have no intention of forgiving him. And don't trot out your "If anyone strikes you on the right cheek, turn the other too."'

'Why not?' Jesus wondered.

'Because it wasn't you, or even Matthew, who said that in the first place. People have been putting words in your mouth without asking permission for centuries.'

'Hold on a second,' said Jesus, as indignantly as his temperament would allow. 'It's true that people make up all sorts of things in my name, but what do you know about what—'

That was as far as he got because the receptionist had stepped out of the shack, holding little Hosanna in his arms.

The moment was over.

'Are you talking to yourself?' the receptionist asked in surprise.

At first the priest responded with silence.

And then she was silent for a little while longer. And then she said: 'Yes. I think so. But dammit, who knows?'

AUTHOR'S THANKS

I want to thank the entire Piratförlaget family, with senior editor Sofia and editor Anna at the forefront. Especially Anna this time, for her fantastic single-handed rescue work at the last minute.

Thanks also to Uncle Hans and Rixon for always being there with encouraging comments on the very first version of the manuscript. Brother Lars and Stefan in Laxå, too, provided inspiration and instilled confidence at crucial moments.

While I'm at it, I'll remind my agent, Carina Brandt, of what an outstanding professional and friend she is. And speaking of friends: everyone ought to have an Anders Abenius, a Patrik Brissman and a Maria Magnusson. Together you make my author's life easier.

In a broader sense, but with no less sincerity, I would also like to thank Doctors Without Borders for making a difference in a time when more people than ever fare badly in our world. You care; not everyone does.

Among all of those for whom there isn't space on this acknowledgement page, I would especially like to mention God. Certainly he deserves a thank you for letting me borrow him to use in my story, but at the same time, I think he ought to work harder to convince his most eager supporters not to take him so seriously. So that we can all start being a bit kinder to one another, so that we have reason to laugh more than we cry.

Is that too much to ask? RSVP.

Jonas Jonasson